BRIAN WESTBY

FORREST REID was born in Belfast in 1875, the youngest of a large family. His father died when he was still a young child, and much of his upbringing therefore fell to his rather conventional mother and his elder sisters. As a youth he felt ill at ease with what seemed the narrow piety of his family's Presbyterian faith, and their solid middle-class values. After a local schooling, he was apprenticed at age eighteen to the tea trade. The work was not demanding, and Reid coped with the tedium of commercial life by retreating into a dream world of wonder and beauty, inspired by his reading of the Greek classics.

Reid later disowned his first two novels, *The Kingdom of Twilight* (1904) and *The Garden God* (1905). The latter risked controversy with its portrayal of romantic friendship between two boys; Reid dedicated it to his literary idol Henry James, who was outraged and never spoke to him again. After the death of Reid's mother, a small legacy enabled him to devote himself more fully to his writing, and in the 1910s he published a string of excellent, though not commercially successful novels, including *The Bracknels* (1911), *Following Darkness* (1912) (said to have been an influence on Joyce's *A Portrait of the Artist as a Young Man*), *At the Door of the Gate* (1915), *The Spring Song* (1916), and *Pirates of the Spring* (1919).

The best of Reid's works, though, came later in life, beginning with *Uncle Stephen* (1931), which, with *The Retreat* (1936) and *Young Tom* (1944), made up the *Tom Barber* trilogy, regarded by many as his masterpiece; the final book in the trilogy won the James Tait Black Memorial Prize as the best novel published in 1944. Reid's other mature work includes *Brian Westby* (1934), inspired by his friendship with nineteen-year-old Stephen Gilbert, who also went on to become a novelist, and *Peter Waring* (1937) and *Denis Bracknel* (1947), rewritten versions of *Following Darkness* and *The Bracknels*, respectively. Forrest Reid died in 1947, well regarded by critics, but never having achieved the widespread popular recognition he deserved. When Valancourt Books reprinted *The Garden God* in 2007, all of Reid's books were out of print. Valancourt is now in the process of restoring his best works to print.

ANDREW DOYLE is a playwright and stand-up comedian. His plays include *Borderland* (national tour for 7:84 Theatre Company, Scotland), *Jimmy Murphy Makes Amends* (BBC Radio 4) and *The Second Mr Bailey* (BBC Radio 4). His most recent solo stand-up show was *Whatever It Takes* at the Soho Theatre, London. He has a doctorate in English Renaissance Literature from the University of Oxford where he also worked as a lecturer.

By Forrest Reid

FICTION

The Kingdom of Twilight (1904)

The Garden God (1905)*

The Bracknels: A Family Chronicle (1911)

Following Darkness (1912)*

The Gentle Lover (1913)

At the Door of the Gate (1915)*

The Spring Song (1916)*

A Garden by the Sea (1918)

Pirates of the Spring (1919)

Pender Among the Residents (1922)

Demophon: A Traveller's Tale (1927)

Uncle Stephen (1931)*

Brian Westby (1934)*

The Retreat (1936)*

Peter Waring (1937)

Young Tom (1944)*

Denis Bracknel (1947)*

NON-FICTION

W. B. Yeats: A Critical Study (1915)

Apostate (1926)

Illustrators of the Sixties (1928)

Walter de la Mare: A Critical Study (1929)

Private Road (1940)

Retrospective Adventures (1941)

Notes and Impressions (1942)

Poems from the Greek Anthology (1943)

The Milk of Paradise: Some Thoughts on Poetry (1946)

* Available or forthcoming from Valancourt Books
(N.B.—Valancourt has republished Uncle Stephen, The Retreat, and Young Tom in a single volume under the title The Tom Barber Trilogy)

FORREST REID

BRIAN WESTBY

*'But sometimes the problem is more difficult of solution, when the voice of
duty seems to call in opposite directions, and sympathy and inclination
themselves are divided. In such cases it is well to consider the claims of
the past, for that at least is known, like an old friend; whereas the present
is still untried, and the future may be an illusion.'* Yakovnin.

With a new introduction by
ANDREW DOYLE

VALANCOURT BOOKS

Brian Westby by Forrest Reid
First published London: Faber & Faber, 1934
First Valancourt Books edition 2013

Published by Valancourt Books, Richmond, Virginia
Publisher & Editor: JAMES D. JENKINS
20th Century Series Editor: SIMON STERN, University of Toronto
http://www.valancourtbooks.com

ISBN 978-1-939140-65-4
Also available as an electronic book.

All Valancourt Books publications are printed on acid free
paper that meets all ANSI standards for archival quality paper.

Set in Dante MT 11/13.5

CONTENTS

INTRODUCTION

LATE in the evening on the first day of February 1932, Forrest Reid was writing a letter to his young protégé Stephen Gilbert about an outline for a new novel.[1] It was to be called *Sea Magic: An Episode*, the story of an ageing novelist who encounters the son he never knew existed. Reid had planned all fifteen chapters, but was anxious to secure Gilbert's endorsement before proceeding any further. "Remember," he wrote, "if you don't like the thing I won't go on with it." Reid was profoundly in love with Gilbert, and this was to be his form of literary collaboration, a figurative consummation of their relationship. He had already settled on a distinctive narrative style:

> I've an idea of making the first two chapters overlap, using the same incidents & parts of the same dialogue, but telling it first from Henry Linton—the father's point of view, & secondly through Gilbert Westby. It's only a technical trick of course, but if workable it might be rather good.

When put into practice, this "technical trick" proved to be a masterstroke. The novel, when it finally appeared in 1934, was called *Brian Westby*.

If any of Reid's books are likely to confirm his status as the greatest Ulster novelist, *Brian Westby* must be a strong candidate. It is his most realistic work, devoid of the supernatural elements that characterize his *oeuvre*. The novel makes a virtue of simplicity; the events take place over the course of no more than a fortnight, there are only three principal characters, and the location is confined to the small Northern Irish coastal town of Ballycastle in which the novelist Martin Linton is temporarily staying for a period of convalescence. As an author who is feeling "the drying up of his creative faculty," Linton is now seemingly indifferent to his own existence; at the time of his illness he "hadn't particularly wanted to die, but neither had he particularly wanted to live." But when he meets the

vii

eighteen-year-old Brian Westby his sense of purpose is renewed, and he soon discovers that the young man is his biological son from his failed marriage with Stella. Over the days that follow their friendship develops and Linton comes to the realization that he "cannot live without him." He attempts to persuade his son to join him when he leaves Ballycastle, and ultimately Brian finds himself torn between a sense of loyalty to his mother and a newfound affiliation for his father, a conflict that leads directly to the novel's powerful *dénouement*.

Reid met Stephen Gilbert at the Belmont Tennis Club in Belfast in 1931. As a young man with literary aspirations, Gilbert was only too happy to accept the older writer as his mentor. It was due to Reid's guidance and support that Gilbert was eventually able to thrive as a successful novelist in his own right, producing works such as *The Landslide* (1943), *Bombardier* (1944), *Monkeyface* (1948), and *The Burnaby Experiments* (1952). His last published novel, *Ratman's Notebooks* (1968), proved to be his most commercially successful. This grisly story of a man who trains rats to commit violent acts on his behalf was subsequently filmed as *Willard* in 1971 by director Daniel Mann.

Brian Westby is a fictionalized account of the early days of Reid's association with Gilbert, in which the two friends are recast as father and son. The tendency to read any given text from the perspective of the author's biography can be misleading, but in the case of *Brian Westby* there are strong grounds for doing so. Writing in 1977, Gilbert recalled the peculiar genesis of the novel:

> I got to know Forrest when he had just finished *Uncle Stephen*. After he sent it to Fabers there was a period when he had nothing to write about and was therefore very irritable. He told me that he wanted to use me as a character in his next book. I objected, threatened that if he did, I would have no more to do with him. Months went by and it seemed that I had stopped him writing. At last he came up with a plot, which he felt I might accept. It was the plot of *Brian Westby*, though the ending was still uncertain. Reluctantly I agreed to let him go on. So he began to write. Each chapter, when the first draft was completed, was submitted to me. Would I have acted as Brian had been made to act? If I said, "Yes," the chapter

was passed. If I said, "No," I had to explain how I would have acted and the chapter was re-written.[2]

Having surrendered all editorial control to his protégé, Reid was forced to comply when Gilbert demanded that he completely rewrite the ending.[3] It is reasonable to suppose that the titular character's name was changed from Gilbert to Brian at his behest, presumably to minimize the possibility of biographical identification.[4] The novel may be dedicated to him, but it opens with a disclaimer: "All the characters and incidents in this novel are imaginary."[5] This was no doubt also at the insistence of Gilbert, and it is as disingenuous as the entirely fabricated epigraph to the novel by "Yakovnin."[6]

Gilbert's ambivalence about his mentor's affections might explain his conspicuous absence from Reid's second autobiography *Private Road* (1940). In terms of its chronological arrangement, Chapter XIX is the point at which we might expect an account of their relationship, but instead there appears an incongruous poem called "The Pear Tree" about two friends and Reid's sheepdog Roger.[7] That this poem is an oblique allusion to Gilbert is made apparent by the fact that Reid had previously sent it to him in handwritten form (see Appendix III).[8] The "S.G." that appears in parentheses after the title is not included in the published version, thus concealing the identity of the poem's subject. The conclusion must be that Gilbert wanted to distance himself from his mentor's work as much as possible. Evidence for this appears in a letter from Reid, written at the time he was working on *Private Road*, in which he discusses his friend Robin Perry's plan for a semi-autobiographical story:

> The characters are a ghost, a mother (R's), a boy (R), another boy (evidently not very clear since he wants assistance with him), and a writer whom the boy comes to see (described as myself). Unlike you, I did not cry out that this last must be ommited [*sic*], and so nip a masterpiece in the bud.[9]

There can be little doubt that the inclusion of "The Pear Tree" in

Reid's book was a gesture to Gilbert, a compromise that the young man was prepared to accept.

A recurring feature of Reid's biography is the need to assume a paternal role, one evidently fulfilled in part by his mentorship of Gilbert. Anne Thirlwell connects this compulsion to the death of his father, Robert Reid, when Forrest was only five years old.[10] He was left in the care of his mother Frances who apparently lacked interest in his welfare. It is tempting to see Frances Reid reflected in the characterization of Stella, Brian Westby's emotionally cold and fervently Christian mother. Whatever the psychological basis, it is clear that Reid's paternal feelings for Gilbert are reified in the novel through the father-son relationship. Even before Linton realizes the truth, he is indulging in private fantasies of Brian as his son:

> Linton watched him with the oddest emotion of pride and affection. Odd, because of course it was absurd—just as if the boy belonged to him.... Then he thought:—If only he *did* belong to me; if only he *was* my son—how different everything would be! And instantly he knew that even to imagine this, even to pretend it, was a happiness.

The sentiment is anticipated in the protective tone of Reid's early letters to Gilbert. He refers to himself as Gilbert's "affectionate uncle" and addresses him as "my own dear boy."[11] Reid channelled these parental instincts into an outline for a short story called "The Purple Vulture" (1936) about a boy who is saved from his desperately unhappy existence at an orphanage by an escaped convict.[12] The two leave for Donegal, the location of Reid and Gilbert's holidays together, and the convict adopts the boy as his own. The story was never completed, but the details are revealing nonetheless.

After the outbreak of war, Gilbert wrote to Reid from his army billet. He was depressed and suffering from acute homesickness.[13] That the two men were on intimate terms is confirmed by the emotional candour of these letters. At one point, Gilbert expresses his feelings through an image of childhood regression: "I would like to look out of my window at Tildarg, as I used to do in the morning, pretending to be asleep if Daddy came in to get me up,

Photograph of Stephen Gilbert taken by Forrest Reid (Special Collections, Queen's University Belfast, MS44/7/5/1).

and watch the tree at the end of the garden in the field beyond the greenhouse."¹⁴ In another letter, Gilbert invokes *Brian Westby* in order to explain the degeneration of his physical and psychological well-being: "Do you remember what Alan Monkhouse said about B.W.—it annoyed you a great deal. I at any rate imagine that if he saw me now I would be the development of what he saw in B.W."¹⁵ This is a reference to Monkhouse's review of the novel for the *Manchester Guardian,* in which he described the character of Brian as "a bit of a lout."¹⁶ Reid's reaction confirms that, from his perspective at least, Brian had become indistinguishable from his real life counterpart.

Photograph of Stephen Gilbert, Forrest Reid, Roger and Barker at "Tildarg," the Gilbert family home, in October 1933 (Special Collections, Queen's University Belfast, MS44/7/4).

In this context, the fictive reconfiguration of their relationship as father and son in *Brian Westby* makes perfect sense. Reid displayed all the qualities of a loving parent: he sought to nurture Gilbert's talent, to comfort him in his distress, to defend him against criticism. Furthermore, he attempted to secure a publisher for Gilbert's first novel *The Assailants* (1936) which, in spite of its merits, was unfortunately overlooked. When Gilbert's second novel *The Landslide* was published in 1943, it was dedicated to Reid "gratefully and affectionately … by his pupil."[17] The phrasing of this dedication is particularly apt. For Reid, an inherent aspect of paternal duty was pedagogical, which explains the reference to a classical precedent when Linton first meets Brian and attempts to find a way to stimulate conversation:

> One thing was certain, they had talked enough about Martin Linton. But how to get his young friend to talk about himself? Protruding from his jacket pocket was a roll of manuscript which he had hastily thrust there on their first exchange of words. This seemed a good opening:—one which Sokrates had employed successfully on a summer morning long ago with the youthful and guileless Phaidros.

Given Reid's romanticized view of Athenian culture, the analogy is unsurprising. Reid was determined that Gilbert should realize his literary potential, and there is little doubt that in this respect his mentorship was a success.

The manuscript that Brian is so eager to conceal is the first few chapters of his novel *Nature Suppressed*. His reluctance to discuss the story with Linton is due to an earlier humiliation at the hands of his sister Claire, who finds the document in his bedroom and reads it without his permission. During an altercation over breakfast, she refers tauntingly to "the bit where Edna's father goes mad and attacks her with a poker," which gives us some idea of the melodramatic nature of the story. Later, we learn more details. Edna Kearney wishes to marry her fiancé Eric Grey, but is terrified of the possibility that their children might inherit the psychopathic insanity of her father. When Brian reads his work aloud to Linton, the sense of anticlimax is inevitable:

> What he had written was positively ugly and definitely charmless. And as he watched him sitting there, above the sea, with the grey rocks and heather all around him, and his fair hair bowed over his manuscript, Linton marvelled at the contrast between the creator and his creation. … Linton felt at the same time sorry and impa-

tient, touched and disappointed. And what, when the time came for criticism, could he possibly find to say?

This account is all the more remarkable given that Gilbert had actually been writing a novel called *Nature Suppressed*, the manuscript of which still survives in the archives at Queen's University, Belfast (see Appendix II).[18] The story and characters are virtually identical, although the fragment included in Chapter VII of *Brian Westby* is Reid's invention. He effectively captures the naïve and stilted prose of the young writer without having recourse to direct quotation. Nonetheless, Gilbert's mixed feelings about the publication of *Brian Westby* can be more easily appreciated in the light of Linton's damning verdict.

It is instructive to consider Reid's patronage of Gilbert in the context of his prior association with Kenneth Hamilton (1904-1927). When Reid befriended the Hamilton family in 1916, it was the youngest child Kenneth who became his "constant companion."[19] The tender paternal love that Reid felt for the twelve-year-old boy emerges again and again in his correspondence and in an essay entitled "Kenneth" published in his book *Retrospective Adventures* (1940).[20] Some critics have made the mistake of assuming that Reid's friendships with boys, and his obvious interest in adolescence as a theme for his novels, is indicative of pederasty. Given that there is not a shred of evidence to support this idea, it cannot be taken seriously. As Kenneth's sister Grace later explained, Reid's relationship with her brother was "parental, in an ideal sense, as few fathers have the time to give all the love and attention to their sons, that Forrest gave to Kenneth."[21]

There was also an educational dimension to their friendship. With Reid's guidance, Hamilton was able to produce nine volumes of *Kenneth's Magazine* from 1917 to 1919 with Reid acting as "assistant editor." Each handwritten volume contains a combination of poetry, short stories, illustrations and tongue-in-cheek editorial commentary. Reid's desire to act as tutor to the boy is evident in Hamilton's "An Essay on Mr Forrest Reid":

Mr Reid draws a distinct line between a poet like Shakespeare &

one like Pope. Shakespeare was a poet. Pope was not. Shakespeare
could write poetry. Pope could not. True, Pope was poet laureate
to Queen Anne, but Mr Reid looks at this point sensibly. Poet laure-
ates are not always the best poets. Look at William Butler Yeats. Is
there any better poet living?[22]

That Hamilton adored Reid is evident from every page of *Kenneth's
Magazine*, and is confirmed by the testimony of his sister Grace. For
Hamilton, Reid was not only a best friend, but also an intellectual
role model. "Birth brought him good brains & showed him how
to use them," Hamilton writes. "He is studious but by no means
a 'swot.'"

True to form, Reid tried to protect Hamilton against the
bullying he was experiencing at school and later attempted to find
him employment. After a number of false starts, Hamilton eventually enlisted with the Merchant Service, and the young cadet
spent two years at sea. According to Brian Taylor, Reid's last letter
to Hamilton was sent back unopened with the word "deceased"
stamped onto the envelope, and a Christmas pudding was returned
"alive with maggots."[23]

Having lost his surrogate child, it is no surprise that when Gilbert emerged onto the scene Reid was eager to renew his role as
mentor and protector. But whereas the extant documents relating
to Hamilton reveal a relationship approximating a loving father
and a devoted son, those pertaining to Gilbert are markedly different in emphasis. An excerpt from one of Reid's letters will serve to
demonstrate the point:

> I can't help it, Stephen dear, if I seem horribly soppy, but the fact is
> that I would rather you loved me a little than anything else in the
> world . . . I am writing this in a storm of wind & rain, & somehow
> I feel you very close to me. I love you. I love you in three different
> ways & yet they are all mixed up together. I wish you were here
> now.[24]

Unlike Hamilton, Gilbert was a fully-grown man, and perhaps in-
evitably the spectre of sexual desire had intruded to undermine
Reid's paternal idealizations. Had Gilbert been younger, they might

have enjoyed the mutually beneficial relationship of mentor and
protégé. As it transpired, Reid's emotions were closer akin to that
of a tempestuous, unrequited love.

The extent of Reid's infatuation is made clear in the surviving
correspondence. That Gilbert had tried to dissuade his mentor
from expressing himself so freely is evident from Reid's letter
dated 28 May 1932: "you are very dear to me, and though I know
you don't like me to say so, it is very hard for me sometimes not
to say so. I suppose you think I don't try, but I do, and it *is* hard."[25]
On Boxing Day of that year, Reid expresses his regret at not being
able to control his emotions: "Saying good-bye was rather mixed
up, wasn't it? I'm sure you thought I was very silly . . . I very nearly
wept, which was perfectly idiotic. I apologize. What it would be
like if I was really saying goodbye to you I don't know."[26] Ten days
later we have the following: "I have been thinking about you—
heaps & heaps. Stephen, dear, I do love you. I wonder if you will
ever love anybody like this. If you do, you'll forgive your poor old
F.R."

Reid was not forgiven. "Time and again I wished he would
take himself out of my life," Gilbert wrote in 1977. "I felt bitterly
that he had stolen my youth. I knew that he had given me a great
deal in exchange. I carry these gifts with me yet. And for good or
bad he influenced my writing. For good or bad . . ."[27] After Reid's
death, Gilbert wrote *The Burnaby Experiments* as a form of revenge.
In the novel, the young Marcus Brownlow is lured away from his
parents' home by an eccentric old millionaire, John Burnaby, who
persuades him to stay with him at his house in Donegal so that he
can teach him the secrets of psychic translocation. Burnaby is a
caricature of Reid and, like most caricatures, is far from flattering:

> It was not that Mr. Burnaby bored him—though he did bore him
> sometimes when he talked about Greek ideas of love, or morality,
> or the identity of beauty and goodness: but Marcus was seeing too
> much of Mr. Burnaby. He felt often as if Mr. Burnaby were devour-
> ing him mentally, trying to destroy his individuality, and convert
> him into a reflection of himself.[28]

E. M. Forster, a long-standing friend of Reid, was not impressed by Gilbert's posthumous attack. On 18 December 1955 he wrote to Knox Cunningham about this "disgraceful novel":

> *What* a monument of ungenerosity and ingratitude!—having, as its crowning treachery, his employment of the literary powers Forrest developed in him for the purpose of denigrating Forrest ... I fancy though that his conduct is the result of bad breeding rather than of a bad heart, and that he does not really realise how he has behaved.[29]

Yet Gilbert's letters to Reid also appear to reveal a degree of affection and dependency on the older man's support, particularly during the Second World War when Gilbert was suffering from depression. Theirs was a fascinating relationship and, in spite of their difficulties, they remained close friends until Reid's death in 1947.

It is a truism that unrequited love can produce great art. One thinks of Maud Gonne's influence on the work of W. B. Yeats, Dante's obsession for Beatrice Portinari, or Sir Philip Sidney's thwarted desire for Penelope Rich that inspired his masterful sonnet sequence "Astrophil and Stella." As we have seen, *Brian Westby* differs from these examples insofar as Reid represents his love indirectly by reimagining himself as Gilbert's father. Of course, it could feasibly be argued that this is a device through which Reid is able to indulge in the homoerotic objectification of a beautiful youth without fear of censure. Take, for example, the moment when Linton happens upon a church in the countryside around Ballycastle and decides to go inside. To his surprise, he sees Brian and his sister Claire amongst the congregation:

> Brian, all unconscious of the late arrival, was listening to the sermon, and Linton watched him listening. A thin arrow of sunlight touched the boy's loose fair hair, which was fine, like spun flax, with threads of gold or sunshine in it. And perhaps it was this, perhaps it was the story of Jacob's vision, or perhaps it was everything combined, which coloured Linton's imagination, so that presently it seemed to him that he was looking at an angel.

There is a distinctly Petrarchan quality to this passage, with its celestial overtones and emphasis on Brian's golden hair. Likewise, it is difficult to deny the voyeuristic potential of Reid's description of Brian as he bathes:

> Linton watched his strong young body gliding through the clear green water—first downward, and then in a wide upward curve that brought him to the surface. He shook the water from his yellow hair; his blue eyes were dark and bright with pleasure[.]

Such imagery draws on the tradition of the idealized ephebe, the paradigm of male beauty originating in Greek antiquity. This is made explicit when Linton first sees Brian, and is immediately reminded of "the young horsemen on the Parthenon frieze.... It was as if he had discovered a little bit of that ancient world in the midst of the world to-day."

That the depiction of Brian can so feasibly lend itself to an incestuous interpretation has resulted in accusations of dishonesty on Reid's part. In an essay on *Brian Westby* by the novelist John Mc-Gahern, the father-son plot element is construed as no more than subterfuge, a device to "veil the paedophilic nature of Linton's love."[30] Even if we were to accept the view that Linton's desire is erotic in nature, the use of the word "paedophilic" to describe the love of one adult male for another is somewhat bizarre. Admittedly, McGahern's essay dates from 1977 and to a degree reflects the intolerance of the time. Homosexual conduct between men was only decriminalized in Northern Ireland in 1982, and the age of consent was not reduced to sixteen until 2008. However, even in this context the choice of word does not reflect well on McGahern; the casual yoking of paedophilia and homosexuality has long been a tactic of those wishing to denigrate gay love.

In spite of these reservations, McGahern was a great champion of Reid. He attempted to persuade publishers to reissue *Brian Westby* in the 1960s and again in the 1970s, but was unsuccessful. It is rather Peter Coveney, author of *Poor Monkey: The Child in Literature* (1957), who is most hostile to Reid's supposed "dishonesty" in his depiction of youth. He rails against the "concealed eroticism" of Reid's novels, "scenes where sexuality is thinly veiled by recourse to naturalism or a kind of Renaissance paganism."[31] With regard to

Photograph of Stephen Gilbert taken by Forrest Reid (Special Collections, Queen's University Belfast, MS44/7/1).

Brian Westby he complains that Reid does not employ "the language of a father about his son, but of a lover and his loved one."[32] This is a valid reading. Given that Brian is based wholly on Reid's beloved Gilbert, there was always the danger that *storge* and *eros* might overlap in his portrayal. That said, Coveney's true objection emerges soon enough: "If we really are to have homosexuality treated in the novel, better the directness of Mann's *Death in Venice*, or Gide's *The Coiners*."[33] Gay love, then, should not be dignified by deniability. Much better that it should be overt and thereby readily detected.

But the cynicism articulated by the likes of McGahern and Coveney does a disservice to Reid's artistry. For Linton, Brian comes to represent a fundamental aspect of himself that he has lost. Before their meeting, Linton's "morbid state of mind" has left him feeling as though there is "nothing to live for." "Happiness," he concludes, "is only made by affection. Nothing else in the long run matters." In his review of *Brian Westby*, Monkhouse deems it "a curious detail that the father, a distinguished author, proposes literary collaboration with the son, who appears to be capable of nothing but rubbish."[34] But considering Linton's need to be appreciated and to be loved, his motives are intelligible.[35] Brian's physical beauty further enables Linton's idealization. Linton, like Reid, subscribes to the Platonic understanding of *eros*; that is to say, a form of desire that seeks transcendental beauty whilst not necessarily entailing the satisfaction of sexual desire. This is a consistent leitmotif in Reid's work. In his very first novel *The Kingdom of Twilight* (1904), Reid evokes "the beauty of Plato's ideal world . . . so far exalted above mere physical, sensual attractiveness."[36] Critics who refuse to take Reid's philosophy at face value, who insist on dishonesty where none exists, will ultimately find *Brian Westby* a hollow experience. Such a reading necessitates the complete repudiation of the work's philosophical core. In other words, to see Linton as a predatory voyeur renders the novel incoherent.[37]

Reid was not unaware that his representation of Brian might be interpreted in this way. In a letter to Gilbert dated 22 May 1932, Reid writes of the advice he has received from his friend, the poet Walter de la Mare:

He seems to think the psychology was bound to be all right, but then he believes that *all* love is essentially the same—mother's and father's and lover's and friend's—and that the differences in its external manifestations are unimportant and superficial. At any rate it was encouraging.

This was an important matter for Reid, whose distrust of eroticism verged on the puritanical. This is exemplified in a letter to André Raffalovich in which Reid hints at having composed homoerotic love poetry in his younger days: "I should never dream of publishing them. It is possible to write a poem to a friend, but it must not be a love poem. Even the faintest tinge of eroticism in such a thing would strike me as a deplorable error in taste; & bad taste is always ugly."[38]

Reid's own poems to Gilbert likewise eschew the erotic in favour of a romanticized elevation of the beloved. Take the following stanza from a poem written for Gilbert's birthday in 1935:

> Dearest boy of the spring-time,
> Stephen with hair of sunlight
> And eyes like the sky,
> What can I send with my love song?
> I have nothing to send you:—
> Nothing but love.[39]

Or the following, from a poem simply entitled "S.G.":

> Stephen, to me you have brought all
> That sunshine and the morning bring
> When dew is shining on the grass
> And woods beat with the heart of spring.[40]

The simplicity of the language conveys a purity of emotion and, irrespective of the very real possibility of sublimated eroticism, it is a panegyric to the Platonic ideal that Reid espoused throughout his work. In these lines, Gilbert embodies what Forster called the "indwelling power" of nature.[41] Little wonder, then, that Linton sees Brian as constituting "a part of his surroundings—of the sun-bleached sand-dunes, the deserted shore, the blue tumbling waves, the open sky . . . as if something of the impersonal beauty of sea and sky and shore had passed into him and become human." Brian, then, is the actualization of Reid's animistic creed.

In Gilbert's aborted novel *Nature Suppressed*, Eric Best takes Edna Kearney to Dundonald Cemetery in East Belfast to visit her father's grave. His true motive is to find somewhere sufficiently quiet in order to propose. The plan fails. Much to their mutual irritation the graveyard is overcrowded, and they are forced to leave. Dundonald Cemetery is the final resting place of Forrest Reid, and it seems somehow appropriate that it is also the scene of Stephen Gilbert's first literary effort and, moreover, that it tells a tale of thwarted love. But if Reid's desire for his protégé was the source of much personal agony, *Brian Westby* is the consolation. It is a testament to Reid's unique capabilities as a writer. It is a declaration of faith in the Hellenistic ideals of beauty, truth, and goodness. Above all, it is a profound and important work of art.

ANDREW DOYLE

July 28, 2013

NOTES

1   Letter from Reid to Gilbert dated 1 February 1932 (Special Collections, Queen's University Belfast, MS45/1/14/5). See Appendix I.

2   Stephen Gilbert, "A Successful Man," *Threshold* 28 (Spring 1977), pp. 104-114. See p. 110.

3   The original ending of *Brian Westby* no longer survives, as Reid tended to dispose of early drafts. In the case of his first published novel, *The Kingdom of Twilight* (1904), he was so dissatisfied with the work that he actively sought to destroy every copy that he could find. It is partly due to Reid's antics that the book is now such a rarity.

4   In early drafts of *Brian Westby* held by Belfast City Library and the McClay Library at Queen's University (Special Collections, MS44/2/14/1) the character is called "Gilbert." In both cases many of these have been scored through by Reid and emended to "Brian."

5   In a letter to Gilbert dated 28 May 1932, Reid explains that the disclaimer was the idea of the poet and novelist Walter de la Mare: "Wal-

ter suggested an evasion of the publication difficulties in Linton's story. A note saying:—"all the characters in this book except one are completely imaginary." He says Linton doesn't count, because an author can't help putting his own thoughts & feelings into a book" (Special Collections, Queen's University Belfast, MS45/1/14/9).

6   "Yakovnin" is almost certainly a reference to a minor character from Sergey Aksakov's *A Russian Schoolboy* (1917). See Brian Taylor, *The Green Avenue: The Life and Writings of Forrest Reid, 1875-1947* (Cambridge: Cambridge University Press, 1980), p. 157. See also Michael Matthew Kaylor, *Arch-Priest of a Minor Cult: A Study of Forrest Reid*, published as vol. II of *The Tom Barber Trilogy* (Kansas City: Valancourt, 2011), pp. 353-358.

7   Forrest Reid, *Private Road* (London, Faber and Faber, 1940), pp. 237-238. In truth, Roger was not Reid's dog at all. As he recounts: "though he spent his days with me he was not, strictly speaking, my dog, and returned at night to his owners. Sometimes he returned reluctantly, but after all I couldn't very well take complete possession of him, and it didn't really much matter whether he slept in their house or mine. With Roger therefore it was a case of friendship, and this friendship was established without any preliminary advances on my part ... he was the cleverest dog I have ever known." Ibid., p. 111.

8   Forrest Reid, "The Pear Tree," undated manuscript poem (Special Collections, Queen's University Belfast, MS45/1/14/72).

9   Letter from Reid to Gilbert dated 6 October 1939 (Special Collections, Queen's University Belfast, MS45/1/14/46). *Private Road* was written between January and December of that year. The reference to "a boy, and a dog, and a tree" in the final line of "The Pear Tree" was deleted in the published version.

10 Angela Thirlwell, "Child's-eye View: The Autobiographies of Forrest Reid," *Retrospective Adventures—Forrest Reid: Author and Collector* (Aldershot: Scolar Press, 1998), pp. 17-23. See p. 19.

11 Letters from Reid to Gilbert dated 24 December 1931, 12 August 1931, and 5 January 1933 (Special Collections, Queen's University Belfast, MS45/1/14, items 4, 2, and 12 respectively).

12 Forrest Reid, notes for "The Purple Vulture" (Special Collections, Queen's University Belfast, MS44/3/11).

13 Letters from this period from Walter de la Mare show him consoling Reid over his continued anxiety for his protégé. One letter, dated 18 November 1940, reads: "I wish you could have sent better news of Stephen. It is astonishing to what degrees of physical and mental strain one can manage to survive—without apparent trouble. But this direct

effect on Stephen's memory you refer to is disquieting, this attack on what is called the unconscious. I do hope his leave has been a real rest" (Special Collections, Queen's University Belfast, MS44/1/33/246). See also the letter dated 24 March 1941: "I wish indeed you had better news of Stephen. I am not of course surprised at his general despondency. It breathes up occasionally in my mind without the justification he has for it; but I wish it were otherwise" (Special Collections, Queen's University Belfast, MS44/1/33/255).

14 Letter from Gilbert to Reid dated 22 December 1940 (Special Collections, Queen's University Belfast, MS44/1/47/3). "Tildarg" was a property in Knock, East Belfast, where Gilbert lived until the death of his father.

15 Letter from Gilbert to Reid dated 22 December 1940 (Special Collections, Queen's University Belfast, MS44/1/47/3).

16 Alan Monkhouse, "Father and Son," *Manchester Guardian* (2 March 1934).

17 Stephen Gilbert, *The Landslide* (London: Faber and Faber, 1943).

18 Stephen Gilbert, *Nature Suppressed*, undated typescript (Special Collections, Queen's University Belfast, MS45/2/16). The typescript was presumably in the possession of Reid; the words "Stephen's novel" appear at the top of the first page in Reid's handwriting.

19 Forrest Reid, *Retrospective Adventures* (London: Faber & Faber, 1940), p. 212.

20 Ibid., pp. 207-212.

21 Quoted in Robin Bryans, *Let the Petals Fall: An Autobiographical Sequel* (London: Honeyford Press, 1993), p. 351.

22 Kenneth Hamilton, "An Essay on Mr Forrest Reid," *Kenneth's Magazine* vol. 4 (Special Collections, Queen's University Belfast, MS44/8/1-9). These opinions on the supremacy of Yeats and the relative merits of Pope and Shakespeare are echoed in *The Milk of Paradise: Some Thoughts on Poetry* (1946), the last of Reid's books to be published during his lifetime. Given Reid's educational instincts, it comes as no surprise to learn that this book was initially entitled *The Child's Guide to Poetry*.

23 Taylor, op. cit., p. 101.

24 Letter from Reid to Gilbert dated 16 August 1931 (Special Collections, Queen's University Belfast, MS45/1/14/3). Given Reid's affinity for the philosophical ideals of Greek antiquity, it is tempting to see his "three different ways" as an allusion to the concepts of *eros*, *philia*, and *agape*.

25 Letter from Reid to Gilbert dated 28 May 1932 (Special Collections, Queen's University Belfast, MS45/1/14/9).

26 Letter from Reid to Gilbert dated 26 December 1932 (Special Collections, Queen's University Belfast, MS45/1/14/10).

27 *Threshold*, op. cit., p. 106.

28 Stephen Gilbert, *The Burnaby Experiments* (Kansas City: Valancourt, 2012), p. 128.

29 Letter from E. M. Forster to Knox Cunningham dated 18 December 1955 (Public Record Office of Northern Ireland, Belfast, MIC/45/1).

30 John McGahern, "Brian Westby," *Threshold*, op. cit., pp. 37-50. See p. 44.

31 Peter Coveney, *Poor Monkey: The Child in Literature* (London: Rockliff, 1957), p. 226.

32 Ibid., p. 227.

33 Ibid., p. 228.

34 Monkhouse, op. cit.

35 In fact, Gilbert had refused an offer of collaboration from Reid. See letter from Reid to Knox Cunningham dated 14 October 1937: "I wish he would let me collaborate with him on his new book. Perhaps I'm wrong here too. He thinks that if it was a success I'd get all the credit for it. But constructive criticism *is* a kind of collaboration & not the best kind since it leads to compromise & you don't get the best of either writer—It's very difficult. I suppose I'd better not interfere. On the other hand if I don't and it's a flop it will be perfectly awful" (Public Record Office of Northern Ireland, Belfast, MIC/45/1).

36 Forrest Reid, *The Kingdom of Twilight* (London: T. Fisher Unwin, 1904), p. 134.

37 Such interpretations would be more convincingly applied to Francis King's novel *An Air That Kills* (1948), a deliberately eroticized variation on *Brian Westby*.

38 Letter from Reid to André Raffalovich dated 20 May 1920 (Special Collections, Queen's University Belfast, MS44/1/106B/5).

39 Forrest Reid, "For a Birthday," manuscript poem dated 22 July 1935 (Special Collections, Queen's University Belfast, MS45/1/14/23). See Appendix IV.

40 Forrest Reid, "S.G.," undated manuscript poem (Special Collections, Queen's University Belfast, MS45/1/14/73). See Appendix V.

41 "Address by E. M. Forster," *Forrest Reid Memorial: Addresses Delivered at the Unveiling of the Plaque at 13 Ormiston Crescent and Afterwards at the Luncheon* (Foxton: Burlington Press, 1952), pp. 3-6. See p. 4.

Acknowledgements

Much of my research has been based on material from the Forrest Reid and Stephen Gilbert collections at Queen's University, Belfast. I would like to thank Deirdre Wildy, Brenda Robinson, Diarmuid Kennedy, and the whole team at Special Collections. Thanks also to the staff at the Public Record Office of Northern Ireland, and to Catherine Morrow at Belfast City Library.

In addition, I owe debts of gratitude to the following people for their feedback and support: Tom Gilbert, Patricia Craig, Brian Taylor, Philip Doherty, Martin Gourlay, Dameon Garnett and James D. Jenkins at Valancourt Books.

BRIAN WESTBY

Note

All the characters and incidents
in this novel are imaginary. F.R.

TO

STEPHEN GILBERT

Part First

A CHANCE ENCOUNTER

*

*As in water face answereth to face, so the
heart of man to man.*   Proverbs.

Chapter I

LINTON

Martin Linton, after a restless wakeful night in which he had lain listening to the sea, and a more drowsy morning, came downstairs late. In the big bright empty hotel dining-room he breakfasted alone except for Susan, the young woman who waited on him, and Micky, an ancient smooth-haired fox-terrier, who during Susan's brief departure to fetch tea and toast had waddled in and taken up a position beside Linton's chair. Not very hopefully perhaps, for Micky was fat and clumsy and no good at working magics, and even if he had succeeded in making himself invisible he would still have been audible. As a matter of fact Susan's sharp eyes detected him at once. "Shoo! Get out of that!" she cried, setting down her tray and flapping a napkin.

Linton intervened. "It's all right," he murmured. "I like dogs."

Susan stopped flapping, though reluctantly. "He knows he's not allowed in here," she said. "He'll sit there waiting in the hall till your back's turned or your hands full of dishes, and then he'll slip past you and get under a table. There's a smell off him too. It's only last week he took away a lady's appetite."

"I haven't any appetite," Linton answered mildly, "and I don't object to his smell."

"Well, I'm sure!" Susan said.

But Micky divined a temporary truce and emerged from his shelter. He raised two tremulous paws in an attitude of prayer, watching intently Linton's every movement as he cut up his toast. Breakfast shared and finished, he followed him out into the hall and as far as the porch. It was friendship at first sight, though in the porch Micky stopped, and Linton himself only crossed the road, where he stood with his hands in his pockets, gazing out to sea. Micky hesitated; he even got up from his mat in the sun. If the walk was only to be as far as that! But Linton had begun to stroll on again, so he lay down, sighed, stretched his two white forepaws straight out, tucked his black muzzle down between them, and shut his eyes....

Linton took the path between the sunken tennis-grounds and the sea. He crossed a narrow wooden bridge spanning the mouth of a river and reached the golf-links, with the long sandy crescent of the beach stretching away on his left to a dark line of rocks beyond which rose the headlands. It was a nearly windless morning, yet big waves were rolling up and pounding on the yellow strand with a swirling backwash of foam and gravel. It was the same sound he had listened to last night, but this morning and in the sunshine it had a different meaning, not sad at all, though still lonely. Linton's pace slackened; he was even thinking of sitting down when a golf-ball flew by his ear and he realized he was walking along the fairway. He drew closer to the edge of the bank.

It had been his plan, made while shaving, to walk to the foot of Fair Head, but now he found he had underestimated the distance. He had thought of it as about two miles, whereas it must be nearer five. Strange that he should have made such a mistake, for when he had been here before, as a young man, this had been his favourite walk. And otherwise the place was just as he had pictured it. Pictured it six months ago in a nursing home in London, when Dr Cardan had advised him to take "a complete rest in some quiet spot by the sea". Instantly the spot had been there, like a vision in a crystal—the long stretch of beach, the wide expanse of grassy hummocks running inland, the dark steep cliffs—Ballycastle. It was odd, for in all the twenty years since he had last visited the place he did not suppose he had thought of it twice. Yet there it was.... And all through the spring and early summer, while he had pottered about the south coast of England in obedience to Dr Cardan's recommendation, the vision had haunted him. He had known that in the end he would yield to it: and now he had done so....

It was the second promise Dr Cardan had extracted from him,

and he had kept them both. The first had been more fantastic, very queer indeed. Dr Cardan had grumbled that Linton wasn't helping him, wasn't doing his share; and this had been true. Linton hadn't particularly wanted to die, but neither had he particularly wanted to live. The desire to live *had* been there—very strongly there—but after his operation it had vanished. He had no regrets, no fears, no wish to come back to former friends; he was just tired and content that it all should be ended. But it was this state of mind Dr Cardan found so discouraging. One night he had made an appeal, though not on grounds of sentiment. It had been rather in the half-impatient manner of a schoolboy extracting a promise from a chum. Would Linton do something for him? It wasn't a big thing: it was a very small thing in fact—merely not to let him down, to give him his word that he would hang on till the doctor's early morning visit.

Linton had smiled feebly, but given the promise. The doctor was watching him closely. "That's agreed then?" he said a little grimly. "You've given me your word that you'll still be alive when I come in the morning."

"Yes," said Linton, "that's agreed."

And the gaining of those few hours must have been of vital importance, for having gained them, straightway he had begun to recover. Now he was here to complete the recovery....

But not to write. He had never felt less like writing in his life. His writing days, he fancied, were over.... It was not a cheerful thought—especially when he remembered his last visit. He had then been writing *Hippolutos*, and it had been like some absorbing exciting adventure, filling all his mind, and even his dreams at night. *That* kind of thing could never happen again.... At least he thought not. He had returned to this place, not to try to renew a lost inspiration, but merely because it was quiet and pleasant—a place where nobody would know him, where he would be free from the inquiries of acquaintances, where he would not have to simulate a sociability he did not feel, where he would be quite alone. And apart from the few necessary words concerning his room he had not yet spoken to a soul except Susan and Micky,

though he had arrived two days ago. That was what he wanted. He
had taken the precaution not to sign the visitors' book, he was
practically safe; it was most unlikely he would come across anybody in this part of the world who knew him or would recognize
his appearance....

As for Stella—in whose company his earlier visit had been paid
—he was no more likely to meet her here than elsewhere. She
might, for all he knew, not even be living now in Ireland, though
it was to Ireland she had gone back after their separation. He had
never seen her again, never wanted to see her, the whole thing had
been—and for her more than for him perhaps—a tragic mistake....

Linton had found this out within a very few months of their
marriage, but it had not been till the publication of *Hippolutos* that
he had realized how hopeless the situation was, and actually two
further years had elapsed before the final crisis was reached. He
had known, of course, very soon after he had got to know *her*, that
their views of life were utterly different, but he could never have
guessed that she would come to regard *his* view with so intense
an aversion. Perhaps she had been slow in understanding, perhaps
the book really *had* been a revelation, perhaps unconsciously,
in trying to please her, he had given her a wrong impression of
himself. Anyhow, he now saw that secretly from the first she must
have believed she could influence him, bring him round to her
way of looking at things, ultimately to her faith; while on his part
he had never suspected the existence of that streak of fanaticism
in her which disappointment had brought to the surface. He did
not understand it now. Granted that his creed was not hers; why
need this have wrecked their life together? Yet it had. She could
not or would not accept him for what he was. They had ceased to
be companions and from day to day the estrangement between
them had deepened. True, there had been brief periods of reconciliation. But a reconciliation of dubious quality, born of mere
bodily promptings and leaving behind it a feeling of resentment
and humiliation. A third person might have detected nothing beyond a certain coldness. And indeed there *was* nothing for some
time except a gradual emotional and spiritual withdrawal. Stella
had a profound sense of duty, and in the superficial ordering of

their life all was as before. There were no scenes, no recrimina-
tions, no reproaches. His physical comforts were punctiliously attended to, and after her first and last expressed loathing of it she
had never again referred to his book. But this had meant that she
had never referred to his work at all. As if anyone could write in
such an atmosphere! One morning, as they faced each other across
the breakfast-table and carried on a perfunctory conversation for
form's sake, he had realized that they must either separate or he
would begin to hate her....

She had agreed at once. Indeed, without affection, what was
there to bind them together? They had no interests in common;
there were no children; and Linton at least had ceased to expect or
hope there ever would be. There was not even a financial problem
to be considered, for at her father's death she had been left comfortably off. What object, then, in carrying on a life which brought
out the worst qualities of both—in her a capacity for cold and sustained silence, in him an increasing nervous irritability? So he had
remained in London, while Stella had gone back to her mother's
house near Dungannon. From there, a year and a half later, had
come, like a thunderclap, the letter telling him she wished to marry
Westby. He had been genuinely amazed. Not because he had never
heard of Westby before—that, after all, was natural enough—but
because he could not, even with this letter staring at him, imagine
her suing for a divorce. Yet a divorce must be what she was after,
since still less could he imagine her contemplating bigamy. His
first thought, when he had emerged from a temporary stupefac-
tion, was that she must be extraordinarily fond of this Westby; his
second, that she was asking a good deal. She explained nothing,
told him nothing; he could even see that it had cost her a struggle
to write to him at all. As to the point of view which made such
a request possible—that, he knew, he should never comprehend.
Probably, with her idea of him, she considered the sacrifice of his
moral reputation to be of little importance. At any rate, he had
made it—had told her to bring her action, told her he would fake
sufficient evidence; and he had done so, done everything he could
to enable her to make good her case with the minimum amount of
unpleasant litigation. This accomplished, and before the case itself

could come on, he had set out for the East, where he had remained
for eighteen months. Doubtless, long before his return, she had
married Westby, but he had never inquired and had never learned
indirectly. Deliberately he had closed that painful chapter in his
life, and avoided anything that could remind him of it. In all the
years which had gone by since then he had heard nothing further
either from or of her. Stella had passed out of his existence, and
after a while pretty well out of his thoughts also, for it was only
because he was here, in this place where once he had been with
her, that a mild curiosity had begun now to stir in him as to what
might have happened. He even found himself wondering if she
had been happy with Westby. Perhaps it would have been more
appropriate to wonder if Westby had been happy with her. But
Linton's memories were far too dim and ancient to be accompanied by bitterness. He decided that it was most unlikely she should
have married the wrong man twice. And with the right man, and
with children....

Chapter II

LINTON

He strolled on in an apathetic mood, not really interested in
these thoughts, not interested in anything. It had been like
this ever since his illness. He had returned to life, only to find that
the drying up of his creative faculty had left him nothing to live
for. That should not be. It was wrong—all wrong. It showed that,
somehow, somewhere, his life had failed. And he knew, when he
looked deliberately back over the years, just where it had failed.
Happiness is only made by affection. Nothing else in the long run
matters. The responsibilities and anxieties that accompany affection are in themselves blessings. He had no responsibilities, no
anxieties, and he felt that he had lived long enough....

Linton felt it here and now—an odd accompaniment to a superficial sense of the charm of his surroundings. It was a morbid
state of mind, he told himself, and one which would disappear

if he could get back to work. As a matter of fact his work had never been sufficient for him, though certainly it had helped, had covered over and hidden away his loneliness. Yes, he *must* get back to it. But how? *Something* was wrong; *something* was gone; and that 'something'—whatever it was—appeared to be essential. At present an idea might occur to him at night, might even seem full of promise, but in the morning, as if touched by a secret blight, it would have wilted and faded till he wondered what he ever could have seen in it. Before his illness he had written nearly two-thirds of a book, and to-day the mere thought of completing it filled him with a sort of bored distaste. Possibly if he could find a subject sufficiently fantastic it might inspire him, but nothing else could, and subjects were not to be found by seeking for them, they sprang up mysteriously from some dark region of subconsciousness into the world of dreaming. Those frail, fugitive ideas that had visited him had perished because they had no root in his emotional life, were wandering seedlings of fancy, too weak to come to flower and fruit.... He supposed he had written himself out. It was an ugly, unpleasant phrase, but the fact was less pleasant still.... And through all he had the sense of a stream of beauty flowing endlessly by him, a beauty he was powerless to arrest, yet which, unless he could grasp and perpetuate some moment of it, would be lost for ever....

Beauty could be wasted or betrayed or shared.... The beauty of that fair-haired boy, for instance, sitting with his head bowed over his manuscript in a hollow he had chosen between the sand-dunes and the sea—it was there now only because he, Linton, was there, and after he had passed it would be gone. For there was no such thing as beauty apart from a human interpretation of it. The beauty Linton saw in that seated figure was relative to himself. For those seagulls it did not exist; for the next person who went by it might not exist: and it was the feeling it aroused in him which he was no longer able to express. It was not that his imagination and power of observation were dead. He knew it was not that. But through some failure of creative energy, some spiritual or mental disintegration, the broken fragments would no longer coalesce....

The boy lifted his head and looked at him absently; then bent

down once more over his work. A book lay unopened on the thin
dry grass beside him. Linton recognized its cover and paused, but
the boy did not look up again, and after a brief hesitation Linton
passed on.

He walked more slowly now. His whole impression had been
spread over three minutes perhaps, and yet he felt that something
strange had happened. Doubtless this feeling would pass as quickly
as the rest, but for the moment it was like an awakening. The
sound of the waves was intensified; the salt smell of the sea was
fresher, keener; the sun warmer; the whiteness of the seagulls and
the greenness of the grass were more vividly white and green. And
everything was closer to him—had acquired a new value. He
stopped to watch the gulls searching for food among the pools and
seaweed left by the retreating tide. Their harsh voracious cries had
now a naked discordant music. The whole scene had acquired an
interest. Yes, it was that. The brown, ribbed sand was wet and firm,
and he could make out a line of footprints between the water's
edge and the bleached looser sand under the hollow where the boy
was writing....

He had been so absorbed in his writing that he had stared Linton
in the face without really being conscious of him. He had been in
another world, and Linton wondered what that world was like. It
must be, he thought, his first work which had held him so spell-
bound, for he could not be more than seventeen or eighteen....

It seemed a strange coincidence that the book lying beside him
should be Linton's own first novel, though of course he had been a
good deal older than that boy when he had written it. Still, it was a
definitely juvenile performance, and the greater part of it was bad.
He cut at a thistle with his stick. He felt an absurd desire to return
and tell the boy not to read it, to read one of his later books instead.

He stopped, drew a deep breath into his lungs, and sat down
on the rough stone wall facing the road under the cliffs. *Should* he
go back? What could he say if he did? You can't simply rush up
to people and say, "Look here! I wrote that novel you're reading.
Wouldn't you like to talk to me?" Particularly when you've already
determined to keep your identity a secret, and when you've no
grounds for supposing the person *is* reading your novel, hasn't

given it up as a bad job after the first chapter. Nevertheless Linton got down from the wall. These doubts and diffidences were absurd at his age. Three minutes conversation would either destroy for ever or confirm the impression he had received, and at the worst could commit him to nothing more than a future nodding acquaintance....

He began slowly to retrace his steps, and when he came once more within sight of the hollow the boy raised his head, and Linton imagined there was a faint recognition in his eyes. He himself immediately halted and half turned round, as though to admire the long curving sweep of shore and sea. A silent dialogue began to whisper and murmur within him, at the end of which he again glanced at the boy, and this time a strange thing really did happen. For his first impression, the corporeal impression, vanished. The boy's eyes were fixed on him, and it was as if a spirit—happy, not unfriendly, but shy and a little surprised and curious—were looking straight out at him through their unclouded blueness. Linton had an odd thrill, as from something hoped for, hardly expected, and then suddenly and beautifully found. It *was* there—what he had half imagined, half divined—his instinct, his vision, had been true after all.

He said good-morning and the boy said good-morning—two words, but sufficient. Linton had now heard his voice, and it fitted in with all the rest.

After those first words, which sounded somehow not conventional, but quite sincere, the surprise vanished from the boy's face, though the shyness remained. Linton, for that matter, felt shy himself. Also he felt an impulse to pass on his way, as if just this were enough, and by prolonging the encounter he would risk spoiling it. It was only by an effort of will that he held his ground. He pointed with his stick to the book lying in the grass. "How do you like it?" he asked. "Or haven't you tried it yet?"

The boy looked at him and then down at the book with a quick raising and lowering of his eyebrows. The trick was unconscious, and unexpectedly at variance with his accent and manner, which pointed unmistakably to an English public school. But English boys rarely have this mobility of feature, and Linton decided that probably he was Irish. "Yes, I've tried it," the boy said. "I'm reading it for the second time."

They both now were gazing at the book, and Linton even gave it a tentative push with his stick, as though it were some dubious geological or botanical specimen. "I suppose that means you do like it," he said. "On a first reading, anyway."

"Yes," the boy answered, and after a moment asked, "Don't you?"

Linton shook his head. But not wishing to give the impression of being a superior person, he immediately qualified his dissent. "I don't like it as much as I once did," he said. "I think it's the kind of book you grow out of."

All this time they had been standing, for the boy had risen to his feet when Linton had first spoken to him. He now murmured, dropping his voice in a momentary return of shyness, "Won't you sit down?"

Linton smiled. He hadn't in the least expected this invitation, which seemed to him extremely gracious. It had been given, of course, chiefly out of politeness; but still the fact that it had been given at all might in a measure be regarded as a response to his own friendliness. They sat down side by side, and the boy asked him, "Don't you like any of Martin Linton's books?"

It was a question Martin Linton had been asking himself only that morning, so he was able to answer it at once. "Yes, I like two of them;—the two last. And I still like parts of *Hippolutos*, which is one of the earliest." After this he was silent, and remained so until he realized that he must have been looking for a long time at his equally silent companion. He hastened to complete his meditation aloud. "Do you know what might be an interesting experiment? I expect it was suggested to me because you've got hold of the first book of all—one he afterwards tried to suppress—I think it might be interesting to read the books in the order in which he wrote them. In that first story, you see, he's only feeling his way—pretty blindly too—yet there *is* something, even in it, which he's trying to express. It's not exactly a meaning, or an idea, or a message: at least it's not quite any of these, though in a way it's all three. I don't know what to call it; but it's there, and with each book it ought to become clearer. Mind you, I don't say it *does*. I should have to read the books over again myself to be sure of that. Nobody can do more than feel his way till he's acquired a method, learned his job, so to speak; and Linton was uncommonly slow in learning his. Besides, he often chose the wrong kind of subject; and in the beginning the writing itself was often bad. Still, after a fashion the books do fit together. I mean, he's got an ideal; and each of his books is an attempt to express it. So far as it *is* his book, that is to say, for the subject sometimes won't allow it to be. That's what I meant when I said he chose the wrong subjects. There's only the faintest glimmer of what he's really after in op. one, for instance; and in none even of the latest books, perhaps, is it there all the time. If he *could* bring it off, *could* produce it naked and complete—then I should think he might make a bonfire of the earlier things. They'd be only sketches and studies for the finished work.... Which *may* mean—you know—and I can't help thinking really *does* mean, that he isn't a novelist at all.... Or do you think that's to take him quite too seriously?"

"No," the boy answered. "But I can't say very much, because I've only read three of his books. *Hippolutos* was one of them, and I'm afraid I liked it least. I only came across them in my last term at school. My housemaster lent them to me."

"I don't think it was very clever of him to lend you *this!*" Linton exclaimed, taking the volume up, and immediately dropping it again. "He must have known it's the worst of the lot."

The boy watched him with a broadening smile. "I wonder why you dislike it so much," he said. "What's wrong with it?"

"It's all wrong," Linton answered. "It's untrue to begin with: —invented, not imagined. I'm not talking of the actual writing, though that would ruin it even if it *were* true; but the whole thing is based on a psychological impossibility."

The boy's face at once showed a lively curiosity. "What do you mean?" he asked. "What is the impossibility?"

Linton was delighted to have interested him, and beamed with a sort of happy contentment. "The impossibility is that Bernard —for the sake of the story—is made to feel simultaneously two powerful emotions; whereas in reality he could only have felt one. You can see that the author knew this himself by the immense pains he takes to try to make it plausible. That's rather feeble, don't you think? In fact it's worse than feeble, it's insincere; and I hate insincerity. I hate it in life; and in art, of course, it's fatal."

The boy dug his hands into the dry white powdery sand. He lifted the sand up abstractedly, and let it trickle through his fingers. The tiny grains glittered in the sun.

Linton looked at him as he sat there, nearly in profile. He was very untidy and very attractive, with his flaxen ruffled hair breaking into loose curls over his forehead, and his fair skin. He was wearing a rough brown jacket, a tennis-shirt, and an old pair of baggy grey flannel trousers held up by a knotted scarlet necktie instead of a belt. He gave Linton the impression of being a part of his surroundings—of the sun-bleached sand-dunes, the deserted shore, the blue tumbling waves, the open sky. He gave him the impression of being more *in* nature than anyone he had ever before met. He looked as if the cleanness of the sea-wind was in his blood; he looked as if something of the impersonal beauty of sea and sky and shore had passed into him and become human. And suddenly Linton found himself thinking of the young horsemen on the Parthenon frieze, riding by in proud humility. He was like *them* too, although his features were quite unlike. Or rather it was that both were like the same thing. And now he knew that this was what had first struck him. The boy had reminded him of the world he loved best, the spirit he loved best, the beauty he loved best, the only beauty that had the unspoiled freshness and simplicity of nature. It was as if he had discovered a little bit of that ancient world in the midst of the world of to-day. It was like finding a green well in a desert.

"They're quite different emotions," the boy was saying. "I don't see why he couldn't have felt them at the same time."

Heavens! he was still thinking of that wretched book. Linton with reluctance brought his own mind back to it. It was like returning to a stuffy room after a tramp over the heather. "I know they're different," he agreed, "but their difference is less than their similarity. They're at any rate both absorbing, which was all I meant. What's-her-name—Amy—oughtn't to be in the story at all: she's too little in it for the part she has to play, and too much in it for anything else."

"I think she ought to be in it," said the boy.

Linton was surprised—both at this opinion and by the so decided expression of it. He looked at his companion wonderingly. "Do you?" he said. "Don't you agree that she's chiefly there to make the tragic ending still more tragic?"

"Of course she does do that," the boy admitted. "But still I think she ought to be there. At any rate it would be a quite different story if she wasn't."

Linton chuckled. "It would," he answered; "it would be some thousands of words shorter for one thing. The first version was supposed by the publishers to be *too* short."

The boy pricked up his ears. "*Is* there another version?" he asked. "I'd like to see that. It would be interesting to compare them. You see, I'm—I'm writing a story myself."

"I thought you were," Linton said. "But I'm afraid the first version no longer exists." Then, noticing that the boy's ingenuous gaze was now fixed questioningly upon him, he felt he had perhaps said too much. "I happen to know Martin Linton pretty well," he explained. "At least I've known him for a long time, if that helps you to know a person well. And I know he invariably destroys his preliminary notes and drafts:—I expect most writers do. He once destroyed a full-length novel after putting in a year's work on it—and it was by no means his first, either. He wrote it, revised it, had it typed, read it over, and then made a bonfire of it. Nobody else ever saw that novel. But perhaps this kind of gossip bores you?"

"It doesn't," said the boy. "All the same, I think it's very silly to burn things just because they don't satisfy you. I'm not going to burn anything *I* write. Why couldn't he have put it away?"

"I don't know. I suppose because he's like that."

"Like what?" the boy asked.

"Well—rather impulsive."

There was a silence. Linton, glancing at his companion, saw that his face had grown strangely still. His whole body was stilled, and his blue eyes were gazing at the sea, but with no consciousness in them of any material thing. He might have been rapt in a vision. Possibly he was. At all events, so far as Linton was concerned, he was 'gone', and his departure was so unexpected and complete that Linton felt at first astonished and then uneasy.

For it was not mere vacancy; he *was* looking at something; and something which for Linton was not there. He felt inclined to give him a shake, to wake him up, but he did not do so.

"What's he like?" the boy asked abruptly, and Linton started, for there had been no transition between dreaming and waking. Next moment the boy turned, and reading the perplexity in Linton's face, laughed. "Sorry," he said, "I'm afraid I was thinking. But it was about what you told me, so it wasn't as rude as it must have seemed."

"Rudeness hadn't occurred to me," Linton replied. "I was only wondering where you'd got to."

"I was just thinking," the boy repeated. "I'm sorry. What *is*— Martin Linton like?"

The hesitation—the faintly self-conscious pause before the name—puzzled Linton. But the question turned the conversation into a channel he did not want it to take, and from which he determined to divert it. So he replied vaguely, "Oh, very much like other people."

The boy looked surprised, disappointed, and sceptical—sceptical probably of the life-long friendship he had just been told about. All he said was, "He isn't very like them in his books."

But there was a dryness in his tone which Linton found pleasing. It suggested that his own lack of enthusiasm had slightly jarred. Then, through his pleasure, he felt a sadness, which had its origin in the very charm that so attracted him. It was because that charm made everything else seem dull and futile, and because in a little while he would be left alone with the dullness....

One thing was certain, they had talked enough about Martin Linton. But how to get his young friend to talk about himself? Protruding from his jacket pocket was a roll of manuscript which he had hastily thrust there on their first exchange of words. This seemed a good opening:—one which Sokrates had employed successfully on a summer morning long ago with the youthful and guileless Phaidros. Two minutes later, however, Linton discovered that it was anything but a good opening. Either he lacked the adroitness of Sokrates or the boy was more bashful than Phaidros. He flushed faintly. He answered indeed, but it was in a slightly frozen voice, and the expression in his eyes grew alarmingly aloof. The change was disconcerting. He had become all at once the incarnation of coldness and stiffness, and as he sat bolt-upright, with his mouth obstinately closed, he looked to Linton about as unapproachable as anybody *could* look. It might be only shyness, but it might be that he resented questions; people who liked asking them very often did. Linton, at all events, felt conscious of a rebuff, and on any other occasion he would have drawn back immediately into his shell. Yet he did not do so now. It was as if a deeper instinct prevailed, the instinct which had already lured him so far from that defensive shelter. And presently the barrier of reserve disappeared as suddenly as it had arisen. There seemed to be no reason why, but the boy turned to him, his face cleared, and he began to talk easily, happily, and frankly.

In fact Linton had no need to ask further questions, for it was as if, displeased with his own reticence, the boy had now made up his mind to tell him all he could possibly wish to know. He told him that he was eighteen, very nearly nineteen, that he had left school and was at present looking for a job. But it was jolly hard to find a job—or at least a suitable one. He didn't want to go into business, and there seemed to be nothing else to do. His mother's people were all in business. One of them had offered to give him a start, but he knew he should hate it—stuck in an office all day long. He was interested in birds and in animals; he was interested in botany and had worked a little at it, and sometimes, on half-holidays, had gone out botanizing with the housemaster who had lent him Linton's books. He was interested in politics and in history. He was particularly interested in writing, though up till now, except for winning a prize for an essay, he hadn't been successful. The prize, too, had been only a school prize, so it didn't count. Still, the Head had suggested that he might go in for writing. His mother didn't think much of this plan, but she had been quite decent about it. So he was taking out a correspondence course in journalism, and in the meantime had made a study of magazines and newspapers and had written exactly the kind of things they printed when other people wrote them. They hadn't printed his, however. He had written quite a lot—short stories, articles, and paragraphs. The short stories and articles had been returned, and all the paragraphs except one, which had been accepted just before they came down here. It had appeared in a local paper and he had been paid five shillings for it.

Linton listened, half amused, wholly sympathetic. Perhaps it was the eagerness and enthusiasm of their author which inspired it, but he felt a profound interest in these short stories and articles— was even curious about the paragraphs. If they at all resembled the being who had produced them!

Commonsense whispered that they didn't. The works of too many beginners had been thrust upon him for him not to know that if there is one quality which the writings of the very young rarely or never express, it is the spirit of youth. Or at any rate the attractive side of that spirit. Yet in spite of this warning, Linton's interest remained. There was always the possibility that the boy beside him might be an exception, and he believed he was, whether he possessed a literary gift or not. Linton was even inclined to believe in the literary gift. "What were you working at when I interrupted you?" he asked.

Instantly he regretted this return to dangerous ground, though even now he could not imagine why it should be dangerous. But the boy blushed, and Linton perceived a further peculiarity. The suffusion of blood, as it mounted from his cheeks to his forehead, hardly altered his colour, so that Linton had the odd impression of feeling rather than seeing him blush. For just half a minute it looked as if a relapse into uncommunicativeness were imminent; then, perhaps aware of this himself, the boy faced him quickly and smiled. "I was working at my novel," he said.

Linton, taken aback, murmured a rather tactless "Oh!" He found himself frowning, but hastily corrected that. It was the word 'novel' which carried with it such dire implications. All the old submerged Linton came to life and rose in protest against it. Short stories—yes: but a novel! He had said it so innocently too—as if it were natural to write a novel—as if it were possible, as if it were easy. The correspondence course, the paragraphs—these were all very well and merely amusing, having nothing whatever to do with literature.

The short stories might have to do with it, were at least within the bounds of possibility—but a novel! Linton abruptly pulled himself up. He was being stupid. Everybody began like that; he had begun like that himself, and at an even earlier age. In fact, if it weren't for this virginal innocence, this blissful optimism, who would ever begin to write at all? Besides, what did it matter? These first novels never were completed—were doomed from the very moment of conception. They gasped painfully through a chapter or two and then expired; to be able to complete one would be the worst sign imaginable. Thus Linton pursued his thought, for he regarded precocity as being of all qualities the least promising. Then he decided that it might be as well to learn something of the facts before elaborating a theory, and certainly before pronouncing an opinion. "I wish you'd tell me about it," he said.

The ensuing silence was long enough for him to wonder whether the boy wanted to tell him or not; whether his hesitation were due to disinclination or merely to shyness. "I haven't written much of it," he began, "and I haven't reached the part I really want to write. The part I'm doing now is pretty sloppy, but of course you have to put in what people like; and I don't mind so long as I can do the parts I want to do later."

Linton seemed to recognize the dismal counsels of the correspondence course. "I don't understand," he murmured. "I mean about putting in bits for people to like. There's your subject, and your treatment of it: I don't see how there can be anything else."

"It is part of the subject," the boy replied. "It's introductory, but at the same time it's necessary. I have the whole thing in my head, only I don't think a description of the plot would give you any idea of it. The plot, you see, isn't really what matters. I have to have it because I want to be read, but it isn't what I'm writing the book for—if you understand."

"I wish you'd try to give me some idea of it, all the same," Linton said. "You don't mind, do you?"

"No: it's only that it will sound rotten told like this."

Linton hesitated—disappointed and uncertain. "Then perhaps you'd better not tell me," he agreed at last.

"I'm going to," the boy replied, revealing an unsuspected streak of obstinacy. "I wasn't waiting because of that: I was only thinking how to begin."

He continued to think, while Linton leaned back and half shut his eyes, stilling his mind to a receptive quietude. However baldly the idea might be expressed, he knew he shouldn't miss it: the danger was all the other way—that he might read too much into it—expand it and mould it after his own fashion. And in the silence, while he waited, he hoped the novel wasn't going to be realistic. A rather frailer hope was that it would be lovely and strange, have perhaps magic in it. No, not exactly magic—but a suggestion of both worlds; be, in short, his kind of story. After all there was no reason why it shouldn't be, why this boy shouldn't imagine such a story even if he were incapable of writing it. He *looked* like that. And the hint, the suggestion, would be enough for Linton; his own imagination would do the rest.

With very nearly the first words, he knew that it wasn't going to be his kind of story. Nor the boy's kind either, for that matter, or else he was very much mistaken in him. What apparently he had meant by an idea was simply a desire to express his personal views: the story was to be a kind of safety-valve through which a lot of pent-up steam would emerge. It represented, Linton strongly suspected, a reaction to the less beloved aspects of home influence. Well, so did *The Way of All Flesh*, if it came to that:—only this book was at the same time to have a popular appeal. It was to be good of course, but mysteriously also, it was to reach the hearts of those whose tastes definitely *weren't* good—to contain bribes and allurements to captivate the baser sort of reader while satisfying his betters—to contain, in short, something for everybody. Naturally it was to make a splash;—the bigger the better. A splash meant fame, fortune, and power. Rather splashy, too, the conception of fame,—distinctly spectacular and exciting! Linton was treated to a rapid sketch of a successful author. It meant that when you entered a place of public amusement a whisper ran through the audience: it meant that in trams and restaurants you caught fragments of eager discussion of your works: it meant bookstalls laden with cheap editions; it meant interviews, articles, references from the pulpit, a motor-car driven at the highest possible speed, and perhaps, later on, an influential voice in the government of your country.

How far he ought to attribute all this to the boyish exuberance
of the moment, and how far to a genuine ambition, Linton did not
know. He listened—shocked, disappointed, amused—and extraordinarily attracted. It reminded him a little of an extremely youthful
Arnold Bennett, and it had the same disarming qualities of gaiety
and vitality, high-spirits, energy, and determination. It was most
unlike the frieze of the Parthenon, but it dispersed the last cloud
from Linton's spirit, and it made him laugh. It did more than this: it
gave him an exhilarating feeling of renewed life. At the same time
an intense desire grew up within him that this their first meeting
should not be their last. Only the strength of that desire, indeed,
enabled him to overcome his shyness and the fear of a repulse, and
to ask the boy, as he now did ask him, if he would come out with
him—somewhere—anywhere—in the afternoon. "We could drive
somewhere and walk home. Or we could keep the car waiting. We
might walk over Fair Head and down into Murlough Bay."

He was acutely disappointed when the boy said, "I'm afraid I
can't. I promised to play tennis with my sister this afternoon."

And as he spoke he looked away from Linton and out across the
sea. "Thank you very much," he presently added, with a quaint
effect of having remembered his manners. "I suppose you're staying here?" was a still later thought.

Linton seized on it as an encouragement. "Yes," he answered at
once. "At the hotel."

Then he waited, but the boy, contrary to his hope, did not
suggest a further meeting on another day. He merely said, with
a wave of his hand in that direction, "I'm staying in a house up
on the hill—the second house from the top. I'm staying with my
mother and sister.... Mother sprained her ankle yesterday, going
round the rocks. You know—the rocks beyond the pier."

Linton murmured a polite regret.

"It *was* rather bad luck," the boy agreed. "Because she was by
herself at the time, and managed to make it a lot worse hobbling
back. Now she may be crocked for all the rest of our stay. At least
the doctor told her so. You see, we came down here only for this
month."

Again Linton expressed condolence. He also allowed a decent pause of perhaps eight seconds to elapse before changing the subject. "I may see you to-morrow?" he then suggested.

But the boy did not answer and Linton felt himself colouring. Didn't he *want* to see him? He wished now that he hadn't mentioned it.

"Yes," said the boy, without looking at him, "if you're sure it won't bore you."

"It won't bore me," Linton said simply.

"Are you sure? I don't want to take up your time, you know."

It was Linton's turn not to answer. Somehow this reluctance, or diffidence, or mere politeness, depressed him. It had the effect of reducing everything to that plane of conventionality he loathed. His proposal had been genuine, all he had said had been genuine, he had shown the boy pretty plainly that he liked his company—if anything too plainly—and he must have seen this, therefore why pretend he hadn't? All the same, he couldn't leave it there; it was suddenly become too important to him; and he made a further effort. "We might talk things over," he said. "A good many of my friends are writers, and I might be able to help you in some way."

"Thanks," said the boy slowly after a pause—as if the idea of being helped had its less attractive side.

He *was* odd, Linton thought; and the whole situation was beginning to border on the ironic. It became more ironic still when he thought of the number of appeals he had received in the past—appeals to read manuscripts, to criticize manuscripts, even to assist in the revision and placing of manuscripts. And now, the one author he felt an urgent desire to assist seemed to prefer to be left to his own devices! It did not alter Linton's determination, but it puzzled him. He had no idea whether the reluctance sprang from self-sufficiency, or unbelief. It might be from neither. Then all at once he remembered that the boy knew nothing about him, and perhaps regarded him simply as an officious person fond of interfering. It would be pretty awful if he thought that, though Linton did not quite see how he could. After all, his criticism of that wretched novel had been fairly competent. In fact, for perfect safety, for perfect truth to his rôle of mere amateur, hadn't it been just a little *too* competent, *too* professional? "I don't intend to advise you *not* to write," he said. "I don't think anybody could give you such advice at present:—it's too soon. I may tell you that I think what you've written isn't good, but that's a very different matter. And I really would, you know," he went on persuasively, "very much like to see something you've done."

The boy became lost in thought: apparently it took time to reach a decision.

"*Will* you bring something?" Linton asked, with the sense that this was final.

Then the boy made up his mind. "Yes, I'd like to," he said.

Chapter III

BRIAN

B rian Westby, seated at the breakfast-table, frowned, unscrewed a fountain-pen, pursed up his lips, took a dumpy little leather-backed notebook from the inside pocket of his jacket, and made a note in it. The note led to another and yet another—quite a lot of notes—and between each of them he frowned severely.

They were notes for his book, for the chapter he was going to write that morning, ideas which might be lost if he didn't record them at once. There was something he had thought of in his bath, too:—it was gone, but he must get it, for it was important. He frowned still more deeply till he caught the ironical glance in his sister's narrow brown eyes (Chinese eyes really, he thought). "Your sleeve's in the marmalade," she said.

Brian looked down quickly. Judging from the state of the table-cloth his sleeve must have been in the marmalade more than once, and he glared at her. "You might have told me sooner," he said.

"I did tell you."

"Yes.... You took jolly good care to wait till I'd made as much mess as possible."

"Not as possible," Claire replied. "You're making more now with your handkerchief."

He muttered something, but stopped using his handkerchief.

"You'd better change your jacket," Claire went on, smiling a faintly superior smile. "Give the dirty one to Mrs Belford and ask her to sponge it for you. She'll understand: her own little Herbert is always plastering himself with something unpleasant."

Brian rose from the table. There were times when he detested Claire and this was one of them. He would have liked to pour what was left of the marmalade over her sleek brown head, but the days for that kind of retort were past. Once, when they had both been a good deal younger, he had boxed her ears, and the memory of the howl she had then set up before running to tell their mother still gave him a retrospective satisfaction. He wished the incident had occurred oftener, for in the merely wordy battles that were all they had now she invariably got the best of it.

He saw her looking at him with a malicious enjoyment of his discomfiture. He knew, too, what was making her so disagreeable. It was because he had refused to play golf with her and the Grahams. Well, he wasn't going to play golf if he didn't want to:— not to please Claire, anyway. They could pick up somebody at the club-house or on the links, or play a three-ball match.

"When you *are* upstairs," Claire continued, "you'd better ask mother if she'd like some more tea."

He did not reply. He knew she wanted him to refuse, or to tell her to go herself. Then she *would* go, and without actually complaining manage to let their mother know how disobliging he had been. That was her favourite method, and he supposed it was because she was a girl. Privately he regarded his own sex as definitely superior.

With a gratifying sense of having scored by his silence, he walked to the door and opened it. But his triumph was brief. Before he had time to shut the door Claire's voice reached him: "The first three chapters of *Nature Suppressed* are on your dressing-table. I found them on the floor beside your bed. I didn't know whether you meant them to be thrown away or not, so I picked them up."

Brian came back into the room. His mouth had closed tightly and his eyes were dark with anger. "What were you doing in my room?" he asked in a voice so restrained that it was almost a whisper.

Claire looked surprised. She raised her delicate eyebrows. "I went there to look for the clothes-brush," she answered composedly—"the one that belongs to the hall. If you'd put things back when you've done with them, people wouldn't have to go to your room."

He remembered about the clothes-brush, but at the same time knew that the allusion to his manuscript had been made with a purpose. Possibly he *had* left it on the floor beside his bed, for he had been reading it over before getting up; but that wasn't why she had mentioned it. He looked at her fixedly. "Did you read it?" he asked in the same low voice.

Claire smiled. "I didn't read it exactly. I dipped into it. I got as far as the bit where Edna's father goes mad and attacks her with a poker."

She suddenly laughed, and Brian stood there, his arms held stiffly at his sides. He waited a moment or two and then said, still without raising his voice, but with an appalling sincerity, "You *are* a little beast.... I wonder if anybody else knows *how* beastly. A sneak too, for if you'd do that you'd do other things—read people's letters, or a private diary—it's exactly the same."

"Is it?" Claire answered sweetly. "I must give you a diary for a birthday-present."

"Oh, shut up."

"That's very polite!"

He turned away: there was no use talking to her. She was almost certain to tell the Grahams about his novel—make fun of it, describe the poker incident—but he wasn't going to ask her not to. Nor, since she had suggested it, was he going to ask Mrs Belford to sponge his jacket. He carried it upstairs over his arm and washed it himself with hot water and soap. Then he went to his bedroom.

He put on an old brown jacket, pulled a suitcase out from beneath his bed, unlocked it, and took a book from it. He left the book on the floor while he stood up and gazed out of the window. There was no use pretending; he did hate Claire having seen his novel, and he hoped she wouldn't tell Derek and Eva Graham about it. Whether she told or not depended on how much she was annoyed with him, yet he was determined to do nothing to conciliate her.

Of course the Grahams knew already that he wrote things—everybody did, for that matter—only they didn't know he was writing a novel, and they were the last people in the world he would dream of taking into his confidence.... He knew that the scene between Edna and her father *could* be made ridiculous. He didn't care much for it himself: it was too melodramatic. It was absolutely necessary for the plot, however, and melodramatic things often happened in real life. Then, with a sudden apprehension, he wondered if this were all Claire had read? He hoped so. It was bad enough that she should have read even this, but it would be much worse if she had read the love-scene in the third chapter. If she had got as far as that (and how could he be sure she hadn't?), she would be almost certain to tell the Grahams. And they would tell Jimmy Garratt—in fact any of their friends who happened to know him, Brian. He was perfectly aware that they all regarded him as peculiar, and the very idea of his trying to write a love-scene would strike them as highly amusing. There would be jokes and allusions without end—especially from Derek. If Claire did tell, he would never forgive her.

Facing the window and still as a post, he stood pondering his love-scene. He had always had his doubts about it, been pretty certain it wasn't right, though what exactly was wrong with it he couldn't see. Otherwise he would have changed it. But there was no use changing it unless he could make it better. It was a pity that these introductory chapters were so indispensable, for once Edna was married he would be on comparatively safe ground. The struggle in her mind, her fear lest her children should inherit their grandfather's insanity—all that, he was sure, he could make really powerful. And it would be quite true to life, for naturally she wouldn't want to have children, and equally naturally she wouldn't be able to tell her husband why. Having married him with this guilty secret weighing on her conscience, she would never find the courage to reveal it. For of course she oughtn't to have married him; it was pure selfishness. Or at least she ought to have told him the truth first, and given him the choice either of breaking off their engagement or of agreeing to do without a family. As it was, he would want to have children—everybody did—and she would have to invent false reasons for her refusal. Brian felt a further misgiving. It mightn't do to be too realistic here: the subject had its awkwardnesses and must be treated with extreme delicacy. He stood for several minutes considering this new problem. What reason *could* Edna give? He was afraid he didn't know. It seemed to him that it would be jolly difficult for her to discuss the matter at all. All memory of his quarrel with Claire had by this time vanished from his mind. Then, as he moved his foot, he accidentally kicked the book he had taken from his suitcase. He stooped, and lifting it from the floor, crammed it into the side pocket of his jacket. Into the other pocket he stuffed a roll of blank paper, and both these actions were performed automatically, for he was still thinking of his novel: he didn't want it to contain anything which could be regarded as unpleasantly sexual....

Not, really, that there was much danger of this. Where he would be far more likely to shock people was on the subject of religion. In fact, if the novel ever did reach the stage of publication, it might be better to publish it anonymously. Or under an assumed name. He was thinking now of his mother, of the impression it would make upon her, and he didn't see how she could possibly like it. Viewed dispassionately, it was a repudiation of nearly everything she *did* like. He wondered if other authors had these domestic dilemmas to bother them. One ought to ignore them, he supposed, but it wasn't easy to do so without at the same time feeling rather a beast. Fortunately his mother had expressed no curiosity so far, had never once asked him what he was writing about; and though this might not be particularly flattering it was distinctly an advantage....

Really, she took very little interest in books—particularly novels. It was not that she disapproved of fiction, but simply that imaginative literature had little attraction for her. The books she preferred were records of actual experience, and nearly always of religious experience. She took them so seriously too! He had never taken religion quite like that, though there had been a time, in the years of his 'prep' school—and even later—when he had been definitely 'pi'. The marvel was that he had never actually been saved! Claire had—or at least she said she had: Brian held his own opinion about that. Suddenly he remembered his mother's tea.

It was rather late, he was afraid; nevertheless he went to her room and knocked on the door. A faint voice told him to come in. He puckered up his nose and stood hesitating. Why should she answer in such a tone! Hang it all, it was a bit thick! she wasn't ill in *that* way; she'd only crocked her ankle! He pushed open the door gingerly, but remained on the threshold. The blinds were down, the room was in a kind of yellowish twilight, the breakfast-tray had been removed, and his mother was now lying with her face turned from the door. Brian stood gazing with alarmed eyes at this depressing interior.

There was only one thing to be done, however, and he entered with a burst of cheerfulness. He crossed over to the window and stood looking down at her. "I came to ask you if you'd like some more tea," he said encouragingly.

Mrs Westby raised herself slightly on the pillows, but did not sit up. "You were a rather long time coming," she murmured. "I heard you going to your room a quarter of an hour ago."

"Oh, not so long as that!" Brian argued optimistically.

"Yes, quite as long as that," his mother replied.

For the moment it brought their conversation to a stand-still. Brian smiled amicably and began to fiddle with the blind. Then he tried to explain what had happened. "I really did come upstairs to see if you wanted anything, but I began thinking of other things and forgot about it."

Abruptly the blind—one of those spring contraptions—shot up like a rocket, and Mrs Westby uttered a startled cry. Brian got a start himself, though he laughed. "Sorry!" he exclaimed, and tried to pull the blind down again, but each time he released it the spring failed to catch and the rocket performance was repeated. Brian watched this extraordinary behaviour with round eyes which had acquired an innocent, serious, and astonished expression. He was not discouraged.

"Do leave it alone, dear," Mrs Westby sighed after the fourth ascent. "Why you *will* fiddle with things, when you know what invariably happens when you do, I can't imagine!"

"It's not my fault," Brian defended himself. "It's the spring that's weak. Just look at that!" This time, however, he left the blind where it was. "It ought to be up anyway," he declared. "It's not good for you lying in the dark."

"It's very strange that you should be so clumsy," Mrs Westby continued, though less in reproach than perplexity. "Your hands are big enough one would think, but they seem to be more like paws."

Brian inspected them in the light of this criticism. "They *are* rather big," he admitted with a slight frown. "Rather square too." He looked at his mother as if she might have an explanation to offer, but she only laughed.

"Never mind," she said. "I like them just as they are. And I don't see why you need stand at the furthest possible distance from me, as if I had chicken-pox or measles. You haven't even said good-morning."

"I did when I came in," Brian reminded her. He knew what she meant, all the same, and crossing the room, kissed her lightly on the cheek.

The sunlight streamed straight in upon them, and it occurred to him that his mother looked remarkably young. The effect of time was chiefly visible in a bleaching of her hair and complexion, but her hair had not turned grey, its flaxen yellow was only faded, and her face even in this strong light was very little lined. What it lacked, he thought, was——

Abruptly he checked this train of speculation, and asked himself if his having started it meant that he didn't love his mother. He became lost in this interesting question, while she watched him, half-amused, half-resigned, wondering how long he would remain without speaking if she just left him alone. His eyes were fixed abstractedly upon her. He was very fond of her of course. Only sometimes he thought it was easier to love things than people— things like the sea. At least there were times when you didn't want people, when you were happier by yourself: he believed he could be perfectly happy by himself.... Yet maybe this wasn't true: and suddenly he remembered that when his mother had been ill a few years ago, the thought that perhaps she might die had been awful. It had kept him awake and miserable half the night, though there hadn't really been the slightest danger. He had been only a youngster then, but still—— And if they didn't get on quite so well together now as in those days, wasn't it chiefly because then he had accepted all her views? In this last year—and still more during these last six months—he hadn't accepted any of them: he had merely given in to them to avoid rows....

The worst of it was that this docility by no means satisfied her. He might go to church twice every Sunday, and lead all the time the most blameless life, yet still it wouldn't satisfy her. For his mother there were only two alternatives—either you were saved or you weren't; and he definitely wasn't. She couldn't see that people must develop along their own lines: in fact her firmest conviction was that they mustn't. It meant, of course, that he had to keep most of his thoughts to himself, and all his deeper thoughts. It meant even more than that: it increased in him a natural reserve and tendency to fight shy of any display of affection. He was perfectly aware now, for instance, that if his manner had been a little more demonstrative it would have pleased her. Yet it was quite impossible for him to be demonstrative: he never had been, never would be, he supposed. Still—he wasn't sure. There had been times when he had longed for something different and thought that if he could only find the right person——

"Don't you think you ought to get up?" he suddenly suggested, emerging from this self-examination with characteristic abruptness. "Would you like me to carry you downstairs? I'm sure I could, you know; you're not very heavy."

Instantly he saw that this speech had pleased her. She smiled back at him and patted his hand. "Of course I'm going to get up," she told him, "but I'm not going to be carried, and certainly not, Brian dear, by you."

"Why?" he persisted. "I'd be frightfully careful."

His mother laughed. "Yes, I know you would," she said.

"Then why? Of course if you can't trust me!"

She hastened to reassure him. "I think it's very nice of you, and it's not that I shouldn't like you to carry me; you know that. It's only because I can't help feeling that Mrs Belford and the banisters would be safer."

Brian had risen to his feet, but he still hovered between the bed and the door. "They may be safer," he remarked, "but they won't be nearly so exciting." He took another step forward and again stopped. "Have you anything decent to read?" he asked. "There's a lending-library in a stationer's shop in the town and it wouldn't take me a jiff to go on my bike. Would you like an Edgar Wallace story? You know you enjoyed the one you read."

"No thank you," Mrs Westby replied. "You needn't worry about me, dear," she added gently. "I shall be all right."

But for some reason Brian felt impelled to worry. "Won't you find it dull?" he persevered. "Shall I ask Mrs Graham to come round?"

His mother shook her head. Then she changed the subject. "What are *you* going to do?" she asked.

It was naturally the one question he hadn't wanted, and too late he regretted his persistence. He tried to adopt a casual tone, with the result that his voice sounded particularly stiff and self-conscious. "I thought of going round the shore," he answered slowly, "and perhaps writing a little." He gazed fixedly at her as he spoke—a sure, though unconscious sign that he felt ill at ease.

"Don't you think it would be nicer of you if you went to play golf with Claire?" his mother suggested. "She asked you to last night."

"No," answered Brian firmly, "I don't."

His mother looked at him. "Well, I think it would be. You oughtn't to allow your writing to make you selfish."

Brian became indignant. "I *have* to write," he said. "That is, if I'm ever going to be a writer. If I was in business you wouldn't think it selfish of me to attend to my work. But because I'm at home it's supposed not to matter how much time I waste."

His mother listened to him, though she did not look impressed. "I don't think it's ever a waste of time to consider other people," she said.

Brian's expression altered. It was at this point that a likeness between mother and son suddenly emerged where there had been none before. "Claire's got plenty of friends," he returned coldly. "She never wants me except when it happens to suit her convenience. Anyway, I'm going to play tennis with her and the Grahams this afternoon, and I don't see why I should spend my whole time with them.... I *told* her I wanted to work this morning."

His mother was no longer looking at him. "I know you told her," she answered slowly, "and I suppose you'll go your own way. But some boys are fond enough of their sisters to *like* obliging them."

She added nothing further, however; nor did he. In silence, and with his head up, he left the room, feeling he had been treated unfairly. On one point he was resolved; he wasn't going to give in. That would be to admit he was in the wrong, whereas he was in the right. If it wasn't selfish of Claire to want to play golf, then it wasn't selfish of him to want to work. His working didn't even prevent her from playing; it only meant that she had the slight extra trouble of finding somebody else to make up a foursome. The Grahams knew lots of people; Derek could easily get somebody. But there was no use pointing this out to his mother: she always took Claire's part.

Still glowing with a sense of injured rectitude, he left the house and walked down the hill in the sunshine. Just as he reached the corner by the Marine Hotel he *saw* the Grahams—about a hundred yards away—coming along the road from the town. It was the kind of thing that would happen! They were carrying golf-bags: they waved their hands. Brian waved back, but he was determined not to stop; he wasn't going to begin his explanations all over again. He turned through an open gate and hurried along the path above the tennis-grounds. Then, when he had crossed the bridge, he ploughed through several yards of soft white sand and ran over the firm brown sand beyond it till he reached the water's edge. Here he progressed more erratically, because he wanted to keep as close to the waves as possible, and every now and again had to skip back when a bigger one than usual rolled in, broke, and suddenly rushed at him with a playful hiss of bursting foam. The waves, he discovered, were alive. They knew he was there and tried to take him by surprise. They pretended to be slow and sleepy, until all at once, like a huge blue dragon, one would dart out its frothing tongue at him with unexpected swiftness. Several times he was nearly caught in this way. Once he *was* caught, and the blue-green water with its swirling covering of foam lapped over his shoes, while he stood, trapped, in the middle of a shallow lake. A solitary collie, perceiving that a game of some sort was in progress, raced up to take part in it before it should be over. *He* didn't care whether he wet his feet or not—though he seemed to think it wasn't a proper game without sticks or stones. He said as much to Brian, who had begun to walk on again. But the collie, in order to explain about the sticks, had to proceed backwards, looking up into Brian's face and leaping from side to side, barking sharp staccato barks of encouragement. Brian threw some pieces of driftwood for him, and then began to throw the driftwood up the bank while at the same time he ran on as fast as he could, but the collie always caught him up in a minute. Both by this time had forgotten everything else, and it was the dog who remembered first. He may have had a master somewhere on the links: at any rate, having come nearly to the end of the bay, all at once he turned abruptly and tore back at full speed without so much as a parting glance.

Deserted by his playfellow, Brian began to practise long jumps. This made him hot, and being hot reminded him of bathing, and with that he suddenly realized that he had come without his bathing-things. "Damn!" he muttered—rather to his own surprise, for in spite of eight years of school, swearing did not come natural to him. All the same, it was a beastly nuisance about his things, and it was his mother's fault—and Claire's. Now he would have to go home earlier than he had intended to, and bathe off the end of the pier, which wouldn't be nearly so good as going in off the rocks.

He walked on a little further and then, leaving the sea, scrambled up the loose sandy bank and began to search for a place where he could write. He soon found one—a rounded hollow—almost at the end of the links. The thin, vividly-green grass pierced through the soft white sand, and the hollow itself was warm and dry and sheltered, so that his papers would not be blown about. He pulled the book he had brought out of his pocket—not to read it—he would only read if he got stuck in his writing—but to make himself more comfortable: then he sat down. And he sat for a while in idleness. Now that he *was* here, he felt a strong temptation not to work but to dream. It was queer how the sea invariably put him in this mood. But it wouldn't do—especially after all the fuss he had made at home. He looked over the notes he had scribbled at breakfast and added one or two more; but this wouldn't do either—it was only another form of slacking. So he spread out his papers on his knee and wrote in capital letters at the head of the top sheet:— Chapter IV. Edna Learns Her True Value.

His eyes rested on the scene before him, and the sound of the waves was in his ears. It was a very lovely world, but gradually it dimmed and faded, while Edna's world of town and houses, of crowded noisy streets and congested traffic—with the Queen's Bridge for some unknown reason stuck in the very middle of it— slowly spread out before him. At the same time his mind began to take the colour of Edna's, to be filled with anxieties and doubts, unpleasant memories of the past, and a nervous dread of the future....

For the position of Edna was this. Having lost both her parents and been abandoned by a callous brother, she was at present faced by the alternative of either finding a job or starving. In a way, when you came to think of it, it was not frightfully unlike Brian's own position!—though of course ever so much more urgent. Eric, the young man who had proposed to her in the previous chapter, had been turned down. But she had turned him down only because of that secret knowledge of her father's madness, not because she didn't love him. It was rather a bore, in fact, because it meant that there would have to be a second love-scene, in which she accepted Eric, and Brian couldn't very well stick in all that kissing business over again. It had been bad enough doing it once, and as for a rep- etition——Perhaps it was because it took place in the open air, on a bank beneath a hedge, that he couldn't help thinking it somehow suggested those real love-scenes you hastily pass by with averted eyes when you are taking a short-cut home through the fields at night....

However, he needn't bother about it now. This morning's task was to make Edna look for a job—as a typist, he thought—a typist on the whole would be best. He *ought* to be able to do this. He had looked for a job himself and knew exactly how ghastly an experi- ence it was. The actual interviews weren't so bad; it was the period beforehand, when you were screwing up your courage.... Brian began to write.

He wrote in sudden spurts, with intervals of reflection, but while he was actually writing the sentences came fluently. If he couldn't find the word he wanted he put down another one; during the intervals of thought he was considering ideas, not their expression. And in a few minutes he was completely absorbed.

He wrote on—page after page. Half an hour passed—an hour— another half-hour. A shadow glided across his manuscript and he glanced up. He was vaguely conscious that someone was there—a man—but before the texture of his dream was broken only the sea was there, its lonely and unresting voice crying out of an unimaginably remote past and on into an unimaginable future. For half a minute, perhaps, the idea of endless time made him afraid. Then, like a dark bird winging across the sky, it was gone.

Yet when he tried to continue Edna's adventure, somehow it was not the same, it had become trivial and unreal. He knew he was writing now merely to finish what he had begun. Edna was in the middle of her third unsuccessful interview—this time with the manager of Robinson and Cleaver's—and suddenly Brian felt that he didn't care a straw whether she got a job or not. He must be getting stale: he had better stop. He yawned, stretched himself, and once again wished he hadn't forgotten his bathing-things. He began to calculate how many words he had written. Fifteen pages, with about sixty words to a page:—not so bad, considering it wasn't yet twelve o'clock. And he would be able to have another go at it this evening if the Grahams didn't come in....

Something—though he had heard no sound—caused him to look up. It was his stranger returning. No: he had stopped—stopped to gaze at the sea. He stood at a distance of some ten yards from Brian's hollow, on the edge of the bank, lost in contemplation, like an artist meditating a picture. It was a good chance anyway to take a note, and Brian produced the little black book. But unfortunately he could only take a mental note while the man was actually standing there—couldn't put it down in writing, or he might think a drawing was being made of him. Brian began to compose the note: it might be useful; for as it happened he needed several more characters in his novel, which was at present rather thinly populated. Minor characters, of course—friends of Edna's and Eric's. The drawback was that this particular 'character' didn't look in the least as if he would be a friend of either Edna *or* Eric. He didn't belong to their world—which was definitely commercial, not to say sordid. Lower middle-class at any rate, and for a moment Brian wondered why he should have chosen it, since it wasn't his world either, or in any way attractive to him. Quite the reverse indeed, in spite of the fact that he had lately become a socialist. He refocused his attention on the man and tried to think how he could describe him.

He was middle-aged to begin with—rather late middle-aged—round about fifty, say—for his hair was streaked with silver where you could see it. And he had lived a more or less unactive life—unactive physically.... Sedentary—that was the word he wanted—a sedentary life. He was a bit slouchy, too, and his complexion was sallow, not sunburned. He didn't look awfully well, and—not awfully happy either. Brian felt a distinct satisfaction at this last deduction, which he inwardly characterized as a rather 'peppy' effort, being based not on mere observation—though as a matter of fact the lines on the man's face were fairly deeply marked—especially near the eyes and mouth. But he hadn't got it from that: it was a much more subtle impression—extremely subtle—acquired almost telepathically.... What next? Well, the next was more commonplace: anybody could see that he was careless about his clothes, which needed brushing at this moment.... Brian got no further, for just then the man turned and he found himself looking straight into his eyes, which were dark and intelligent, and at the same time both old and young, tired and very much alive.

They were observant eyes, too, and at present they expressed an interest, and that this interest was in *him*, Brian immediately knew. Hastily he turned away. He felt suddenly very shy, and also quite certain this his 'new character' was going to speak to him. He hadn't time to wonder why, but, with his face averted, simply sat waiting for it to happen. Without hearing him or seeing him, he knew the man was approaching, and next moment he heard his voice. "Good-morning."

Brian sprang to his feet. It was as if a tension suddenly had been broken.

"Good-morning," he returned; and then there followed a silence till the man, pointing with his stick to the book lying in the grass, asked in an odd, but very friendly way, "How do you like it? Or haven't you tried it yet?"

The question for some reason didn't sound a bit like an ordinary conversational opening. It didn't, on the other hand, sound as if he really wanted to know about the book: it sounded definitely as if he wanted to make friends. Which was why, perhaps, it had the effect of making Brian feel a good deal more at ease than he usually felt with strangers—particularly when there was so great a difference of age to be bridged. His first impulse was to say that the author of the book was his father, though he had been brought up as Brian Westby, not Brian Linton, but on second thoughts he kept this information to himself. He wasn't given to making rapid confidences, and moreover, in the last year or two, he had been coming gradually to realize how unusual the possession of more than one surname was, and how inconvenient it might easily become. He had not spoken to his mother about it yet, but merely because he found the subject embarrassing. He *ought* to be told what lay behind it all: it was absurd to treat him as if he were a child.

At the very start, for instance, it was strange that there wasn't one of his father's books in the house. His mother had never actually forbidden him to read the books, but he felt pretty sure that if they weren't there it was because she didn't want him to read them. Evidently she disapproved of them, and this was why he had kept the one he was reading now locked up in his suitcase. At all events, so long as he used the name of Westby, Brian felt he had no moral right to claim Linton as his father. If he wasn't good enough to be acknowledged in one way, he oughtn't to be boasted about in another. Yet he *did* want to discuss the book and to know what the stranger thought of it. So he asked him, and at the same time invited him to sit down. Unluckily, he seemed to think very little of it, which was disappointing, though Brian was not sufficiently sure of his ground to put up much of a defence. The stranger's objections, indeed, were of a kind that made this particularly difficult, being concerned chiefly with points that had never entered Brian's head. He didn't know whether they were right or wrong, and presently he ceased to care, for what interested him infinitely more than any literary criticism was the fact that he had at last met somebody who knew his father.

Somebody from the outside world, that is to say, for obviously his mother's people, though they were careful never to allude to him, must have known him. With his father's people Brian had no acquaintance whatever. *They* must be English, and doubtless lived in England. Even of his father himself he knew next to nothing. This was partly, indeed largely, his own fault. He had been feeble and diffident when he ought to have been energetic and determined. True, for years he had believed Brian Westby to be his real name, but even after he had known it wasn't, he had done little except ponder and speculate in private. He had first learned his true name by accident, through a chance remark let drop by one of the servants. Until that afternoon—it had been in the Christmas holidays, he remembered—he had had no idea that his mother had been married twice, that Claire was really only his half-sister, that his father (Brian still couldn't think of him as anything else) was really only his step-father. The revelation had not merely worried, but in some obscure way had shocked him as well. Yes, he had been shocked, and that was why he had kept it—as he was later on to keep so many things—to himself. The single outward result of his momentous discovery had been that for two or three weeks, until he had gone back to school in fact, his manner to his step-father had been more affectionate than before. It was maybe an odd manifestation in the circumstances, but he had liked his step-father, and had wanted somehow to express his loyalty to him. Then, with his return to school, the whole thing for a long time had sunk into the less visited regions of his mind.

Later—a good deal later, for it had been after his step-father's death—he had been told a portion of the truth by his mother. But she had told him only what she considered sufficient—in other words as little as possible—and even that in a way which had at the same time made him sorry for her and loth to question her. He had simply accepted her brief account of the situation, and had continued to accept it until one afternoon, in his house-master's study, when he had seen on a shelf a row of books by Martin Linton and had taken one down, and when he was leaving borrowed it. He had not really cared much for the book—at least he had only liked bits of it—yet it had altered everything. Everything except his profound reluctance to re-open the subject with his mother. He had opened it with his housemaster instead, though Mr Campion, as was hardly surprising, knew nothing about Martin Linton's private life. He had a great admiration for his writings, but he could not even show Brian a photograph. He had heard, or read somewhere, that Linton had never allowed one to be published—had what amounted almost to a kink in regard to interviews, photographs, and publicity methods in general. All that kind of thing he appeared to detest.

There remained *Who's Who*, which had supplied a few dates, an address, a list of books, a school, a university, a club—and that was all. The address, however, had suggested a letter, and Brian had thought several times of writing one. He would have done it, too, only it seemed to him that he must first tell his mother, and he had not found that easy. Besides, if his father had wanted to hear from him, had taken the least interest in him, wouldn't he have written himself? Brian couldn't make up his mind what to do.

It was surely an amazingly lucky chance, then, that had brought him face to face with one of his father's friends in so unlikely a spot as Ballycastle. For his father's friend also was an Englishman, and English visitors at Ballycastle were rare. Brian felt he was at last going to get exactly the sort of information he wanted—information of a personal kind, and at first hand, and unprejudiced....

But presently he grew more doubtful. He certainly *wasn't* learning much. The friend was ready enough to talk about Linton's writings, his way of writing, and such things as that; but on the subject of Linton himself he was singularly evasive. And it was not, Brian felt, because he had nothing to tell: that remark about his father's being just like other people, for instance, obviously was a fabrication; it had been deliberately intended to put him off.

Suddenly he stopped asking questions. He also stopped talking, and sat digging his hands in the warm dry sand, and letting it trickle in a white powder through his fingers. If nobody would tell him about his father, it must be because there was something to conceal—and something pretty bad, though it was difficult to imagine what it could be. A fantastic idea occurred to him, that his father might be out of his mind, might be shut up somewhere in a lunatic-asylum. If that were the truth, they possibly *would* hide it from him. The more he considered it the more plausible it appeared. Yes, it must be that. And it was jolly queer, therefore, that he should have chosen something not unlike it as the subject of his novel! Brian believed he had solved the mystery. As a solution it explained everything—even the changing of his surname.

Then abruptly the theory collapsed. He remembered that no matter *how* mad his father might be, if he were still alive his mother could not have married again. Brian didn't know much about the divorce laws, but he knew you couldn't get a divorce simply because your husband or your wife is mad. The whole plot of *Jane Eyre* was based on that—based on the fact that Mr Rochester couldn't marry Jane while his wife was living, though *she* was as mad as a hatter. What were the things for which you could get a divorce? He had an idea there were only two: cruelty and—going with other women.... And with this he became uncertain as to whether after all he wished to know more. It was like prying into somebody's secrets. No; he wouldn't ask....

All the same, it was strange that he should be thinking like this. Or maybe it was only strange that he should never have thought like this before—never nearly so—so definitely. He supposed it was because the silence of his present companion had impressed him in a way his mother's silence hadn't. His mother was so strict about a lot of things which didn't really matter. But the man beside him gave him just the opposite impression—as if he would be tolerant and understanding—if anything *too* tolerant. He struck Brian as being sympathetic and kind; he presently even struck him as being the sort of person who might himself have written Martin Linton's books.

That he seemed a bit odd didn't really clash with this impression: the books, too, were a bit odd. And he wasn't odd in any unpleasant or irritating way, though he certainly was unconventional and remarkably inquisitive. The combination had already produced several awkward questions which Brian had found it difficult to answer. And when you didn't answer he either asked them again or else looked disappointed. It was a little unreasonable; for after all you can't, just in a moment, get on confidential terms with somebody you've never seen before in your life. At least *he* couldn't. For one thing, he didn't want to. For another, he was doing his best. That was because he couldn't help feeling that the stranger's curiosity wasn't mere curiosity. At least it was different from ordinary curiosity. Brian had the feeling that for some reason this man was interested in him, was even pleased with him, and though he had no idea why he should be, he none the less liked it. People weren't in the habit of paying much attention to him. He had always known —indeed there had been precious little attempt to disguise it—that most of the people who came to the house preferred Claire.... Yes, he certainly liked it.... Otherwise he wouldn't be talking so much about himself and his work. He had told this man more in a single morning—really only half a morning—than he had ever told anybody else in his life. Far more, for instance, than he had told Mr Graham when Mr Graham had asked him round to talk about his work. But then, Mr Graham, though he professed to be interested, really wasn't. At any rate this was a quite different kind of interest—extending, Brian thought, beyond his writings, and including himself. This last, even in his own mind, was a whispered thought, and he wouldn't have uttered it aloud for worlds. Nevertheless he became practically certain of it when his new friend invited him to come out again in the afternoon.

He wanted to accept, and he would have accepted if he hadn't promised to play tennis. Having explained this, he still stood considering it. But he must go now if he was to bathe before dinner, and the sea, with the sun glittering on it, looked extraordinarily attractive. He watched the waves rolling up the long wet beach. Suddenly he became conscious of his silence and said, "Thank you very much," in a voice which sounded dreadfully stiff and formal. He wished he wasn't so stupid about saying things. They rose up in him, almost came out, and then turned tail and scuttled back into hiding like startled rabbits while he said something entirely different. He wanted to make a suggestion now about their meeting again. Ought he to make it? Oughtn't he to wait till it was made to him? Well, he *would* make it, whether he ought to or not. He

struggled for another moment and then heard himself muttering
"I suppose you're staying here?"

"Yes, at the hotel."

And nothing more followed. What Brian had really meant had
not been understood; or if it had been, was not taken up. Merely
to break the pause and to hide his disappointment he began to
explain where *he* was staying, and to talk about his mother's accident.

He noticed that his companion, who had been looking at him
before, was now looking at the ground, and that he appeared to be
feeling some difficulty or embarrassment. Perhaps he *had* understood, and didn't *want* to make a definite arrangement. In the end,
all he said was, "I may see you to-morrow?"

And he said even that half-heartedly, it wasn't much more than a
mumble. Brian didn't know what to make of it. People sometimes
invited you to do things simply out of kindness, and he would hate
to take advantage of that. The very fact that this man seemed to
show a particular inclination to be kind to him increased his diffidence. He hesitated, fumbled, said something about not wanting
to take up his time; and the moment he had done so knew he had
blundered. There followed a chilling interval during which he
waited—he could do nothing else but wait—for everything now
was going wrong. Then unexpectedly the man said, "We might talk
things over. A good many of my friends are writers and I might be
able to help you in some way."

It was very decent of him, and Brian thanked him again. Only
he wasn't quite sure that he wanted this kind of help. He would
rather, he thought—at first at any rate—see what he could do by
his own unaided efforts. In imagination he had always pictured
himself fighting his own way. He did not want a short-cut to success; he did not want anything he had not earned entirely by his
own merits. Still, this need not prevent him from showing something he had done. What *had* he to show! Certainly not the stuff
he had written for the School of Journalism. He had really nothing
except his novel—and not a great deal of that....

"*Will* you bring something?"

It was rather pressing—the way he said it. Brian was ashamed of hesitating so much; it seemed so ungracious. He suddenly made up his mind, and his face cleared. "Yes, I'd like to," he answered.

And for some queer reason, as soon as he had said it, it became true; he felt he *would* like to. He thought about it all the way home, as he ran over the golf-links. He felt excited and pleased. On the whole it had been a jolly good morning, and just to finish it off suitably he hoped dinner would be late. For if it were, there might still be time for a bathe off the pier.

Chapter IV

LINTON

For half an hour after he was left alone Linton sat dreaming. Then he got up, and walked back in the direction of the hotel.

A small whitish figure was lying in the porch. On Linton's approach the figure rose stiffly, wagged the stump of a tail, and followed him to the foot of the stairs. There it remained until Linton returned, when together they entered the dining-room.

They were late; lunch was in full swing, and Susan was over by the window handing round the vegetables. But she saw them, and Micky, who had assumed the air of a private dog, an individual pet, not an hotel property, kept as close to his adopted master as he could. In this way progress became difficult, at times dangerous, nevertheless they reached their table without an accident. Here Micky retired into a sound strategical position, from whence, protected by the legs of the table, the legs of the chair, and Linton's legs, it would not be easy to dislodge him.

Linton gazed round the room. He saw that there were more people than there had been at dinner last night, but probably some of them were not staying, had only dropped in for lunch. He regarded them benevolently, and opened a magazine which must have arrived by the midday post. His walk had given him an appetite. The Ballycastle air, he thought, agreed with him, for already he felt much better—felt a different person. He had been uncertain yesterday as to how long he should stay, but now he decided that it would be foolish to cut his visit short; he would see about it after lunch and if possible book his room till the end of the month.

With this purpose, as soon as the meal was over, he sought out the manageress in her private den. He was as eager now as before he had been apathetic, and breathed a sigh of relief when Miss O'Casey told him she was sure the matter could be arranged. She consulted a ledger and found that she might have to change his room; but that would be all, and even that, she hoped, would not be necessary.

Linton remained for five minutes chatting with Miss O'Casey, during which he praised the food, praised the hotel, praised the climate and the scenery, and praised Micky. There was nothing left to praise, indeed, except Miss O'Casey herself, and though he stopped short of this, he left that lady wreathed in smiles and with an entirely altered impression of him. He closed the office door behind him, and returning to the hall, paused to tap the barometer. He did this, not because he distrusted the weather, but in a spirit of sheer friendliness. He felt well; he felt younger; he felt what he had not felt for months, a hope, a tremulous belief, that he might get back to work. Not the stupid, pottering kind of work—revisions and annotations—which was all, since his illness, he had been equal to; but the old creative stuff:—the impulse was stirring within him like the whispering of forest leaves, like the soft fluttering of wings. Only it wouldn't, this time, be a novel. Why shouldn't he try his hand at something quite new—or new for him at all events—an adventure story—better still, a children's story? It would be a story and nothing but a story—done for the fun of doing it—something which would be all lightness and happiness and irresponsibility. He even saw the beginning of it—in the hall of a big house in the country, on a wet afternoon. A grandfather's clock was ticking; through the open door came the warm splash of rain on leaves. And a small boy who had grown tired of read-ing——Well, he could think it over better out of doors; and first he would see what this fellow had to say....

This fellow was not his small hero, but the author of an article in the current number of an American review—the magazine which had arrived while he was out for his walk. At lunch he had had no more than time to glance at it and to see that it contained an essay on himself, but he tucked it under his arm now.

In the porch of the hotel he filled his pipe, said good-bye to Micky, and turned to look up the hill-road. There was no one in sight—or rather the person he was looking for wasn't in sight—so he strolled on, taking the direction he had taken in the morning, though this time he did not go farther than the bank overlooking the tennis-courts. Here he sat down; but the courts were at present empty, he seemed to be too early, so he opened his review. He read on until he had finished the essay, which he found well-written and sympathetic. Subtle, too, in its way, and up to a point understanding; which made it all the stranger, Linton thought, that it should miss what he himself would have made the very nucleus of such a study. But he supposed it was too much to expect even the most sensitive of readers quite to grasp what you were after—the primal idea, that is to say, which to you means so much simply because it is the spiritual reality of which your work can at best be only a symbol. And yet this fellow, whose name was unfamiliar to him, and who probably was young, really must like the books, and certainly he seemed to know them backwards. His criticism was not only appreciative, but Linton fancied he could detect in it a note of affection also. Affection for the writings naturally—but then, as he had pointed out to that boy only an hour or two ago, the writings were unusually personal....

And the essay, even if it had not discovered the deepest intention of them—had ransacked the temple, as it were, only to miss the lighted votive lamp burning at the heart of it—nevertheless pleased him. It was graceful and well-thought—and very likely much too kind. But that wasn't really why it pleased him. The true reason was that it had come at exactly the right moment. It might almost have been sent on purpose to encourage him—to remind him that he *had* accomplished something, *had* gained his own little niche, and written several things of which he need not feel ashamed.

Just there Linton paused, and his brows drew together in a slight frown. A question had presented itself to him. Why was it the right moment? Why should praise which would have left him completely indifferent yesterday, to-day give him pleasure?

It was strange; but he had analysed too many states of mind not to be able now to analyse his own. It was all part of the same thing. Why had he decided to stay on at Ballycastle till the end of the month? Why had he sat down in this particular spot, which was very far from being the most attractive or the most comfortable he could have chosen? The answer was that he had booked his room for a month because that boy had said he would be staying here for a month, and had perched himself on this bank because it overlooked the tennis-ground where he would be playing. Would his American critic, the appreciative exponent of his writings, think this foolish? Very likely, for how should he understand? But Linton knew—knew that the interest he had suddenly begun to feel was the only genuine interest he had felt in anything for a long while. He could not account for it, and there was the chance that he might be mistaken, the chance that his first impression was based merely on a charm of manner and appearance, that the boy did not really in the least resemble his idea of him, and that on closer acquaintance he would find they had nothing in common. Only he did not think so, and in any case why anticipate disappointment? Was it not at least as foolish to do this as it would be to build a dream-castle on the slender foundation of a single meeting?

Linton closed his magazine and sat thinking. It is to be feared that the glimmering outline of a castle did indeed begin to take shape in the air before him—to rise wall by wall and tower by tower, with the sun touching its roofs and bastions, its diaphanous turrets and gilded spires....

When he came back to earth again, he saw that the courts had begun to fill up. A good many people had arrived and others were arriving, though among them he did not see his young friend. Then he saw him—coming down the green wooden steps on the opposite side of the ground, the last of a party of four, composed of two girls, an older youth, and himself. They came straight across the ground towards Linton, in single file, the boy bringing up the rear. He was now in white flannels, with a striped school blazer, and looked different and yet the same. Linton was prepared to wave a greeting; he expected at least some sign of recognition; but to his surprise none was forthcoming. Surely the boy must have seen him, for Linton was directly in his line of vision, and moreover was perched in a distinctly conspicuous position, which he shared at present only with a couple of nurses and perambulators. He was puzzled, loth to believe that he had been cut, and yet far from certain that he hadn't. The boy carried a racquet and a small net containing half-a-dozen tennis-balls. He had an air of shyness and reserve, and though he spoke with his companions as they stood all four close to the wall above which Linton sat, he looked a little out of it.

The others were enjoying themselves; their voices and laughter reached Linton's ears quite distinctly through the general babble; and he wondered which of the girls was the boy's sister. He could not even guess, for neither in the least resembled him. Their conversation—at first somewhat subdued owing to the presence of so many strangers—grew more and more vivacious, but the boy did not enter into it; and presently he withdrew a few paces and stood by himself, watching a sett, though not as if he took much interest in it. He looked bored and lonely, not at all as he had looked in the morning, when he and Linton were sitting by the sea. And Linton felt a sudden desire to transport him, 'through the vehemency of his spirit', out of that place and company, as the angel of the Lord had transported Habakkuk. "The angel of the Lord took him by the crown, and bare him by the hair of his head," he whispered to himself.

He wondered if there had been some disagreement on the way, or what it was that held the boy aloof from his friends. They didn't appear to amuse him—in his present mood at any rate—and he showed this rather plainly. Even while he noted it, Linton with a slight shock realized that the boy's attitude was by no means displeasing to him. It ought to have been, for surely he wanted him to enjoy himself. Only he couldn't help feeling glad that he had seemed so much happier in the morning: he had struck Linton then as extraordinarily happy, animated and gay....

Meanwhile he had rejoined his party and said something which caused the others to turn and gaze in one direction. Linton turned too. The sett on the court farthest away, over by the groundsmen's shed, appeared to have come to an end—at least the players were standing in a little group at the net—and the boy and his companions, after a brief consultation, began to walk slowly in that direction. Would it do to follow them, Linton asked himself, but immediately decided that it would. He let them get a little ahead and then sauntered after them along the bank.

Again he sat down. He was absolutely certain now that the boy must know of his presence, though he still obstinately refused to look at him. They paired off—the dark thin hatchet-faced youth—whose glistening head, suggestive of a preparation of lamp-black and molasses, no angel would willingly have touched—remaining on Linton's side of the ground with the smaller and slighter of the two girls. *She,* then, must be Claire, the boy's sister, and he looked at her with an increased interest. She was small and slim and agile—and strikingly pretty in a demure and dainty fashion. Her features were much more delicate than her brother's, and her skin, though not really dark, had an olive tinge dark in comparison with his exceptional fairness.

The game started. Claire (it seemed odd that he should know her name while still not knowing that of his young friend) was quick and neat, and a much better player than her brother. So, for that matter, were the other two; but then Linton's boy played marvellously badly. Endearingly badly to Linton, who was reminded as he watched him of a bull-pup he had once possessed. There was the same recklessness and clumsiness, the same eager impetuous lungeous quality, which had sent mats skidding over floors, and the cat, for safety, on to the sideboard or the chimney-piece. It was now his service—first a tremendously hard ball into the net, and then the mildest of lobs, which soared loftily into the air and dropped in the middle of the court with a gentle bounce. Linton watched him affectionately: his partner, he imagined, with less affection—in spite of the word 'sorry' which was repeated so often. But then he didn't look sorry, and apologies didn't alter his tactics, prevent him from rushing up to the net—always with disastrous results—prevent him from poaching, from falling, from getting in her way and leaving his own side of the court unprotected. No, she didn't like it. She said little, but when she did expostulate her voice had an edge. Linton on the other hand liked it extremely: it was exactly right; it was all part and parcel of the impression he had received—or at least he imagined that it was.

Only he would have liked it a good deal better if after the sett was over—and it ended rather rapidly at 6-o—the boy had come and spoken to him, or even looked up and nodded. Surely he ought at least to do that.... But he didn't. He stayed with his friends, and they didn't interest Linton at all, except that he noticed that the boy seemed now to be getting on much better with them and to have begun to enjoy himself. He was demonstrating certain strokes with his racquet and the others were laughing. Then all four began talking at once, putting their heads together, discussing something eagerly.

Linton wondered what it was, for opinions appeared to be divided. Claire wanted it, he saw, and so did the tall dark youth: the other girl was more reluctant, the boy most reluctant. But evidently he gave in, for a sudden decision was reached, and with one consent they moved over to the opposite side of the ground where several tables were laid for tea.

Linton sat on alone. Quite alone now, for his few fellow-spectators had wandered away, and even the nurses and perambulators were gone. Two or three belated games were still in progress, but most of the players had gathered round the tables, and the remainder were only waiting to finish before joining them....

The boy *might* have come. It would have been nicer of him to have come and said just a word or two. He needn't have done more than that, and Linton once again asked himself why he hadn't. It looked as if he intended to repudiate their acquaintance, yet he didn't for a moment believe this. Probably he was shy—though he could at least have nodded when the others had their backs turned.... No, it wasn't very civil; and in the morning he had seemed to have such pleasant manners. It left Linton, too, in the uncomfortable position of not knowing whether his advances—for certainly he had made advances—were welcome or not; whether he ought to go on or to retreat. In the meantime he could do nothing except wait—wait and see. It would have been wiser, he supposed, not to have come to watch him. Yet why shouldn't he come? Other people had come—several from the hotel. Still, if his presence was embarrassing to the boy, he had better relieve him of it. So he got up, and carrying his magazine under his arm, went on his way.

Chapter V

BRIAN

B rian sat at the window turning over the pages of his manuscript; Mrs Westby and Claire were playing bezique. It had begun to rain about six o'clock, and he was glad, because he wanted to work and knew that if it had been fine he would have been tempted to go out.

He was only revising at present—altering a phrase here and there, with a view to the reading to take place next day. He felt nervous about this reading, and probably would be more nervous still when the time came, yet on the whole he did not regret his promise. On the way back from the tennis-club Derek Graham had said something about seeing him in the morning, and he had put him off, though perhaps a little too vaguely, with a general remark about being busy in the mornings, which Derek might or might not accept as final. Still, he couldn't very well say he had made an appointment with an unknown person from the hotel. At any rate he *hadn't* said it, and wasn't going to mention it at home either: they were all so inquisitive and would at once begin to ask questions.

Brian didn't want questions: not just now at all events. He wasn't sure how his mother would regard the matter and it was quite possible that she mightn't approve of it. Not that she could have any reasonable grounds for disapproval; but there were always the unreasonable ones; the man knew his father: yes, she might very easily object.

That was the chief reason why he had avoided looking at him or going to speak to him at the tennis-club. He had thought it wiser not to, though now he had an uneasy feeling that it really wasn't wisdom which had prevented him, and that it must have seemed very strange. The true reason was that it had been quite plain to

Brian his new friend had come for no other purpose than to watch *him*, and if the others had guessed that they would have thought it so queer! It *was* queer, too. Brian thought so himself, though he had not been surprised, and even, in an odd way, had expected it. But there was a peculiar streak of timidity in his nature which caused him to shrink from anything likely to attract attention or make people talk. He would explain his behaviour to his friend at their next meeting, tell him who he was and about his mother. Probably he already knew about her, but there was just a chance that he didn't know very much, a chance that his father, like his mother, had adopted a policy of silence....

It suddenly struck Brian that in all this he was assuming they were going to see a lot more of each other, which might not be the stranger's intention at all. He thought it was; he even thought they were going to be friends; but he could not be sure. And by 'friends' he meant really friends—not friends as he and Derek were friends, but in the way you only can be with somebody who is definitely of your kind. Brian had never met anybody of his kind before....

He stared out of the window; then knelt down and put his head and shoulders out. The rain was nearly over, but the air was saturated with a cold salt damp mist and everything was soaking wet. He could hear the waves breaking far down on the pebbly beach, but he could not see them. The house stood some thirty or forty yards back from the cliff's edge so that all view of the shore was cut off and he could see only a wide, heaving expanse of greenish-grey water, sullen and desolate under the livid clouds.

When the rain stopped he would go out. The dark broken sea, spume-flecked and overcast, had an obscure fascination for him. He would go along the road beneath the cliffs, over the rocks where his mother had sprained her ankle; he would go round the cliffs as far as he could. The shore would be deserted, there would be nothing but the rocks and the sea, with the steep cliffs towering above him. He would go whether it stopped raining or not.... In the room behind him his mother declared a sequence and Claire exclaimed at her luck.

Brian had a sudden feeling that they were completely cut off from him and outside his life. He wondered how they could go on

playing that game night after night without getting sick of it. Now
and then *he* had played, but his mother didn't enjoy playing with
him, because in the middle of the game his thoughts would sometimes wander. Then she would accuse him of taking no interest in
it; and it was true, he didn't.

He looked down the empty streaming road and saw two people,
waterproofed and umbrella'd, climbing the hill very slowly—the
Grahams—Mr and Mrs. He guessed at once that they were coming to inquire after his mother, which would mean that he would
get no more work done unless he retired to his bedroom. But if
he did do this, Claire probably would be sent to bring him back,
because Mr Graham was supposed to take an interest in him. He
didn't really, but he was supposed to, and to like to talk to him
about books.

Brian detested the talks about books. Yet he couldn't very de-
cently avoid them. That was the worst of it; he had brought the
whole thing on his own head by oiling up to Mr Graham in the first
instance, under the impression that he might be useful. He hadn't
known him then, he had merely heard his mother and Claire talking about him—saying that he wrote for some paper or other and
was a friend of the editor. Brian had accepted this (he would be a
jolly sight more careful in future!) and after his last term at school
had called on him. He certainly *was* literary—the most literary
person Brian had ever met. 'Where do you place Matthew Arnold?'
—'Where do you place Shelley?'—that was the kind of question he
fired at you—always about people you had never read. And it wasn't
as if he himself really had anything to say about them: it was just
one name after another.

Mr Graham was a bore and a humbug, and he had done nothing for Brian at all. He had talked about getting him books to
review, so that he had come away from his first visit with the highest hopes, but after the fourth or fifth these hopes had subsided.
There had merely been a repetition of the same vague promises to
introduce him to the editor of *The Book-Lover's Weekly*, and when
Brian had discovered that Mr Graham's own contributions to this
wretched rag weren't even paid for, he had felt like sending him in
a bill for all the time he had wasted.

The contributor to *The Book-Lover's Weekly* was ringing the hall-door bell now, and Brian, who had drawn in his head at first sight of the approaching visitors, announced the fact. His mother glanced up to see him standing with a rather shocked expression on his face, but she was used to her son's peculiarities, and merely murmured, "Oh!" Then she added, "You'd better run down and help them off with their wet things."

"I'll go," cried Claire, jumping up from the table.

She had reached the door before Brian could make a movement, and he heard her rushing downstairs and greeting the visitors brightly and effusively. It was like her!—always the little ray of sunshine—or intended to be. He listened morosely. And in a minute or two they came up, with Claire hovering in the rear, and there followed the usual fuss of inquiries and sympathy, of pulling out chairs and getting everybody settled, in the midst of which Brian retreated to his old position at the window.

Mrs Graham sat down on the sofa beside his mother, and for a while they held hands and cooed little speeches at each other, like a pair of wood-pigeons on a branch. They always did this, but tonight it lasted longer than usual because of his mother's accident. Mrs Graham was fond of holding hands, and sometimes, if she hadn't seen you recently, she would take your hand between both of hers and pat it softly. Now, after the preliminary cooing was over, as was her custom she said little, and that little very slowly and gently. Her white quiet voice had a queer little break in it, a kind of huskiness, and its lingering slowness made the almost infantile simplicity of her remarks the more noticeable. Brian liked her. She was the kind of person you got fond of without any interchange of ideas. She was older than his mother, whom she was inclined to pet—but then she was inclined to pet everybody: and her silver hair was beautiful. So, he thought, was the expression in her mild uncritical face. She wasn't clever, but on the other hand you never thought of her as stupid, and you knew she was kind and good.

What seemed to Brian queer was that she should have chosen a husband with much of the manner and all the appearance of one of the less tolerant of the minor prophets. He couldn't believe she *had* chosen him. Mr Graham was tall and gaunt and bony, with a deep voice, grey unkempt hair, and a grey unkempt beard. He had the irritability and egotism of a prophet too, and must have been as difficult to live with, though just now he was making himself agreeable. The conversation turned on sprains, doctors, masseurs, and methods of treatment—topics which, if not enthralling, were at least comfortably remote from Matthew Arnold and Shelley. Yet no sooner had Brian reached this conclusion than he saw the prophet's gaze seeking him out with a dreadful purpose behind it. Instantly he stiffened himself into a bolt-upright position, while his own blue eyes grew round with expectation, defiance, and alarm. Thus they sat glaring at each other across the room. He knew it was coming—the exasperating, the inevitable question:—'Where do you place——' As a matter of fact, when it did come, it was a question he ought easily to have been able to deal with, being merely that very old stager, whether he preferred Thackeray to Dickens; but Brian was so absorbed in staring at Mr Graham that it never occurred to him to answer. There was a silence while everybody looked at him. Then his mother said, "Why don't you answer Mr Graham, dear?" and with a violent effort he managed to mumble out, "Oh, I don't know."

It was meant as his contribution to the Dickens and Thackeray quandary, but it didn't sound like it. Mr Graham expressed his own verdict: he preferred Thackeray—which was of course what he would do. Only he wasn't content to let it go at that; he insisted on eliciting Brian's view also. And Brian had no view; he had never thought about it, and was suddenly angry with the others for listening. Why couldn't they go on with their own conversation, or else join in this one, instead of leaving it all to him? Mr Graham ignored the others completely. He mentioned *The Newcomes*. Where did Brian place *The Newcomes*? Brian didn't place it anywhere, he hadn't read it. Actually he had placed it back on the shelf again after struggling through the first chapter, but though this reply entered his mind he was much too diffident to speak it aloud. From *The Newcomes* they passed speedily to *The Virginians*: and then to quite unknown works—*Philip, Lovel the Widower, Men's Wives, Catherine*: —Brian doubted if half of them were by Thackeray at all....

Mr Graham had risen from his chair and was coming to join him at the window when Mrs Graham stopped him. "I don't like to interrupt you and Brian, Wilfrid," she said, "but I think we ought to be going. I told Derek and Eva to be in for supper at nine, and you know how slowly I walk." She turned to Mrs Westby. "I'm afraid it's a very short visit, dear, but really we only looked in for a few minutes to see how you were and to bring a message from the children: they want Claire and Brian to play tennis with them to-morrow morning at half-past ten. They say the courts are usually ready then."

"Thanks awfully," Claire accepted at once; but Brian was silent for a minute, and then said, "I'm sorry I can't."

Claire flushed, bit her lip, and turned away: his mother looked at him persuasively. "Why can't you, dear, if they want you to, and if it's fine?" she murmured.

"Whether it's fine or not, the courts will be wet," Brian replied.

"They won't," Claire snapped. "They dry up in an hour or two after far worse rain than this."

But unexpectedly his mother came to his rescue. "Brian likes to work in the mornings," she explained to Mrs Graham. "He's very much interested in his writing."

Brian was surprised and pleased. His manner immediately altered. "I told Derek I was always busy in the morning," he said apologetically.

"Unless you were to write in the afternoon instead," his mother suggested. "Perhaps you could do that?"

He shook his head. "I don't think so." But the others were looking at him and he hesitated. The fact, too, that his mother had taken his part made him unwilling to be disobliging. "It's not just my work," he explained. "I have an engagement: I promised to meet somebody."

These words created quite a sensation. Everybody stared at him as if he had said something extraordinary, and Brian could only stare back. Why shouldn't he have engagements as well as other people? His mother was the first to recover from her astonishment. "Who is the somebody?" she asked, and they all waited eagerly for his reply.

"I'm afraid I can't tell you who he is," Brian answered stiffly. Then his dignity vanished as he began to feel a little foolish. "I can't tell you, because I don't know myself. I mean I don't know his name."

At this the sensation was renewed, and even Claire looked more curious than annoyed. "Where is he staying?" Mrs Westby asked. "And how did you come to make friends with him?"

"I didn't say I had made friends with him," Brian replied. "As a matter of fact I only met him this morning—and he's staying at the Marine Hotel."

His mother considered a moment, while her eyes—still faintly perplexed—rested thoughtfully upon him. "Couldn't you let him know?" she then suggested. "Very likely the afternoon would suit him just as well."

"How can I let him know?" Brian exclaimed. "I can't go to the hotel and ask for somebody whose name I don't know; and even if I could, I could hardly tell him that I won't be able to meet him because something better has turned up."

"It wouldn't be necessary to put it in that way," his mother said quietly. "You could find out first if the afternoon *would* suit him. And as for asking for him, there aren't likely to be so many boys staying at the hotel that they won't be able to guess who you want."

"He isn't a boy," Brian answered.

"Do you mean he's a *man?*"

"Naturally."

But at this point, with characteristic kindliness, Mrs Graham herself intervened. "I do feel Brian is right," she said mildly. "If he has made an engagement he ought to keep it. It's not as if the other was of the least importance: they've all day long and every day to play tennis."

Mrs Westby gave in at once, but Claire said, speaking in a dry little voice, "Then I suppose I'd better not come either."

Mrs Graham had not meant that at all. "Of course you must come," she declared. "Derek will find somebody to take Brian's place, and if he can't, he'll let you know first thing after breakfast. But he's sure to be able to. There's always the Garratt boy. He and Derek were working at their bicycles this evening—taking them to pieces the way they're so fond of doing. Eva went to the Rectory to listen to some new gramophone records the girls have got."

She rose to say good-night, and a general movement ensued.

"Have you got a title for your novel yet?" Mr Graham asked Brian in a deep sepulchral voice while he shook hands with him. "I heard them saying to-night you were writing one."

Brian darted a furious glance at Claire, which became angrier still when from behind the others she protruded the tip of her tongue at him. "No," he muttered, and turned away.

Then, to avoid further questions from his mother, he followed the Grahams out of the room and downstairs; and when the visitors were gone and the door closed behind them, he still remained standing in the hall, waiting to give them time to get a good start before himself putting on his waterproof and going out.

He walked slowly, knowing the Grahams' snail's pace and not wishing to overtake them. Presently he caught sight of them and stopped. He stood gazing out to sea. His mood was already changing, he was beginning to feel that he would like to play tennis in the morning, and a few minutes later he decided that he ought to play. After all, he could see his hotel friend any time. There were always the evenings, when there was nothing else to do, and, as his mother had said, it couldn't make much difference to him when they met.

Having satisfied his conscience, Brian moved on again until he reached the hotel. Here he paused, but was too shy to follow Mrs Westby's advice and go in. Instead, he loitered about at the corner, walking up and down, which, as he knew, was futile. He took out his watch. It was half-past nine; supper was at ten; so if he was going to do anything about to-morrow he must do it soon. And he had just made up his mind to go into the hotel when he saw his stranger in the distance, coming along the road from the town. This was lucky, and Brian hastened to meet him, in his sudden relief smiling and waving his hand. "Hello!" he called out. "Where have *you* been?" Instantly he felt that this greeting was far too off-hand and familiar. He felt himself flushing. He didn't know *why* he had spoken like that. But next moment the visible pleasure in the dark, rather tired face turned to him told him that all was well. His discomposure vanished: at the same time, just because the pleasure *was* so visible, he found a greater difficulty in saying what he had intended to say.

Meanwhile they both had stopped in the middle of the road and Brian's question was being answered. "I've been exploring the town," his friend said. "It didn't take very long and wasn't very interesting. Everybody appears to have gone to bed."

"I thought I might see you," Brian declared. "That's why I was hanging about. I didn't get much chance to speak to you this afternoon."

As an excuse, he felt it sounded rather weak, but it was accepted —at any rate was not challenged. All the stranger remarked was, "It's a pity it's so late. If we go into the hotel now there won't be a spot where we can talk comfortably. The lounge and the drawing-room and the smoking-room were all occupied when I left: nobody else, I suppose, thought it an attractive evening for a walk."

"Well, it *has* been pretty wet," Brian smiled. "If it had been fine I'd have come earlier. Now, I'm afraid, I'll have to be getting back. I'm supposed to be in at ten."

"May I come with you?" the stranger asked.

Brian demurred. "It's an awful climb," he pointed out, "and I think it's going to rain again: in fact it's beginning now.... Of course, come if you want to," he hurriedly added. "I mean, if you don't mind."

The stranger answered simply, "Then I think I will."

They walked on in silence, turning the corner and proceeding along the sea-front. A thin drizzle had begun to fall, the road was quite empty, and through the blinded windows of most of the houses lights shone. Suddenly the stranger said, "I'm very glad you came."

Brian glanced at him. He was glad too, but he knew he was receiving credit for a motive he had not had, and was tempted to let it go at that. Only, if he did, he would have to keep his appointment in the morning. On the other hand, if he played tennis he would be pleasing Claire and the Grahams—and himself. He walked on for a few yards thinking it over. Then he said, "I wanted to see you—about to-morrow morning."

There was a brief pause. "Yes?" said the stranger.

But Brian still kept silence.

"Well?" the stranger urged him, with a faint smile.

Brian did not smile. "It's nothing," he replied. It hadn't occurred to him that their arrangement to meet to-morrow might have been looked forward to with a good deal of pleasure. Now he knew it had.

"You would like to do something else—you don't want to come —isn't that it?"

"No, it's not exactly that." Brian waited a moment: he found it difficult to explain, because now his own wish had altered. "It's only that I was asked to play tennis in the morning. But I'm not going to."

"Why not? I thought perhaps you meant that you didn't want to come at all. The afternoon will suit me quite as well and give us just as much time. I don't suppose you want to play both morning and afternoon."

"No, but—I want to go for a ride in the afternoon—to Carrick-a-Rede.... And in the evening we're going to the pictures."

"I see."

"I don't think you do see," Brian went on uneasily. "You think I'm trying to put you off. Anyway, I'll meet you in the morning: I don't really care about the tennis. As a matter of fact I had already refused."

"Then why did you mention it?"

"I don't know. I oughtn't to have mentioned it. I really want to come and to bring my MS." He had halted, and his gaze was fixed on his companion's face. He wished this to be definitely settled before they proceeded further. "I oughtn't to have mentioned it," he repeated.

There was another pause. "I wish——" the stranger began; but the sentence died away and Brian never learned what he wished.

They climbed the hill without speaking. It was distinctly queer: they hardly knew each other, and yet somehow an odd indefinite relation seemed to have sprung up between them. Brian had felt it before, towards the end of their first meeting, but he felt it much more strongly now. It was puzzling; not a bit like his relation with anybody else. He felt, too, that it was not really of his making—at any rate, not chiefly. Its unusualness interested and even a little excited him, though he was not sure yet how much he liked it. What he knew was that in some mysterious way he mattered to this man, and that also was what was strange. For why should he matter? It was pleasant of course to feel that he did, but on the other hand he didn't want to feel it too much, not to feel that everything he *did* mattered. And then—it was so extraordinarily sudden! He now was quite sure of what an hour or two ago had only seemed a possibility—sure that they were going to be friends....

They had begun to walk on again and were approaching the house. Brian pointed it out, and at the same time his pace once more slackened. It might appear ungracious, but he did not want the stranger to come right up to the hall-door, did not want his mother and Claire to know they had walked home together.

The rain had thickened gradually and was mingled with a fog which floated in from the sea. The salt air left a moist clinging stickiness on Brian's hands and face and clothes. He could taste it on his lips, and its smell was everywhere, like the smell of wet seaweed. The low roar of the waves breaking on the beach, the long swirling backwash of water and sand and gravel, had a strangely melancholy sound in the darkness. And yet it had another quality too, a quality which made for intimacy. Never before had he felt quite like this—so completely in sympathy with another person's mood.

"Shall I call for you?" he asked. "I mean to-morrow morning."

The stranger was looking at him and Brian wondered what he found to make him look so pleased. Yet the words he spoke were commonplace enough. "Just as you like."

Brian laughed—he didn't know why—except that he felt happy. "Then I think I'd rather meet you somewhere outside. I'll walk on round the shore in the direction of the place where you first saw me, but I won't go past that."

"Very well," the stranger agreed, "I'll keep a look-out for you.... I suppose about half-past ten?"

"Yes," Brian said. Then he said good-night, and added in a low shy voice, "Thank you for walking home with me."

Chapter VI

BRIAN

Coming into the sitting-room, Brian thought it looked very homely and cosy after the wet and darkness outside. A lamp was burning softly in the middle of the table at which Claire and his mother were seated. Mrs Westby glanced up on his entrance, but to his surprise and relief no questions were asked, and in silence he got his book and sat down to read.

He read little, however, and that little only with his eyes, for he found it impossible to fix his attention. From time to time he looked at the others, and they appeared to be absorbed—Claire in *The Strand Magazine* and his mother in a game of patience. Presently he found himself half wishing that they *would* say something. On Claire's part the silence was unnatural, and he came to the conclusion that she must be acting under instructions from his mother, which meant that they had entered into a conspiracy together—a conspiracy to humour him. Yet neither at supper that evening nor at breakfast next morning was a word uttered concerning his mysterious stranger.

Breakfast was later than usual, and Derek when he arrived found them still at the table. He had come on his motor-bicycle, and must have been primed not to forget to inquire after Mrs Westby's ankle, for he began to do so before he was well inside the room. Then almost in the same breath he said to Claire, "I've got a fourth—Jimmy Garratt. He was going to play golf, but I told him he'd mess up our party unless he came along. So he's coming. When can you be ready?"

"I'm ready now," Claire replied.

"Good egg!" said Derek. "Another thing is—about pills. Eva thinks the courts will still be fairly wet and that it's a pity to use new ones."

Brian, who had been eating stolidly, stopped at this. It struck him as being, even for Derek, pretty cool, and he waited to hear what it would bring forth.

"I'll bring ours," Claire said meekly.

Still with a piece of bread poised on its way to his mouth, Brian spoke. "Ours are new. I bought them the day before we came down."

Claire ignored him, but Derek laughed. "Good old Brian! Bring them along, Claire, and never mind the big brother." He glanced at his wrist-watch. "See you in half an hour: I've got to do two or three messages first." He waved his hand from the door, and then, suddenly catching Brian's eye, grinned broadly. "How's *Nature Distressed* getting on? Pretty hot stuff from all accounts!"

He was gone before Brian could think of a retort, and a little later a rapid series of detonations reached them through the open window, in the midst of which Claire rose from the table.

Brian, though they had finished breakfast, sat on. "She's told him," he announced grimly to his mother. "She's told them all."

Mrs Westby was noting down on the back of a used envelope a list of things she wanted to be sent from town. "Told them what, dear?" she murmured absently.

"Told them about my book."

Mrs Westby added yet another item to her list before she looked up and saw the sombre expression on his face. She smiled at him, but received only a deeper frown in response. "Was there any secret about it?" she asked soothingly. "I should think they must all know by this time that you write."

"They didn't know I was writing a novel," Brian answered gloomily. "And they didn't know its name. Claire told them that."

"But Mr Graham asked you about it last night," she reminded him. "Surely their knowing the name can't make much difference!"

"It does make a difference. I didn't want anybody to know."

"*Nature Distressed,*" his mother repeated innocently.

He glared at her, but swallowed down his wrath. "It's *not Nature Distressed,*" he said impatiently. "As if anybody would choose such a title!"

"Well then——" his mother was beginning: but he interrupted her. "He called it that because he was trying to be funny."

Mrs Westby still seemed not quite to understand, though she did her best to smooth things down. "Does it matter?" she asked gently. "I mean, you worry yourself so over trifles."

"It isn't a trifle," Brian replied. "And she'd no right to look at it in the first place. If I had read anything private of hers there'd have been fuss enough! You allow her to do exactly what she likes. She only told the Grahams out of spite—because I wouldn't play golf."

He could say no more, however, for Mrs Belford had come in to clear the table. So he went to his room, and when he came down with his bathing-things and his manuscript, Claire was in the hall, about to start.

They walked down the hill together, but not from choice. Brian had no intention of speaking to her, and Claire on her part seemed quite indifferent to his sulkiness. It certainly did not perturb her, and when they were passing the turning down to the pier she asked him where he was going to bathe.

He did not answer: as a matter of fact he had not consciously heard her, having at that moment—and by no means with plea-sure—caught sight of his stranger, who was seated on the low wall in front of the hotel, with his back turned to them. Why couldn't he have walked on as he had said he would! Brian felt the blood rising to his cheeks. He turned his head quickly and pretended to be looking at the sea, but Claire, whether because he had not answered, or through some feminine gift of divination, immedi-ately knew of his embarrassment. "What's the matter?" she asked curiously, and then gazed round to discover the answer for herself. She instantly found it, as he had known she would. "Gracious, is *that* your friend!" she exclaimed.

Brian had stopped, and was bending down, fumbling with his shoe-lace. "You go on," he muttered angrily. "I've got a stone in my shoe."

But Claire waited for him. "If the stone's imaginary," she said, "I shouldn't trouble about it, because for one thing he's not look-ing at us, and for another I shan't expect to be introduced."

Brian retied his lace and stood up. As he did so the Grahams and

Jimmy Garratt came round the corner of the hotel. They were still nearly a hundred yards off, but Claire hullooed to them, and they came on to meet her, running or pretending to run a race. Eva Graham had already begun to scream at Brian. "You *are* a slacker!" she cried, grabbing him by one arm while Jimmy Garratt grabbed him by the other.

Brian vainly struggled to free himself, and Claire murmured in an undertone, "He had another engagement. That's his friend— sitting over there on the wall."

Brian was immediately released, and the two Grahams and Jimmy Garratt turned in silence to stare at the seated figure, who had not looked round in spite of the noise they were making.

Brian hoped he wouldn't look round. He wished he hadn't waited there. Of course he had done so in complete innocence and with the best intentions, but that didn't make it any the less irritating. What was the use of making arrangements if you weren't going to keep them! He said good-bye to the others abruptly, but had a feeling—perfectly justified—that they were all watching him with the liveliest interest as he crossed the road.

Chapter VII

LINTON

L inton knew he was there; he had heard his voice; but he knew the others were there too, and purposely did not look round. Besides, he got an odd pleasure from waiting like this. It was a childish pleasure doubtless, much the same as that which makes a small boy with a brown-paper parcel, which he knows to contain a present, refrain from opening it, while he examines its exterior, feels its shape, shakes it and weighs it in his hands in excited anticipation. So Linton remained, still and expectant, until he heard a subdued "Hello!" behind him. Then he turned.

"It's exactly half-past ten," the boy said. "I'm absolutely punctual."

"I was more than punctual," Linton answered.

"That means you were *un*punctual. To be punctual is to arrive at the time you said you would, neither before nor after."

Linton stood up. "All right." His eyes rested on the punctual person and for a minute or two he remained thus, saying nothing, but feeling very happy.

Then the boy made a movement. "Hadn't we better go on," he suggested, and Linton smiled.

"Yes," he said. "I suppose so."

The boy left the narrow path to him and walked on the grass. Presently he gave Linton a sidelong look. "What's the joke?" he inquired.

"I don't believe there is a joke," Linton answered. "Why should you think there is?"

"Well, you seem to be laughing—or at least smiling—so I suppose there must be a joke of some kind."

"Not necessarily."

"Why are you smiling, then?"

This time Linton laughed outright. "I don't expect I can tell you: it's very difficult."

"Why?"

"Because it's so complicated.... To begin with—until you mentioned it—it hadn't occurred to me that I was smiling."

"Well, you were—all over—beaming in fact."

"Don't you think the weather might account for it?" Linton said. "The sunshine—or possibly the view? The view, as a matter of fact, I'm sure had something to do with it."

"What view?"

"*My* view.... You needn't look," he went on: "you won't be able to see it, because you're part of it.... Anyhow, I think it's a mistake to inquire too closely into these things. When some comfortable old tabby asks herself why she's purring she at once ceases to purr. Which is the same thing as—If the Sun and Moon should doubt, they'd immediately go out.... I don't want them to go out."

The boy puckered his brow for a moment; then changed the subject. "Where shall we go?" he asked in an expressionless voice. "I mean, if you want me to read to you I suppose we'll have to sit down somewhere, and the grass will be wet."

"We could go back to the hotel and get a rug," Linton said.

The boy was looking down at the tennis-ground below them, where his friends were already busy on one of the courts, raising and lowering a net to get it at the right height. "It seems hardly worth while," he said.

Linton waited a moment: the sun and moon were obviously flickering: they hadn't lasted very long. Then he asked, "Do you want to play tennis? Because, if you do, it's still not too late."

But he knew it was too late—especially when suggested in that tone. The boy merely shook his head. "Anyhow, they've got a four," he added simply; and though this was true it was none the less discouraging.

Linton looked at him doubtfully. Things weren't working out so well after all. Yet he could not think what was the matter, except that the boy was certainly different from what he had been at their last meeting—was less animated, perhaps faintly bored. His unresponsiveness was creating a barrier between them. Linton felt that the only thing to do was to pretend not to notice it, but he wasn't much good at pretending, and by the time they had crossed the bridge and were walking along the sand at the sea's edge they both had relapsed into silence.

And then, to his surprise, the boy's mood all at once altered. Perhaps it was because they had left the tennis-ground behind them and were now alone—Linton had no idea. He only knew that his own state of mind instantly reflected his companion's. He had no perception of what had happened, or how it had happened, or why; but it was quite clear that they had somehow got back into their former relationship, and that the barrier was gone.

It was their true relationship, he reflected—the only one that made for any permanency: it must be either this or nothing. And it seemed to him to spring from a spiritual affinity which existed below the wide difference of age and experience. Between his temperament and the boy's there was a marked resemblance, though there might (he was not sure) be a marked dissimilarity as well. It was too early yet to see where the likeness ended and the unlikeness began, for they were still only at the stage of mutual discovery. But, below all disparities, he was convinced there was something essential and vital which they shared—a point of view, a sympathy, an understanding....

The boy had begun to talk about his school—of his life there, of masters and other boys—and through his talk, like a natural accompaniment to it, sounded the breaking of the waves. And, as always, with the sound of the sea there floated into Linton's mind fragments of poetry. They were only fragments; he was listening really to the boy's chatter: but woven through his chatter were these golden threads of poetry and music—making it mysteriously lovely and intimate, as if they had known each other for years....

The boy took off his shoes and socks. His stout, square-toed shoes he slung round his neck by their laces: his socks he stuffed into his pocket. And he walked in the shallows by the water's edge.

"Don't you think it would be better to go right round to the rocks?" he proposed. "Then I could bathe.... I don't mind whether I bathe before or after reading, but I want to bathe some time."

"I think it ought to be after," Linton said.

The boy seemed to read his thoughts: at all events he smiled. "I won't catch cold," he promised. "I'm used to the water, and if I feel cold I'll go for a run.... Let's wait and see anyhow," he added. His eyes rested on Linton's. They were extraordinarily young eyes— faintly inquiring: they could not have been very different, Linton thought, when they had looked out at an unknown, surprising world from his cradle.

It was going to be a true summer's day. The wind had dropped; the last fleecy clouds had melted; and by the time they had reached the black line of rocks which jutted out into the sea where the crescent of the bay ended, the sun was flaming in a sky of deep dark blue. Here was the bathing-pool, though no other bathers had appeared. It was a natural creek, some twenty yards in width, and a good deal more than this in length. Linton and the boy clambered over the flat, barnacled rocks, which were now only two or three feet above the sea level, and about half way out they reached a kind of stone platform where the living rock had been smoothed artificially with a layer of concrete. The water lapped against the edge with a low sleepy sound. The water looked quiet and immensely strong—deep and green and clear—as it slowly rose and sank, its surface smooth, though beyond the jagged entrance to the creek they could see the waves breaking in white showers of foam. The tide was nearly full; there was no seaweed except the little that clung to the rocks themselves; and ten or twelve feet below the surface was a smooth clean floor of sand.

The boy stood at the edge of the diving-platform, gazing down through the water. "I *must* go in," he said. Then he added half coaxingly, "Mustn't I?"—and he smiled back at Linton over his shoulder. Linton immediately answered, "Yes."

He had a strange feeling of dreaming. The question seemed to have come to him out of the happiness of a dream, and in a dream he had answered. He had a thought, but it was for nobody's ears. He had a longing to make time stand still, for everything to remain just as it was now for ever more.

He sat down and dangled his feet over the edge, while behind him the boy undressed and put on his bathing-suit. Soon he was ready. There was no timidity about his bathing—no preliminary trial of the water's temperature such as Linton himself would have made—he plunged in at once. Splash!—a shower of glittering spray —and Linton watched his strong young body gliding through the clear green water—first downward, and then in a wide upward curve that brought him to the surface. He shook the water from his yellow hair; his blue eyes were dark and bright with pleasure; he turned and shouted back something—then swam out towards the entrance of the creek. He swam powerfully and easily, with rhythmic unhurried strokes, and Linton watched him with the oddest emotion of pride and affection. Odd, because of course it was absurd—just as if the boy belonged to him.... Then he thought:— If only he *did* belong to me; if only he *was* my son—how different everything would be! And instantly he knew that even to imagine this, even to pretend it, was a happiness.

He sat imagining it, he sat pretending it, and all the time his eyes never left the swimmer. Then abruptly he realized that the boy was approaching, and had almost reached, the rough water outside. Linton sprang to his feet, made a megaphone of his hands, and shouted to him to come back. Every now and again the boy raised his head and shook the water out of the hair that straggled down over his forehead. Suddenly he disappeared from view.

Linton sat down again. He didn't like it; it gave him a most unpleasant sensation; but he knew it was a trick and he wasn't going to be fooled. When the swimmer's head once more emerged it was considerably nearer, and Linton pretended to have noticed nothing.... But he wished he could have a picture of him, something that would keep this hour, this scene, permanently with him, for it could never—just in this way, just like this—happen again. The boy swam up to the iron ladder, climbed it, and stood on the rock, the water streaming from him. The sun streamed on him too, as he stood motionless gazing out across the water....

"It's pretty cold," the bather said. "It's nearly always cold round here, I don't know why. Something to do with the gulf-stream, I suppose—its absence, I mean. I'm going in for one more swim—a very short one—and then I'll come out."

"If you're cold I think you'd better come out now," Linton advised.

It sounded elderly and fussy, but he couldn't help that: he was feeling fussy—and probably looking it too. The boy shook a few drops of water over him.

"Just across to the other side and back," he said, clapping his hands to his thighs. His black bathing-suit had a white line round its edge and round the waist. It clung to the shape of his body, smooth and wet and shining, like the skin of an otter. He raised his hands above his head and bent forward slowly, like a young, growing tree in the wind. Then he dived.

But he kept his word and was soon scrambling up the ladder again. He began to dry himself vigorously, his skin taking a faint glow from the rough towel. "What time is it?" he asked.

"A quarter to twelve, I'm afraid," Linton replied.

"Goodness! I won't be able to read very much. It's frightful the way the time goes, isn't it!"

"You're not to read at all until we've taken a walk," Linton said.

The tone of authority was wasted, however, because the boy didn't seem to perceive it. "Oh, I'll be all right," he answered; "I'm nearly warm now. Anyway we'll have to clear out from here, because people will be beginning to turn up. They come about twelve: that's the usual hour for bathing."

"We'll walk for ten minutes—fast," Linton said.

The boy, who was putting on his shoes, replied, "Five—slow." He finished tying the laces and stood up. "I mustn't be late for dinner."

Linton also got up. "What time have you to be back?" he asked.

"Half-past one, and it will take us nearly half an hour. More if we go at the rate we came. We'll really only have about an hour for reading."

Linton had what seemed to him an extremely happy thought. "It would be much better if you lunched with me at the hotel," he said.

But the happy thought failed. "I couldn't," the boy answered, as he looked all round to make sure he had forgotten nothing. "They wouldn't know at home where I was."

"Nonsense," said Linton. "They'd know very well where you were. Your sister knows at this moment that you're with me."

The boy smiled, but he answered none the less firmly, "It isn't nonsense.... Thank you for asking me," he added. He picked up his bathing-suit and rolled it inside the towel. Then he began to make his way back to the shore, jumping from rock to rock, while Linton followed a good deal more cautiously.

The boy waited for him, and the fast walk began—along the deserted coast-road, between the cliffs and the sea. When they had gone about half a mile the boy halted and leaned over a low wall of unmortared stones. "What about stopping here?" he proposed. "It looks rather nice."

Linton took off his hat and wiped his forehead.

"I say," said the boy, "you look pretty hot! Why didn't you tell me I was walking too fast?"

"For one reason, because I hadn't sufficient breath," Linton replied. "But I think perhaps we *have* come far enough."

"And now you're sure to catch cold or something," the boy went on reproachfully. "We'd better sit in the sun—or at least *you'd* better. *I* feel like another bathe."

"No," said Linton definitely, "you're not to."

The boy glanced at him half teasingly, but with a happiness that had an extraordinary charm. "Why not? Well," he added, "I didn't really mean it."

He clambered over the wall and proceeded to assist Linton, who allowed him to, though he felt perfectly capable of climbing worse walls than this. Then, in a hollow just above the sea—half buried in the dry heather and bracken—they settled themselves, and the boy produced his manuscript. He spread it out on his knees and stared solemnly at it. "It's very bad," he said. "I was looking through it last night, and it's worse than I thought. In fact I'm not sure that I ought to read it at all."

Linton took no notice—partly because he was blowing into the stem of his pipe, which had got stopped up.

The boy waited a few moments and then repeated, "I don't believe I ought to read it."

Still Linton said nothing, and the boy glanced sidelong at him. "I *won't* read it, you know, if you go on like this."

Linton gave a final blow and replied, "I don't see that I've been going on in any way. As far as I know, I haven't even opened my mouth."

"Yes, that's just what I mean: you haven't bothered to open it, because you think that really I'm dying to read. I'm not. I'm much more the other thing. Anyhow, you've got to promise that you'll tell me as soon as you begin to feel fed-up."

Linton struck a match and held it over the bowl of his pipe. "I've already told you that I won't be fed-up," he said between puffs of smoke. "Nor am I anticipating a masterpiece."

The boy looked as if this wasn't quite the answer he had expected. "No, but honestly," he began: then checked himself and frowned. "The good part doesn't come at the beginning," he said. "I haven't written it yet. I don't mean that any of it will be good.... But you know what I mean."

"Yes, and you ought to know what *I* mean."

"Oh well," said the boy, "I suppose there's no use wasting time."

And he began to read rapidly, and in a voice which, except for a slight nervousness, was utterly devoid of expression:— "'Nature Suppressed. A novel. Chapter one. Broken Bliss.... As

Edna Kearney approached her father's office she felt pleased with all the world, and particularly with Eric Grey. This was because she was sure Eric intended to ask her to marry him that evening, and, since she loved him, she had already made up her mind to accept. But for the reader to understand Edna it is better to explain who her father was and how she came to be working in his office instead of going about enjoying herself like most of the girls she knew.'"

"Not so fast," Linton interposed, and the boy stopped.

"Sorry," he murmured. "Shall I begin again?"

"Yes, and try to read it in the way you wrote it, not as if it were a leading article."

The boy made another start, and this time he read very slowly. "'As—Edna Kearney—approached—her father's office—she felt pleased—with all the world—and particularly with Eric Grey....' Is that better?"

But in a minute or two he had slipped back into the old pace, and Linton, after a brief inward struggle, resigned himself to it. Already he saw that it didn't much matter, for no reading in the world could make this novel sound anything but what it was, or breathe into it the remotest semblance of life.... Well, he hadn't expected it to be good, though he had hoped it might be bad in the right way. It wasn't: it was bad in the wrong way.

It wasn't so much that it was stilted and absurd (though it was both) as that there was nothing whatever of the boy himself in it. What he had written was positively ugly and definitely charmless. And as he watched him sitting there, above the sea, with the grey rocks and heather all round him, and his fair head bowed over his manuscript, Linton marvelled at the contrast between the creator and his creation. How could he have written this stuff, with its echoes and imitations of the cheapest kind of fiction? But it was its ugliness that chiefly impressed him. It contained not one gleam of imagination or poetry. Linton felt at the same time sorry and impatient, touched and disappointed. And what, when the time for criticism came, could he possibly find to say?

Suddenly the boy said it for him. He had looked up, and his blue eyes were fixed on Linton's face, which was perhaps less inscrutable than he intended. "You hate all this," he said. "I can see you hate it. I'm not going to read any more."

His cheeks had flushed; his eyes were dark with disappointment. Linton did not reply, and the boy fumbled for his watch. "It must be time we were going anyway," he said. "Yes, it is."

"It's only half-past twelve," Linton answered softly. "We've only been here half an hour."

The boy hesitated. He plucked at the heather and remained silent. Some kind of secret colloquy was going on within him, and when it was ended he said in an entirely different voice. "Well, I can stay for another twenty minutes."

It was distinctly nice of him, Linton thought; he definitely must be a very pleasant person. "I think," he began slowly, "part of the trouble is that you've been writing the wrong kind of thing. You haven't given yourself a chance. I'm afraid you've been *reading* the wrong kind of thing, too."

The boy's face had cleared. "Does that matter? I've read all kinds of books—and some of them were supposed to be good."

"Yes.... Perhaps.... I wish I had——"

"Met me a little sooner," the boy completed. "Which means you think it's now too late."

"It doesn't," Linton answered. "And it wasn't even what I was going to say, though I do wish it—because now we haven't much time left. You see," he went on with a strange hesitation, "after this month we shan't have many opportunities—I suppose. I don't live in this country."

"You think I can't write."

"It's not that. I don't know yet. Very likely you can—or at least have it in you to learn. At the same time I know you will only be wasting your time if you go on with this particular book. It *isn't* your book: you've put nothing into it except what you've picked up at second hand—and even that looks as if it had been gathered from rather dubious sources. I'm not sure whether you've yet formed any idea of life, or had any vision of it.... However, we can't enter into that now; it would take too long. But we'll discuss it later, and meanwhile I don't want you to think that what I've said applies to anything except the chapters you've read to me this morning."

The boy was folding up his manuscript. "All the same—it wasn't very encouraging," he murmured.

"No, I don't suppose it was; though really we're exactly where we were before. I mean, I don't think this book counts at all—either one way or the other. We're not going to let it end here, however; at least I hope not. I'm sure I can help you if you'll let me."

The boy did not answer, but unexpectedly he smiled. He was taking it, Linton thought, uncommonly well. "There's one question I'd like to ask you," Linton said. "I'd like to ask the author's name."

The boy replied at once. "*My* name, do you mean? I'm Brian Westby. It's not my real name, but it's the name I'm always called by. My real name is Brian Linton. I know you'll think I ought to have told you sooner—and I did intend to. For a long time I didn't even know it myself, but Martin Linton is my father. I was going to tell you last night, only we began talking of other things and I forgot. At least, I didn't forget: I put it off.... I say, what's the matter?"

Linton put a strong check upon himself. "Nothing," he answered.

"Are you sure?" The boy's voice was suddenly anxious and incredulous, and it became more so next moment. "Are you sure you're all right? You look awfully queer, you know."

"I'm all right," Linton repeated. "I didn't know—Martin Linton had a son."

But the boy ignored this; he wasn't thinking of Martin Linton just now, he was thinking of the man beside him. He let his manuscript drop and went on with an awkward, ingenuous, and to Linton strangely lovely sympathy, "I'm sure we walked too quickly. It's my fault. I'm a stupid ass. I didn't remember. I forgot you had been ill."

"I'm not ill," Linton answered. "I'm not ill at all. And if I look ill it's only because that's my natural appearance."

He smiled to prove it, and Brian, after studying his face carefully, seemed more or less reassured. Nevertheless he continued to gaze at Linton in mingled doubt and solicitude. "You're certainly looking better than you were," he finally decided. "I expect it must have been a touch of the sun.... All the same, we're going to walk home slowly."

"Very well," Linton agreed. "And in that case I suppose we ought to start at once."

But Brian was now determined to look after him. "No, not at once," he said firmly. "Not for another ten minutes at least. It doesn't matter if I'm late: they can begin without me."

Linton submitted: he moved back a little further in the heather and sat still. Five minutes passed. He knew he was supposed to be resting—recovering from whatever faintness or weakness the boy imagined to have overcome him. Brian himself had taken up his manuscript again and was turning its leaves. Linton looked at him from beneath the pulled-down brim of his hat, and sometimes he looked at the sea. He had very nearly spoken, very nearly revealed himself in that first moment: now the impulse was gone and he was glad he had not yielded to it. He must see Stella first, must think the situation over carefully, and then decide on the wisest course of action....

The whole thing was so extraordinary, and he felt that even yet he had not fully realized it.... It almost seemed that in his mood as he had sat an hour ago watching Brian bathing, there must have been some faint premonition of the truth. From the very beginning, and all *through*, there had been something: it had not been as it would have been between strangers. Or was he only being fanciful now that he knew? He could not tell, and in any case what did it matter? That was *his* boy sitting there! Yes—and hadn't he said so before, without words? He had felt it at all events. Only then he had attached a different significance to the thought, and had merely meant and known that the boy belonged to his world....

He drew and exhaled a deep breath that might have suggested a sigh had it not been for the expression in his eyes. That was his boy, pondering over a manuscript, and looking so serious about it. Not, Linton thought, if he had believed in a beneficent power bent on gratifying the deepest and most secret longing of his heart, could he have hoped for this:—yet it had happened. He smiled, and into his face there passed a strange light, a kind of dreaming stillness. He would not think of Stella; he would not spoil this hour: the rest could wait....

"Feeling better?" Brian suddenly asked, glancing up. "Yes, you are, ever so much better: that's good."

"Well," Linton admitted—"if you say so——" His smile deepened. "Does it mean that it's time we were going?"

"Perhaps we ought to," Brian said. He stuffed Edna's adventures into his pocket, sprang to his feet, and holding out a hand pulled Linton to his.

Yet still for a minute or two before starting they stood side by side, with the rough waves breaking below them, and the smell of the sea and heather filling the air. There was a boat, hardly visible on the horizon: at least Brian said there was—Linton himself could not find it. The boy rested his hand on Linton's shoulder while he continued to point it out....

Part Second

THE DAY-SPRING

★ ★

Hence, in a season of calm weather
Though inland far we be,
Our souls have sight of that immortal sea
Which brought us hither;
Can in a moment travel thither—
And see the children sport upon the shore,
And hear the mighty waters rolling evermore.

Wordsworth.

Chapter VIII

LINTON

One strange effect was a sense of timelessness. It had all been so rapid that he could see it as a single hour, and yet everything preceding that hour appeared remote and half unreal. He knew that the hour had lasted exactly seventeen days. It was as if the hands of the clock had begun to whirl round with incredible swiftness and then suddenly had stood still; but no metaphor could convey his impression, because his impression itself was contradictory and dreamlike.

The thing, at all events, which mattered, was that their friendship was now established. Yet no sooner had he thought this than a doubt began to spread like a shadow through his mind. It was established in one way, of course—he saw Brian nearly every morning, and on three evenings in the week—but Brian himself continued to puzzle him. He was even more a puzzle than before, because Linton now knew him so much better, or rather felt he ought to know him better. Only—did he? He certainly knew more about him, but that was not the same thing. If it were, why should he still be so frequently taken by surprise? Linton had imagined that he possessed a wide experience and understanding of human nature, yet he seemed incapable of understanding a boy he saw practically every day, and who talked to him freely of all that entered his head.... Only, again—did he? Linton could not be sure: he was anything but sure. There might be a whole side of Brian's nature of which he never spoke—and in fact he had once hinted, or half hinted, that there was. On the other hand, Linton didn't believe that Brian always understood himself, or for that matter always was the same person. He had moods when he was remote, cold, indifferent; moods when he was responsive, affectionate, and sympathetic. And it was only in these latter moods that Linton could draw near to him—because what he meant by 'him' was a spirit. It might appear fantastic, but he meant it literally. Moreover, he was not only aware of this spirit intellectually, he could actually see it—see it as clearly as he could see the boy's body. And he had a feeling that if he should ever really offend or distress it he would never see it again. That was an awful thought, for he might not be able to help doing so, and at the best he must from time to time disappoint it. This was inevitable. Linton knew he must have acquired narrownesses, prejudices, dullnesses, and that these must become more apparent to Brian as they got to know each other better. His mind was less elastic than it once had been, less open to new ideas: it had ceased to make discoveries or to try experiments. What he feared most was that, the first novelty worn off, he might begin to bore the boy. Then all would depend on whether Brian cared for him sufficiently to tolerate being bored....

It was perhaps absurd that he should feel like this, and it had occurred to him at a very early stage in their friendship that he was allowing the whole thing to gain too deep a hold upon him emotionally. It was just because he took it in this way—more emotionally than reasonably—that he was sometimes hurt and disappointed, and showed it. When that happened he would tell himself that Brian's moods were unreliable as quicksand, and that he gave with one hand to-day what he would take back to-morrow with the other. Yet deeper still than this was a conviction that beneath the boy's changing moods there must be something which remained constant. He had tried to discover what it was, for at present there seemed to him to be two utterly different sides to Brian's nature, with one of which he was in close fellowship, while in the other he could never have any share or part....

Nor was this the only anxiety he felt: he was becoming more and more persuaded that he ought to have told Brian long ago of their true relationship. He had had two reasons for not doing so, but neither satisfied his conscience, and the first had ceased to exist. In the beginning he had wanted the boy to become friends with him spontaneously, uninfluenced by a possible sense of duty. If Brian had asked him his name on that morning of the reading of the manuscript he would at once have told him; but he had not done so—probably had been too shy—with the consequence that

Linton had been given time to think the matter over and to invent the singularly tortuous scheme he had actually adopted. And it was so unlike him to be tortuous; he would never have believed himself capable of hatching such a plot. Yet there it was. On the very afternoon of that momentous day he had wired to Sheldrake to send him a copy of his first book—a volume of poems he had published under a pseudonym while he was still at Oxford, and of whose existence even, few people knew. True, the pseudonym was simply his own name reversed—L. Martin instead of Martin Linton—but Brian, he had been sure, would never think of this. Linton himself did not possess the poems, he had given his only copy to this Sheldrake—an old friend and a collector. And two days later, when the volume had arrived, quite unscrupulously he had removed the inscribed end-paper and presented the book to Brian, telling him he was the author. The trick had worked. Linton had not enjoyed playing it, but it had worked: he had watched Brian reading the title-page—*Poems*, by L. Martin—and on the few occasions afterwards when the boy had not merely called him 'you', he had called him Mr Martin.

No—in no way could it be regarded as a happy stratagem. In fact it now seemed to Linton meaner than the direct lie at which he had boggled. As for his second reason for suppressing the truth—that, he feared, must now be more valid than ever. For his original intention of calling upon Stella, of having the whole thing out with her, had not been fulfilled. He had abandoned it because, on reflection, the risk had seemed too great. He had been afraid of Stella—afraid of what she might do, afraid of the pressure she might bring to bear upon the boy, for he was sure that she would stick at nothing in her determination to keep them apart.

But in deceiving Stella, Linton had a clear conscience. The fact that she had hidden the boy's very existence from him, and brought him up as Brian Westby, justified him, he thought, completely. It had been an outrageous thing to do, and how she had brought herself to do it presented a moral problem quite beyond Linton's experience. It could, at any rate, only have been after a prolonged mental struggle, in which she had seen herself forced to make a choice between two evils. He knew from Brian himself that she had wished to make a parson of her son. In this she had failed, but she had at least been able to bring him up in the strictness of her faith, unhampered by Linton's influence. It was strange, though he was well aware that in the same cause, and with as pure a motive, still stranger things had frequently been done. The irony was that he *felt* no prejudice against Christianity, except when it assumed these warped and unlovely forms.

Well, he had always known Stella to be an extraordinary woman, but he had not suspected that she would go quite so far as that. Actually, she had gone further, for she had told Brian nothing. Very little drawing-out on Linton's part had sufficed to elicit this. She had deliberately left him to face the damning facts of her silence, of her action for divorce, of Linton's disappearance, of the suppression of his name—and to form from these things his own conclusions. What conclusion *could* he form except the worst? Unsophisticated, inexperienced, fond of her and loyal to her—how could he do anything except take her part blindly, condemning the man he did not know? But her conduct had at least freed Linton's hands; if it came to a struggle between them now, he would have no compunction in fighting against her with all his strength for possession of his son....

Not that he supposed, as he pondered over it, Stella to have placed herself legally in the wrong. Linton was entirely ignorant of the procedure in such matters, but it seemed to him morally certain that, since he had not defended the case, she would have been granted custody of the child. Anyhow, he never could have taken that way. But another—yes:—and for the moment it looked as if fate were on his side. Luck at all events. The coincidence in time between his meeting with Brian, and Stella's accident, had made all the difference in the world. If it had not been for that accident, which had confined her to the house and thus left him a free field, he would have been obliged at once to come out into the open and the struggle would have been over long ago—she simply would have gone away, taking Claire and Brian with her. At that stage there could have been no struggle, he would have had no chance. Time had meant everything to him—time which had permitted the boy to get to know him, to get to like him, to form his own impression of him—an impression she might not find it easy now to alter. Brian no doubt would still be loyal to her; but that he would be loyal to him, too, Linton believed implicitly.

With this his thoughts took a fresh turn, and all the bitterness passed from them as he began to dream of Brian's future—a dream into which neither Linton's problem nor Stella's entered. It was, to be sure, the veriest castle in Spain that he was building, for he was imagining Brian's career, the kind of books he would write, and he had only the ghostliest surmises to guide him. He did not think they would at all resemble his own books, but he would like them to be books which, even if they came too late for him to read, he would have been in sympathy with and admired had he been there to read them. He would have given much to have been granted a peep into the future or to have had one of those books brought back to him, though more perhaps for the light that it would throw on Brian himself than for its own sake.

Had it ever happened that both a father and a son were writers? Linton cast about him for examples, and they were not numerous. There were the two Disraelis, the two Arnolds, the two Collinses, the two Jameses.... Perhaps it was as well at this point that his list—which had begun to be faintly depressing—was interrupted by a little girl who wished to know the 'right time'. She looked a very thoughtful little girl—one such as might have been encountered about 1798 in the English lake country, though she did not tell him how many brothers and sisters she had, nor did he inquire. Having mentioned the time, and witnessed her winged departure, he decided that he might as well be making his own way homeward.

So he turned, and began to saunter back towards Ballycastle, stopping more than once to lean over a gate or a stile, and still pursuing his day-dreams. These now had drifted from the future to the past, and he began to think of all the years of Brian's companionship he had missed—years which might have been so rich and full, a storehouse of happy memories. Of that companionship, of those memories, he had been robbed—yet he could not help wondering, and brooding, and guessing. He pictured Brian at various stages of his boyhood, though the only tangible aid to imagination

he possessed was a solitary photograph procured for him one day
when the boy had gone up to town on some business of his mother's. Linton had asked if any early photographs existed, and Brian
had brought one back with him. He had presented it that same
evening—not without amusement:—he didn't seem to understand
why Linton should want it—or at least he had said he couldn't understand. All the same, Linton felt he *had* understood, and had even
been pleased....

The portrait showed him at the age of ten or eleven, dressed in
an Eton suit, and standing at a table, with one hand resting on the
table and the other in his trousers pocket—a rather solemn little
boy, regarding the world with a grave innocence. Linton had studied the picture in silence. Secretly he had been profoundly moved
by it, but he had been careful to hide this and to accept the gift as
lightly as it had been offered. He had studied it again when he was
alone, and it had seemed to him then that that lost little boy might
have stepped straight out of Wordsworth's famous ode. Certainly
he had not yet travelled far from the east, Linton could trace no
shades of the prison-house in his countenance, he did not believe
there were any. Meadow, grove, the earth, and every common
sight, still for the boy in the picture had the glory and the freshness
of a dream. He had tried to catch his gaze, but he could not—could
not make him look at him—always he looked over Linton's shoulder and at something beyond....

He had never known, never could now know, this bygone Brian;
but he could let his imagination brood upon him in dreamland.
There he watched him growing from childhood to youth, gave him
a voice and words and actions—gave him difficulties to overcome,
troubles and happinesses. It was all, doubtless, unsubstantial as a
mist at sunrise, but it was not sad, because he had the real Brian,
whom certainly he would not have exchanged for any earlier one....

This was one of his evenings; Brian would be coming to see him
this evening.... They would go for a walk—a slow and loitering
walk—returning through the dusk. These evening walks were what
Linton was fondest of, so that merely to look forward to one filled
his day with an anticipated happiness. This time, too, he had a plan
to propose. He hoped it would appeal to Brian, and believed it

would, for it had to do with his work, which at least was greatly in its favour. Linton had seen nothing of that work since the morning when he had listened to the novel, but he knew something was being written, though Brian had refused to talk to him about it while it was still unfinished. Linton's plan might interrupt it; but on the other hand he fancied Brian would be pleased; he himself at Brian's age certainly would have been....

Meditating upon it, sunk in a deep and pleasant reverie, Linton walked on through the late afternoon sunshine, which was mild and innocent as his own mood. Sometimes he smiled, though he did not know he was smiling, and all the time he was taking two walks—one in reality and the other in imagination—one along a white dusty road between fields of grass dotted with grazing sheep, and the other in the darkness, by the sea.

Chapter IX

BRIAN AND LINTON

Brian hurried along the road in the dusk. It was Friday evening— one of Mr Martin's evenings—and he was late. He knew Mr Martin didn't like him to be late, and he had never been so late as this before. In fact he would have preferred not to go out at all, but he had thought it better, particularly since they hadn't met in the morning—nor, now he came to think of it, yesterday. But he had been frightfully busy both days—though perhaps rather slack too. To-night he would stay a little longer than usual to make up for it.

Just then he caught sight of his friend, who was turning down the road past the harbour, walking slowly, with his hands in his pockets and the brim of his hat pulled down. Where on earth could he be going to? At this distance and in this light Brian only recognized him from his general outline, and from his gait, which had in it something of a slouch. He broke into a run and at the same time whistled shrilly, but the figure in front of him neither paused nor looked round.

This was queer, and for a moment Brian's pace slackened.... It certainly *was* Mr Martin, and he must have heard and recognized that piercing whistle, which was the only kind of whistle Brian could make. He ran on again, and this time gave a shout. "Hi! I say!"

Mr Martin had stopped, though he still did not look round. "Didn't you hear me?" Brian panted as he came up with him. "I whistled and shouted. I'm sorry for being so late, but I couldn't help it."

There was no reply, and Brian's smile slowly faded. He gazed at his companion in perplexity, trying to discover what was the matter, but he could only see that Mr Martin's face was dark and brooding, and that his eyes were fixed on the road before him. So Brian too became silent, and in this depressing fashion they walked on for perhaps three hundred yards. Then Mr Martin suddenly spoke, and from his first words Brian realized that he was very angry.

It was not exactly that he flared up, but his voice was more like a growl than anything else. "What's the use of coming at this hour?" he said. "You might just as well have stayed at home."

The tone was new to Brian, and so unexpected that for a moment he was incapable of speech. He had come out in the friendliest mood—had come, moreover, at some inconvenience to himself—and this was the way he was received! "Perhaps I'd better go back," he answered stiffly.

"Just as you like: please yourself."

Brian's immediate impulse was to take him at his word. Astonished, hurt, and then in his turn offended, he certainly would have done so had it been anybody else who had spoken to him like this. Yet now for some reason he didn't, though he knew what the sole grievance against him was, and nothing could be more unjust and unreasonable. "I come to see you as often as I can," he said, "and I've explained that I couldn't help being late."

Mr Martin's face grew no more amiable, nor did his manner alter. "You haven't explained anything," he contradicted peremptorily. "You haven't said anything except that you were late, which I knew already, and that you were sorry, which wasn't true."

Brian flushed, and with difficulty repressed a retort. He certainly wasn't sorry. If it came to that, he had nothing to be sorry about, nor was it incumbent upon him to give Mr Martin an account of his actions and motives. They were none of his business. He had apologized once and wasn't going to apologize again. "I was busy," he answered, "and we had visitors."

He might as well have held his peace. "What visitors?" Mr Martin asked as if he hated them, and Brian closed his lips, leaving him to think what he liked.

This was no use either, because Mr Martin wouldn't be left. "Were they *your* visitors?" he went on, with a dark look, and Brian replied coldly, "No, they weren't my visitors."

There was a silence. His voice as he had spoken those last words had been as little conciliatory as Mr Martin's own, yet they still continued to walk side by side, close together, each knowing more or less what the other was thinking. There was plenty of time to think, for the silence lasted for quite five minutes. Then Linton muttered, with a kind of sombre childishness, "If you preferred the society of your visitors to mine, why did you leave them?"

The speech was in fact *so* childish that it had upon Brian a disarming effect, and he might even have smiled if he hadn't determined not to. As it was, he made no reply, but actually submitted to further reproaches.

"You seem to consider nobody but yourself," Linton went on gloomily. "You knew I was expecting you—would be waiting for you—wondering whether you were coming or not—but that didn't matter so long as it suited your convenience."

Brian had by this time quite ceased to be angry, he didn't know why, for he was receiving plenty of provocation. It was partly, he supposed, because Mr Martin really seemed to think he had been badly treated, and if he felt like that, then—he wanted him not to feel it. "It wasn't to suit my convenience," he said in a low voice.

"I don't know what it was then," Linton answered. "What possible difference could it make to your mother's friends whether you were there or not? All you had to do was to say you had an engagement."

"*Am* I to go away?" Brian asked, coming to a standstill. "Do you really want me to go?"

"I've told you to please yourself."

Again Brian was tempted to leave him, and again another feeling prevailed. "You know you won't like it if I do," he said.

"No, I shan't like it," Linton answered, "but that needn't trouble you. You knew I shouldn't like hanging about the hotel all evening, not knowing whether to go out or to stay in; yet it didn't prevent you from making me do it."

It seemed spoken with an ebbing conviction, however, and Brian was quick to note the change. He was also quick to respond to it. "It wasn't to please myself that I kept you waiting," he said. "I would rather have come. But I had to be civil.... And anyhow I *have* come," he added with a sudden smile.

"Yes, for half an hour."

"I can't spend all my time with you."

Linton looked at him, and in that brief glance the reproach died out of his eyes. "I know that," he said, "but——" He broke off, only to continue with a rather forlorn hesitation, "There *isn't* a great deal more time, is there? At the end of this month you'll be going away—and so, I suppose, shall I."

It was almost as if he had a faint hope of being contradicted, but how could Brian contradict him, and how could he help having to go home? It was unfortunate: but it wasn't *his* fault that Mr Martin lived in England, and that they would be unlikely to see much of each other in the future. You had to be prepared for that kind of thing. He himself had seen precious little of any of his school friends since he had left school, yet he didn't get depressed about it!

Nevertheless, through this practical wisdom, he had a dim instinctive understanding that the present situation was different, and that his past experience had very little bearing upon it, his school friendships none whatever. He ought to make allowances perhaps—allowance for this unknown element which, whether he wanted it to be there or not, undoubtedly *was* there. At least he could try, and at least they needn't let it spoil their whole evening—or rather the little of the evening that remained....

Meanwhile they continued to walk on, though the path had ended some time ago, and in the deepening darkness it was becoming increasingly difficult to pick their way over the rocks. Brian wondered what Mr Martin would have done if he *had* left him? Would he have called him back? He wasn't sure, but he didn't think so. Probably he would just have continued on by himself. Yet, even if this *had* happened, Brian told himself, he wouldn't have allowed it to be the end, he would have gone round to the hotel in the morning just as usual. Only he wished he knew what Mr Martin was thinking about, and would have liked to ask him.

As a matter of fact, Mr Martin's chief thought was that he had very little to be proud of. He still felt that Brian had been inconsiderate, but surely he might have told him so without losing his temper. There had been the transient relief of giving way to his annoyance, and that was all. He sat down where the rocks overhung the dark water, and Brian sat beside him. Both felt a little subdued, a little foolish perhaps.

It was the boy who broke the silence. "To-day is my birthday," he murmured, and though he had said it with no such purpose, he could not have found a more effective speech had he searched for an hour.

"I'm sorry," Linton mumbled.

"So am I," said Brian.

"I don't mean about your birthday."

"Neither do I," said Brian.

To a third person the words doubtless would have sounded half comic, but neither of the speakers noticed this. Only Brian wished that Mr Martin wasn't quite so easily offended. He hated offending him, but it was frightfully easy to offend him accidentally, simply by doing or leaving undone something which with anybody else would not matter....

"Mother gave me a typewriter," he went on. "It arrived this evening. It came by train and they didn't send it up from the station till after six. I couldn't help trying it, and while I was trying it the Grahams came in, and then everybody wanted to try it."

So that was why he had been late! Linton felt suddenly ashamed, and at the same time relieved. But he wished Brian had spoken sooner: then their quarrel needn't have happened at all. On the other hand, perhaps he hadn't given him much chance to do so. Mentally he made a vow to be less quick to jump to conclusions in future.

"Will you do something for me?" he asked gravely.

He half hoped Brian would say "Yes," but he expected he wouldn't; and primarily he had put his question in its ambiguous form for the sake of watching the boy's reaction to it. The mixture of cautiousness and impulsiveness in his nature was very odd, Linton thought, and he could not imagine where the cautiousness came from. Not from him at all events, and not, he thought, from Stella. It must come from farther back—like his extraordinary conscientiousness. To Linton both qualities had something incalculable about them, something that would always, he felt, leave him dimly wondering.

Brian was looking at him doubtfully. "Of course—I can't promise that," he began at last. "But let me hear what it is."

"I'd rather you promised without hearing," Linton said.

"And I'd rather you told me."

Linton dug the point of his stick between the stones. The demand he had originally made half in jest he now for some reason felt tempted to urge seriously. "Do you think I'd ask you to do anything you oughtn't to do?" he said.

"Not anything you *thought* I oughtn't to do."

Linton sighed. "Why are you so stubborn?" he asked.

"Why are you? No; I'm sorry; I shouldn't have said that:—though really you're behaving in exactly the same way as I am, and it was you who began it."

Linton pursued his digging while he turned this over. "*I'm* stubborn only because I don't want you to refuse."

"Yes, I know," Brian laughed.

"Why don't you trust me, then?"

Brian wrinkled his forehead. "I do trust you.... We won't get any further that way, because my trusting you or not trusting you has nothing to do with it. I know what you want. What you want is to see if you can make me give in."

"It isn't," Linton denied. "I want something quite different. I want to give you a birthday-present—that's all."

"Well——" Brian hesitated—"if it's not anything big——"

"But it is," Linton answered; "if by big you mean bulky. Only I can't think of anything else."

"You know I don't mean bulky," Brian said. "What is it?"

Still Linton held back. "I don't think you've any right to ask. I want it to be a surprise. People as a rule don't ask what their presents are going to be."

"People as a rule don't have to," Brian replied.

Linton turned away. Suddenly he felt a difficulty in telling him. "It's a set of your father's books," he murmured sheepishly—"and I may tell you I'd thought of it long before I knew it was your birthday.... I could get him to autograph them for you, if that would be an inducement."

"I'd rather you autographed them yourself," Brian answered simply.

This preference was unexpected, and though perhaps not flattering to the author of the books, Linton felt pleased by it. "Is that settled, then?" he asked.

But Brian did not answer. As a matter of fact it was extremely hard to answer—and just now particularly—because just now he wanted very much to do something to please Mr Martin, and he knew that if he accepted his present it would please him. Also he would like to have the books for their own sake.... Unfortunately, he knew his mother *wouldn't* like him to have them, so he searched for a compromise. "Couldn't you give me *one* of the books?" he at length proposed.

"Yes, but I'd rather give you them all," Linton said.

Brian faced him candidly. "I know; but you can't give me them all.... It's not for the reason you think," he went on, determined to make this clear. "It's—— You see, mother doesn't know I've read *any* of them. She doesn't want me to read them. And if she suddenly saw me with the whole lot——"

Linton stared at this remarkable picture, but the smile it drew from him was a little grim. "Yes," he admitted, "I can see it might lead to complications.... It would be rather awkward, I dare say, if she insisted on your returning them—though I'd know it wasn't your fault."

"Whereas if you only gave me one," Brian urged, "she couldn't very well object."

"Couldn't she!" Linton thought, but he didn't say it. "Yes, I'll give you only one," he agreed. "Now, I mean. I'll give you the rest *some* time.... Only it seems such a miserable present," he added. "Isn't there anything else you'd like instead—or as well?"

"No; I'd rather have that, and it's not miserable. I *really* would rather have it," Brian went on positively, "and it would look very queer if you gave me two things."

"Would it?" Linton murmured. "It would look queer, I suppose, if you were to listen to the morning stars singing together, or to sell all your goods and give to the poor. I think you think too much about how things look." He did not pursue the matter, however, and after a moment said tentatively, "There's something else I want to discuss—something that isn't queer." He paused again, and this time for so long that Brian was obliged to say "Yes?" encouragingly.

"It's all very well saying 'Yes'!" Linton returned. "The question is whether you're going to say it later on when the plan is revealed! I'm beginning to have my doubts."

"If the sun and moon should doubt, they'd immediately go out," Brian quoted.

Linton gazed at him in silent speculation. "It's about writing," he began—"writing something together.... What?"

"I didn't speak," Brian said.

"You don't like the idea—is that it?"

"I haven't said I don't like it. I don't know what it is yet. What kind of thing do you mean?"

"Well, perhaps a short story to start with."

Brian pursed up his mouth, which made him look extremely prim and non-committal. He did not definitely reject the proposition, however, and with him that was always something. On the other hand, neither did he accept it; he merely waited until he should have heard a little more.

Linton watched him. He had not expected him to jump at the proposal exactly; but still he had thought it might interest him a little more than it evidently did. He felt disappointed, though at the same time faintly tickled. He wondered, as he had often wondered before, what Brian's opinion of him really was? But he should never know this, he supposed, so there wasn't much use thinking about it. "You don't believe in giving yourself away—do you?" he murmured ruefully.

"It's you," Brian retorted. "It's because you're always wanting to do queer things—or at any rate to say them. I'm not like this with anybody else."

"You mean all the other people are sensible, reasonable beings? I doubt it.... However, I'm still waiting for your answer."

"Why can't you write the story yourself?" Brian asked.

The question had slipped out before he could check it, and his immediate look of dismay made Linton laugh. "Because I'd rather write it with you," he answered firmly.

Brian had known that—known the reason—and he gave it further consideration. "Do you think it's possible?" he asked dubiously. "I never could see how collaboration was managed. It seems to me that either one or other of the collaborators must do all the work."

He had taken out his watch while he was speaking, and now abruptly he jumped up. "I say, it's frightfully late: we'll have to go at once, and we'll have to walk quickly.... Not *too* quickly," he corrected himself, recollecting a previous occasion. "I only mean we mustn't waste time. It's after half past ten, and we've come a long way round."

"Does it matter?" Linton murmured, for he hated hurrying. "Would you like to run on by yourself? I'd rather you did that than get into trouble when you reach home."

"It's my birthday—there won't be a row," Brian said innocently. "A slight ticking-off at most. Besides, I told mother I might be late.... All the same, I don't want to be *too* late.... I suppose you think I'm trying to avoid discussing the story."

"Yes," Linton answered, as he slowly rose to his feet. "And it isn't the slightest use, because nothing can keep me from discussing it."

"Then I'm afraid it will have to be on the way home. Come along."

Linton drew a breath of resignation and came along—inwardly reluctant, and outwardly with not a little stumbling over stones and roughnesses, for his vision at night was poor. Presently Brian grabbed him by the arm, and they proceeded in this fashion—

not really arm in arm, but as if Linton were being dragged on a lead—till the way became smoother. Here it was easier to talk, and Linton began at once: "Well, what about it?"

"What about it, you?" Brian returned. "It was your plan."

"My plan perhaps, but you're the one who's brimming over with ideas and subjects. I want you to produce one."

Brian reflected—which at least had the effect of making him walk more slowly. "I *had* thought of a story," he began, "but I'm not sure that you'll like it: you'll probably think it's morbid."

"I've no objection to that," Linton hastened to assure him—"so long as it's morbid in the right way. Let me hear it at any rate."

Brian continued to think. He knew he would have to speak in the long run or he would get no peace, but he determined to take his own time about it, and not allow himself to be rushed. "It's a kind of ghost story," he said at last—"though not the ordinary kind."

"Then that's all right," Linton declared. "Ghost stories have precious little chance of coming off unless they *are* morbid. *The Turn of the Screw—Seaton's Aunt—The Lost Stradivarius*—they're all morbid—or supposed to be."

Brian having read none of these tales, as illustrations they failed. He proceeded, however, to outline his own tale, and when he had done Linton began to embroider upon it and to make changes. He made so many, indeed, that Brian with difficulty refrained from interruption.

Linton watched him with an increasing amusement. "Don't look as if you had a stomach-ache," he begged at last. "I'm doing my best."

"Yes, but——" Brian expostulated feebly.

Then he told himself that, after all, the part he cared for most had been left untouched, so that it did not matter. Besides, he felt that the plan would never really come to anything, and it was at least interesting to discuss it. And this was true. Even if he didn't relish them, he was interested in Mr Martin's alterations, and particularly in his filling in of details. The opening scene, for example, had become very nearly a short story in itself. At this rate, instead of a couple of thousand words, the thing would run to at least ten or fifteen thousand.

"Let's each write the beginning," Linton proposed. "We'll write it separately and afterwards compare our versions: then we can go on from that. We'd better get our first sentence now. I always like getting first sentences—and last ones.... We have Clayton waking up in his lodgings after the third dream. He has gone to sleep in his chair after dinner, and when he wakes up it's time for him to keep his appointment with the other man.... It's autumn—don't you think?—so his landlady won't have given him a fire. 'Clayton awoke with a slight shiver':—how would it do to begin with that?"

"You mean with those exact words?" Brian asked.

"Yes—provisionally—just to make sure that we'll both be starting from the same point. Then we can——"

"Half a tick," Brian interrupted, stopping and taking out his notebook to jot the sentence down. "I wrote it in shorthand," he mentioned, when he had caught Linton up again.

But Linton was still thinking of the story, and replied absently, "Was that what kept you? The first part——"

"It didn't keep me!" Brian cried indignantly. "I wasn't more than three seconds."

Linton wakened up and apologized. "All right. So long as you can read it——"

"It doesn't matter whether I can read it or not," Brian said ingenuously, "because I know it off by heart."

"In that case I don't quite see——"

"I just wanted to show you who you were collaborating with." He paused, glanced sidelong at Linton, murmured an inaudible sentence to himself, and then repeated it aloud:—"With whom you are collaborating."

Linton chuckled. "Am I to take my choice?"

"I know which is right."

"That's good. Albert, of course, wrote in a hurry. To criticize I scarce presume. But still I think that Lindley Murray instead of 'who' had written 'whom'."

Brian looked at him suspiciously. "What's that?" he asked.

"That's an example of subconscious recording," Linton told him complacently. "It was written by Thackeray in an autograph album —under some lines by Albert Smith about the opening of a new bridge. Albert's verses had ended with 'I don't know who they'll get to cross it.' Albert took it rather badly, I'm afraid—in other words, was furious."

"But where does the subconscious recording come in?" Brian asked.

Linton regarded him benignly. "Well, when I read it I must have been about fifteen, and I've certainly never thought of it between that day and this."

Brian's gaze was fixed upon him. "All the same, you're rather proud of having thought of it," he said.

Linton considered. "Not proud," he qualified. "Self-satisfied, I fancy, would be the *mot juste* here."

"It's much the same thing."

"But not quite the same. When we're collaborating we'll try to give words their precise meaning."

"Yes, I know," Brian grumbled. "You needn't think I didn't know from the beginning that the whole thing was designed simply as a course of instruction for me."

"It wasn't," Linton contradicted. "If that came into it at all, it was quite a minor point."

Brian was still watching him closely. "Do you want me to ask now who Albert was, and who Lindley Murray was?"

"I do rather," Linton admitted. He knew he was being cheeked, but he also knew he liked it. "Everybody enjoys showing off," he defended himself, "even if it's only in this miserable fashion. Albert —since you *have* asked me, Brian—was Albert Smith—a club-mate of Thackeray—not to be confused with the brothers Horace and James Smith, who wrote the *Rejected Addresses*. Albert was what in those days was known as a wit. It was almost a profession—like, I suppose, being a 'professional beauty.' Also he wrote several third-rate novels—*The Adventures of Mr Ledbury, Christopher Tadpole*, et cetera—and contributed to *Punch*. Lindley Murray was a grammarian. They weren't really contemporaries of mine, though I can see you think so. Lindley Murray died in the eighteen-twenties, and I wasn't born till after that. The only person I know who might be regarded as nearly a contemporary is Micky. I've worked out Micky's age, and giving him the human equivalent, it's a hundred-and-five. You know Micky, don't you?"

"You mean the fox-terrier at the hotel?"

"Yes."

Brian sank into a reverie inspired by Micky's span of life. "You know, we might write a short story about *him*," he produced as the result of it. "A hundred-and-five: it's pretty good!"

Linton glanced at him. "You're going to write our story, then?" he asked.

"Yes, didn't you know I was?"

"I thought you seemed a little luke-warm about it."

"So I still am," Brian told him frankly—"though I don't mind beginning it. We'll never get beyond that, of course, but it will be something to talk about.... Honestly," he questioned, "do you really believe in it yourself?"

Linton refused to be drawn. "What I believe is, that at present it will be much better for you to write short stories than to try a full-length novel. You can do short stories out of your imagination, or out of your experience as far as you've gone; but not a novel—unless you limit it to the years of childhood and boyhood; and I don't think it will be very good even then. After all, you must try your wings from tree to tree before you risk a sustained flight. Even if you found a good subject for a novel now, you'd only waste it. Quite apart from anything else, you don't know enough, you haven't lived enough, three quarters of what you wrote would be either imitation or guess-work. On the other hand, you might write a short story of the kind I mean which would be completely successful."

"All the same," Brian persisted, "there *were* things I wanted to say in my novel, which I can't say in a short story.... You needn't be alarmed," he went on, as Linton made an involuntary gesture, "I've given it up. I only wanted to tell you that it wasn't going to be quite so futile as you think. There were a lot of things I wished to write about—religion for one—and I could have done them through Edna."

"But gracious heaven!" Linton exclaimed. "A work of imagination isn't the place for airing your views on religion. If you want to write a pamphlet, do so; but don't mix the two things together."

"It wouldn't have been a pamphlet," Brian maintained stolidly.

"And if the characters in a book happen to have certain views, I don't see why they shouldn't express them. *My* characters had. And in my father's books, which you say you like, he expresses *his* views."

"I never said I liked them," Linton contradicted. "I said I liked one or two of them.... And at any rate, does he? Give me a single example."

But Brian couldn't: that wasn't what he had meant; nor did the lack of quotable examples, he thought, refute his argument. "I don't mean that he discusses Christianity," he said. "But he has a definite point of view: there's even a kind of religion. In fact, in a way, it's *all* that."

"I hope it isn't," returned Linton quickly. Then he laughed. "At least, if it is, he must be pretty bad."

"Well, you said so yourself," Brian reminded him. "I mean, you said there was something in his books he was trying to get at, though he didn't always succeed."

Linton felt momentarily baffled, and wondered how he could convey what he really had meant. But Brian had understood. "What you want me to write," he went on, "is a kind of poetry. I'm to dump down a poem and pretend it's a short story."

"Yes," said Linton eagerly, finding this statement surprisingly apt and reassuring. If Brian knew as much as that, it must be because he had the poetry in him. Or at least Linton thought so. Understanding was the first step to achievement, and a pretty long step, too. Besides, he had felt from the beginning that what he was looking for must be there—the feeling for, the response to, beauty. He had caught glimpses of it in the boy's ordinary talk, in the kind of things he liked—even in the fact that in many ways his intelligence had retained a sort of childishness and freshness of outlook. It was what all along had most attracted him. Yes, it was there; and Linton's mind impulsively expanded these wandering gleams and glimpses till in imagination he saw the pupil far surpassing his teacher—as indeed he might easily do. It had often happened before. It had happened frequently in the other arts. The Italian Renaissance was filled with examples of it. Linton merely saw it happening again.

Chapter X

BRIAN AND LINTON

Immediately after breakfast Brian went to the sitting-room to have a look at his typewriter. He lifted off the cover, slipped in a sheet of paper, and sat down before it.

He had the room to himself; it was a good time for working—particularly as he had not promised to go out with Mr Martin. He began by typing his name—Brian Westby—Brian Linton: then he ran quickly through the whole alphabet....

They had made no plans at all. Besides, he could type the beginning of their story, and that was what Mr Martin wanted....

He took out the spoiled sheet of paper and put in a fresh one. He typed the first sentence. His face grew thoughtful, yet he was only half thinking of his story, though he typed a few more sentences, clicking down the keys slowly and jerkily.

'Clayton awoke with a slight shiver. He was seated in the room he would be giving up to-morrow, for he was going away on a long journey. The fire had died down into a dull grey mass of ashes, and his previous feeling of contentment had left him.'

There wasn't to have been a fire, Brian suddenly remembered. But it didn't matter: he let the sentence stand, and typed on.

'Clayton had dined well and all the world had seemed rosy when he fell asleep. He was a rising man now. His years of hard work were to be rewarded at last. His paper was going to send him out on an important and difficult piece of survey-work in Burma, which showed that they trusted him. Then the dream came and left a feeling of *certain* uneasiness. For it was a dream of death—*his* death. In spite of himself he knew it was true.

'Death! he thought. Why should he die now—now when he was so happy; for all things were right in Clayton's world? In his struggle for work the worst was over, and now he was going——'

Brian's hands dropped from the keyboard. Whether he went on typing or not, he might as well be honest about it. He wasn't doing it because he believed it was what Mr Martin wanted. For that matter, he knew it *wasn't* what he wanted—or at any rate what would please him most—it was only what he, Brian, wanted. He gazed out of the window and his face became strangely still—with the stillness of a lake or a pool. For nearly five minutes he remained thus: then he seemed to awaken. At the same time his whole countenance lighted up, the author vanished and the boy reappeared: he rose and put back the cover on the typewriter.

He ran downstairs, jumping the last five steps, for now that he had made up his mind he was suddenly in a hurry lest he should not catch Mr Martin, who must have finished breakfast an hour ago. Better take a coat; and he slung his waterproof over his shoulder.

It was a gusty, uncertain morning into which he emerged. Cold, too—far more like October than August—but Brian rather liked the cold, and definitely liked the wind. He began to run down the hill, his shoes beating clippity-clop on the puddled road. When he reached the hotel he stopped for a moment to peer through the window of the smoking-room, and was reassured, for Mr Martin was sitting there in solitude, in an armchair before the fire. That is to say, he was alone except for Micky; and he looked as if he were waiting. Brian was glad he had come.

He hurried on to the front door, hurried along a dark narrow passage, and entered the smoking-room with the tumultuous effect of a gust of wind. He brought with him something of its temperature too, and the salt wet savour of the sea. Micky on the hearthrug shivered, but Linton pushed back his chair and half got out of it, as Brian, leaving the door wide open behind him, crossed the room. "Goodness, what a fug!" the boy exclaimed. "It's like coming into a greenhouse."

Linton pushed his chair still further back, while Micky moved away from this impetuous and uninvited visitant from the winds and seas. He had disturbed their peace; they didn't want him; they had been quite happy by themselves; and from beside the coal-box Micky eyed the intruder without a tail-wag. A minute ago the room had been delightful—warming up nicely to something like eighty in the shade: now all at once it was filled with piercing draughts, the papers on the table between the door and the only open window were fluttering madly, the curtains were flapping, and the being who had called up this tempest was straddling there, with his legs apart and his hands in his pockets, occupying most of the hearthrug. Micky watched him uneasily. There was magic about him, he was working magics all the time, he smelled of them, Micky wouldn't be surprised if in another minute they were all floundering in the sea.

Nevertheless, an ingrained religious feeling, deep, dim, and ancestral, began to stir below this superficial rebelliousness. It suggested an act of propitiation, and Micky faintly moved his tail. After all, this was a god—one of that sacred and omniscient race, without whom life in all its higher aspects would be impossible and the world a mere ravening wilderness. He was a young god too; he radiated joy and vitality; he seemed, as he stood leaning back against the chimney-piece, to tower up to the ceiling; his face was lit with divine smiles; his ruffled yellow hair was the wind, and his blue eyes were the sea. "I left the typewriter, the story, a comfortable home, and everything else, just to come to see you," he was saying to Micky's safe old friend, who replied at once, "That, Brian, was very good of you."

"I think so too.... Good dog, Micky."

Micky's tail moved more confidently; he even advanced a few steps and received a pat. Cautiously he approached his nose till it nearly touched one of the grey-flannelled legs. He had not been mistaken; it was certainly a sea-magic: mysterious emanations of winds and waves were still flowing powerfully from him.

"What'll we do? I expect you'll think it's a beastly morning for a walk, but we really oughtn't to stay in here."

"We'll go out, then," Linton replied. "I intended to go out anyway. I was only waiting on the chance that you might turn up. I'll go and put on my shoes."

He got up from his chair while he spoke, and most inconsiderately left the room, so that Micky and the visitor were alone together.

They looked at each other in silence.

"Well, Micky, so you're a hundred-and-five!"

Micky turned away his head. And then a most unexpected thing

happened, for the sea-god plumped down on the hearthrug and put
his arm round him. Even if he had wanted to, Micky could not have
escaped—there was no time. But he wasn't sure that he did want
to. It was very pleasant being scratched behind your ears; it was
still pleasanter having an arm round you, holding you close. All
that about magic and about the sea had been nonsense: this was
just a human boy, and the soft wool of his jacket had lots of other
smells—warm, interesting, animal smells—delicious smells—body
smells—under its sea smell. With a little sigh Micky sank back into
his old faith: after all one must have faith: the tension of his limbs
and mind relaxed: he shut his eyes....

Linton was coming downstairs when Brian reached the hall. He
had put on a ragged old waterproof and crammed his hat well
down over his ears. "We'll go inland if you've no objection," he
said. "It won't be so windy, and when a shower comes on we can
shelter under the trees."

So they took the inland road.

"How much of the story have you done?" Brian began gaily. "I
thought I'd find you working hard at it this morning."

Linton had expected some such question, though he had intended to ask it himself. "Did you?" he replied. "And how do you
know I wasn't?"

"You didn't look like it. You hadn't even a sheet of paper to
write on. It was pretty slack, you know."

A violent gust of wind caught them before Linton had time to
answer. He made a frantic grab at his hat, was too late, and next
moment he watched it bowling merrily along the wet road with
Brian in hot pursuit.

The hat was captured, but only after a prolonged and exciting
chase—unnecessarily prolonged, Linton suspected. He said so, and
was not convinced by the pursuer's accusations of ingratitude. "At
any rate I'm going down into that wood," Linton concluded. "It
may be the conduct of a weakling, but it's going to be mine."

He climbed over a stile, and Brian followed, grumbling because
of the elemental joys they were leaving behind.

"Well, you stay and be blown about," Linton told him. "It won't impress me, and you can't really like it, but if it's a matter of principle——"

"I do like it," Brian protested. "That's just where you're so narrow-minded. You think everybody at heart must share all your particular likes and dislikes, whereas they don't. *I* don't: I merely give in to them."

He gave in to this one at all events, and they descended a grassy slope—wet and slippery—at the foot of which was a narrow copse of hazel-trees and a stream. Broken sunlight pierced between the branches and danced on the shallow water; the wind stormed in tempestuous gusts above and around them; but Linton was able to walk by the water's edge in shelter, while Brian jumped from stone to stone.

"You'll fall in, you know, and that will be the end of it," Linton remarked presently, as Brian's jumps became more daring.

"Why? Why will it be the end of it? Do you think I'll be drowned in ten inches of water?"

"No, but you'll get your feet wet and have to go home.... There now!"—as with a sudden splash his prophecy was fulfilled.

Brian scrambled out, laughing. "It was your fault!" he cried. "You distracted my attention. I believe you did it on purpose!"

Linton sat down on the trunk of a fallen tree and filled his pipe. He refused to budge from this position until Brian had taken off his shoes and socks. There followed, of course, the customary refusals and expostulations, but in the end he had his way, Brian wrung out his socks and, the path being smooth and mossy, did not put them on again. He hid them and his shoes under a blackberry-bush and walked barefoot.

"Now tell me how much of the story *you've* done," Linton demanded.

"Not much," Brian confessed, "but at least I began it."

Linton expressed his approval. "That's good!" he said. "I might have done the same if you hadn't made it so difficult."

Brian found this speech characteristic and unsatisfactory. He frowned to show his disapproval, but directly afterwards spoiled the effect by smiling. "How have I made it difficult?" he said.

"In fact about as difficult as anything could be," Linton went on, disregarding the interruption. "After leaving you last night I tried to remember if I'd ever read a ghost story that was told through the ghost. I couldn't. I don't believe there is one."

"So much the better then!" Brian pointed out. "Ours will be unique.... Besides, Clayton isn't a ghost in the beginning, so your excuse won't work."

"He's a ghost in the most important part—and I don't know how it's to be done."

Brian thought *he* knew: in fact Mr Martin's lack of confidence rather cleared the path, though he did not say so. "Suppose we divide it up," he suggested, "and I do the bit when he's a ghost. It's the bit I always wanted to do, and you can easily do the other."

Linton had stopped to pluck a half-opened wild rose. "Yes," he agreed, "I dare say I might manage the other."

"Of course, it isn't really fair," Brian continued, after thinking for a moment. "I'm bagging the part that will be far the most fun."

But Linton was quite prepared to let him bag it. "If you think it fun," he said, "I suppose it means that you've got your ideas about it." He looked at Brian in an intent though abstracted way before he added, "Only, there must be more than two parts: there are five distinct scenes as we planned the thing last night."

"Five!" Brian exclaimed. "I make it only three. Where do you get the fourth and fifth?"

"The fourth and fifth are to be your share," Linton replied. "There's the opening scene, with Clayton alone in his lodgings."

"'Clayton awoke with a slight shiver'," Brian quoted in an undertone.

"Yes; and then comes the meeting in Derringer's flat.... By the way, the lodgings must be rather dreary and comfortless—if not positively sordid: the flat can be as luxurious as you like."

"O—h!" murmured Brian, drawing out the word. "I'm afraid I've just given him a good dinner.... *And* a fire," he added with a faint smile.

Linton did not smile. "The fire doesn't matter, but you'll have to scrap the good dinner.... I don't believe you're taking this seriously, you know, and I want you to.... It ought to be a typical lodging-house dinner—distinctly dismal.... After all, Clayton's chance has only just come: up till now he's had a hard struggle. Besides, he'd have had to go out to a restaurant to get a good dinner; his landlady couldn't have supplied one. And we want to mark the contrast between his circumstances and Derringer's."

"I haven't described the dinner," Brian said ingenuously. "I can easily change 'good' to 'bad'."

Linton regarded him with benevolence. "Yes," he said.

But the benevolence was not appreciated. "I wish you wouldn't look at me like that," Brian complained. "I don't like it."

"Why?" Linton asked in surprise. "What way did I look? I don't see how it can have been very dreadful."

"Well, it was—dreadfully superior.... And that's the way you were feeling."

"I wasn't," Linton denied. "I was feeling indulgent."

Brian liked this no better: in fact it seemed to him exactly the same thing, because you can't feel indulgent without feeling superior. He reverted to the story, however. "The lodgings and the flat could be worked together in one part, couldn't they? In my version Clayton's just on the point of starting out for the flat, and I've written less than a page—in fact not much more than half a page."

"But have you *got* the lodgings?" Linton asked in astonishment.

"Got them? I've mentioned them," Brian replied. All the same, he knew what Mr Martin meant, and knew he hadn't got them. For that matter, it hadn't occurred to him to *try* to get them; he hadn't thought them of any importance.

"You see," Linton explained, "we'll be able to fix our relation between the two men much better if we've first placed them clearly in their habitual surroundings. Though I think you're right about the two scenes being run together: there's no reason why they shouldn't be, since there's no break in Clayton's consciousness. The third scene, however, ought certainly to have a chapter to itself:—I mean, when Clayton, deserted by his native servants, is dying of malaria in the hut."

"Then that's two chapters," said Brian; "and mine—after he's dead—makes three."

Linton was still thinking it over. "Yes," he yielded temporarily. "Of course you must do it in your own way."

"Which means, I suppose, it will be the wrong way!" Brian grumbled.

"Not necessarily.... It only means that I can't myself see it in a single chapter.... Nor, for that matter," he added, "in a dozen.... It's where I break down—and where you will have to step in. The lodgings and the flat can be done easily enough; and at a pinch the jungle, though we've neither of us ever visited one: but how and by what miracle you're going to get your Limbo is beyond me."

"Oh, I think I can get it all right," Brian answered airily. "I can see it quite well; it's the part of the story I saw first."

"What colour is it?" Linton asked unexpectedly.

"It's grey," Brian said slowly—"grey and damp—with mists and sharp rocks and sand—And there's a sea—yellow and without a tide...."

"Well—if you *can*," Linton mused—"then of course you'll get your story. All the rest in comparison is child's play."

But Brian's confidence had suddenly begun to waver. "You really think it's going to be so difficult?" he questioned. "I don't see why it should be.... Of course——" He did not complete his speech, but instead looked curiously and in silence at his collaborator.

"Yes, that's it," the collaborator replied. "The time problem— and here even worse than usual."

Brian laughed. He had been thinking of something quite different, but the time problem was not displeasing to him. True, just at present he did not quite know what it meant, but he knew he had only to wait and it would be revealed.

"However it's to be managed," Linton went on, "they must be *seen*—or perhaps I should say *felt*—in procession, moving by.... And there must be at least thirty of them—possibly more—to give the other fellow—the friend on earth—Derringer—time to degenerate into the gross, hardly recognizable apparition who emerges at the end of them."

Brian again gave him a rapid look. Somehow, with this concise statement of the story, he felt a misgiving. It was his own idea, but he found that at close quarters it was faintly distasteful to him. "It won't be a very pleasant story," he remarked.

"No," Linton said, "not so far as Derringer's concerned. Derringer isn't a very pleasant person. It's the story you thought of, though, isn't it?"

"Yes," Brian admitted. "In a way——"

"And it needn't necessarily be *unpleasant*," Linton continued, disregarding the qualification. "I mean, it needn't be what is usually meant by unpleasant. Of course it can't be particularly cheerful, but we get our moral values through Clayton, and since it's in Clayton's mind that everything takes place, our whole tone will depend upon what we make of *that*." He paused before continuing in a different voice, "It was there, you know, Brian, that your novel failed. Your young woman wasn't good enough, wasn't sympathetic enough, to support it. If you'd given her sufficient intelligence—including a moral intelligence—and had presented your story *through* her, you might have made your details even more sordid than they actually are, and still have produced something that wasn't sordid."

Brian's gaze remained fixed upon him, and Linton after a moment asked, "Well, what's the trouble?"

But the boy had already found an explanation for himself. "I expect you've discussed these things a lot with my father," he said.

"Why?" Linton wondered—and then immediately guessed why.

"Oh, I don't know. It's just that it doesn't sound as if this was the first story you had written. And it is, isn't it?"

"You've been talking about it as much as I have," Linton prevaricated.

"I haven't," Brian answered simply. "I've done nothing except ask a few intelligent questions. I haven't been talking about 'tones', and 'time problems', and 'moral values'. I might have if I'd ever heard of them before, but I hadn't."

"It's difficult not to use a kind of technical jargon," Linton apologized evasively. "I mean in discussion. Of course, when you're actually working, you work by instinct."

Brian sank into a meditation. He had taken off his jacket and was swinging it slowly backward and forward by its sleeves. He next loosened his tennis-shirt, and it looked as if in absence of mind he might be going to undress completely, when suddenly he put a question which seemed to have nothing to do with what they had been talking about. "What did you mean when you told me I hadn't had a vision of life? You said it that day—after I'd read you my novel."

Linton tried to remember, but his recollection was hazy. "Did I?" he murmured. "I don't think I can have been so definite as that."

"You were," Brian persisted. "At any rate those were the words you used. You *are* pretty definite, you know."

"You mean I'm inclined to lay down the law?" Linton said mildly.

"Yes; and it's a very fixed law."

"That sounds unpleasant."

"Oh, I don't mind it," Brian declared. "I expect everybody gets like that when they're—— When they've reached——"

"I know," Linton helped him out. "At all events, what I intended to say was not that you hadn't had a vision (for how can I tell whether you have or not?) but only that I saw no indication of it in what you'd been reading to me."

"Yes; I understand that: that's not what I meant. I want to know what *you* mean by a vision."

Linton had to think himself. "It's not very easy to explain," he confessed. "I expect at the time I may have meant an *actual* vision —some kind of spiritual revelation such as Wordsworth had in his boyhood among the Cumberland lakes. It's true, Brian, you know; one *can* have such a vision:—something which remains ever afterwards as an influence—which creates an ideal—and a longing that it may come again. An opening of the doors of heaven, you might call it, and it would hardly be far-fetched. At any rate, to those who *have* had it, the memory of it is in everything they afterwards write:—everything, that is, which has been inspired by a genuine emotion."

Brian did not dispute the point, but he did not accept Linton's judgment of its value. "Wouldn't it be very limiting in the result?" he ventured. "Wouldn't you always be writing the same thing?"

"It certainly makes the work very personal," Linton agreed. "But after all isn't that what one wants?"

"I don't know that it *is* what I want," Brian said. "At least I'm not sure that it is."

"Don't you think your work ought to have an ideal behind it; that it should be more than mere reporting, more than a mere chronicle of happenings? You don't want to write the kind of stuff which can't be read a second time until the first reading is forgotten—which depends on mere surprise for its interest. There must be something behind—or rather all *through* your work—a spiritual atmosphere. It seems to me that this alone can give it richness. Art isn't just life in the raw: it is a selection from life: it *is* a vision:—life seen through a temperament, as Zola said. And its quality depends on the quality of that temperament far more than on the material out of which the actual pattern is woven."

Like a fiddler improvising on a favourite theme, Linton was just beginning to enjoy himself when he happened to glance at his auditor. He stopped. Indeed, it would have been rather cruel not to have stopped, for Brian seemed nearly bursting with the restraint he was putting upon himself. "Well?" Linton asked, and instantly the boy began.

"Do you remember what you said last night? I mean, when I told you there were certain things I wished to put in my novel."

"Yes," Linton answered, a little puzzled by this breathlessness. "At least I can imagine what I said."

"Suppose, then, you and I were in a novel." Brian paused to mark the effect of this opening, but since none was visible he was obliged to draw the conclusion himself. "According to *you*, if we'd been made to talk in the way we've been talking, it would have been all wrong. Yet it's the way we *were* talking: therefore it's true; and therefore it can't be wrong."

"I see," Linton murmured. "In other words, I've been refuted out of my own mouth."

"Well, you've certainly been expressing views," Brian said:— "whole shoals of them." But his air was less triumphant, and he even cast a tentative glance to discover how his words were being taken. "I don't mean that I don't believe you," he finished uncertainly. "It's only that I like arguing."

At this, he was astonished to see a flush coming into his companion's face. He watched him anxiously for a moment or two, wondering if he could have offended him; but in the end decided that he hadn't. No, it wasn't that. Brian felt relieved, yet at the same time not a little perplexed.

Chapter XI

BRIAN

Mr Martin's views, though Brian had not quite made up his mind yet as to how far he really accepted them, at least suggested several ideas, and that afternoon, seated before his typewriter, he determined to put them into practice. The first thing was to get Clayton's lodgings, and this surely ought to be easy. But it would have been easier still if Claire and his mother had not been in the room. They each had a book and were supposed to be reading, but that didn't prevent them from carrying on a desultory conversation more distracting than if it had been continuous. The rain was coming down in a deluge, too, so that there wasn't the least likelihood that Claire would go out. He told her that her remarks interrupted him; he was careful to put it most politely; but she merely replied that the clicking of his typewriter interrupted *her*.

"Why don't you go to the dining-room, dear?" his mother asked. "Nobody will disturb you there, and it's rather difficult for us to sit absolutely dumb."

This was unanswerable, Brian's sole reason for not going to the dining-room being that he didn't want to go. All his materials were here on the table in front of him, and it would be a nuisance to have to carry them into the other room. Only he still didn't see why they need talk. When *he* was reading he didn't want to talk. It wasn't as if they had anything to say either, for they hadn't: yet he couldn't help listening, and once or twice actually joining in.

The real trouble, of course, was that his heart was not in this story. It had seemed all right while he was discussing it with Mr Martin: at any rate for the time being he had been interested. Though even then his interest had been more in planning how the thing was to be done than in the story itself. He wondered if he could rewrite his novel in accordance with Mr Martin's theories, but after a brief consideration decided against this. It would be better, as Mr Martin had said, to do something entirely new—a story about his childhood and his prep school: he had tons of material for such a book, and he could read the chapters to Mr Martin as he wrote them. The worst of it was that there was very little time for this—only about another ten days....

Unless he could persuade his mother to stay on.... She might do that.... After all, she hadn't had much of a holiday so far, and even now was only able to go out for drives. On the other hand, Claire would be going back to school, thank goodness!—and—no, there was no use mentioning it.... But if his mother would allow him to stay on by himself for a bit—that would do. Mr Martin had already suggested it, and had suggested his staying with *him*—either at the hotel or at Mrs Bedford's if she could take them.

Brian looked over the top of the typewriter at his mother. It would be far more satisfactory really if Mr Martin got to know her. For one thing, she would never allow him to accept the invitation unless he did. She had already made inquiries about him, which had proved fruitless. Nobody knew Mr Martin, and there was even revealed, on the part of the Grahams and others, a disappointing lack of interest in him, in spite of his friendship with Brian. Supposing, then, he did call upon her, Brian could see no reason why inconvenient facts need transpire. Mr Martin needn't mention that he was a friend of his father's, and certainly Brian wouldn't mention it. Of course, if his mother ever found out, she would accuse him of having deceived her, but how could she find out? *She* wouldn't introduce the subject, and why need they?

Her present theory was that Mr Martin was extremely shy. It was a surprising, but in the circumstances distinctly useful theory, therefore Brian had left it unchallenged, though he had been curious to discover upon what exactly it was based. His mother had simply propounded it, without reason or explanation, and immediately afterwards had suggested that he should be asked to tea.

What she didn't know was that Brian had already asked him, and that the invitation had been refused. Bluntly and plainly refused, with no beating about the bush. Mr Martin—in his shyness—had not even troubled to invent an excuse. He had refused point-blank. Uncommonly queer, Brian had thought it—not to say rude! Besides, it complicated things so—placing him in a most awkward position: because of course his mother had asked him if he had given the invitation, and, without actually telling a lie, he had led her to think he hadn't.

He glanced at the large gilt clock on the chimney-piece and saw that it said half-past three. He wasn't getting on very rapidly with Clayton!—nor would he be able to do anything this evening, because he was going with Claire and the Grahams to the pictures. To-morrow would be Sunday, too, when the typewriter would be tabooed: and he had wanted to have something to read to Mr Martin on Monday morning.

He *would* have something, he resolved; and began to type steadily. The quality of what he was doing mightn't be particularly good, but at least he was covering paper. And presently he got more into the swing of the story; hadn't to pause to think; even ceased to hear what the others were saying....

At five minutes to six he stopped, stretched his arms and legs, which were beginning to feel cramped, and then, as usual, made a hasty computation of the number of words he had written. Five pages—about fourteen hundred words—a pretty fair start. Clayton was now alone in the forest, dying of malaria, and Brian thought it would be an excellent place to leave him. He began to read his work over, not bothering to correct the typographical mistakes. When he had finished he sat staring at the last sheet.

It was really in a way remarkable. What he had written seemed to possess every fault Mr Martin had warned him against. It might—so far as the result went—have been done with no other purpose. Except for a brief description of Clayton's lodgings at the very beginning, it was simply one fact after another, stated in the baldest narrative form, with a few sentences of dialogue obtruding clumsily because they didn't in the least resemble the main texture of the tale. Moreover, though every misfortune he had been able to think of had happened to the luckless Clayton, the effect was exactly as if nothing had happened.

Brian clipped the pages neatly together. It would have to do, he supposed, for there was no time to rewrite it; and perhaps it was better than he imagined. He hoped so, but it made him feel that he didn't want to go on with the story at all—though he would wait to hear what Mr Martin had to say about it, and to hear his version, before finally making up his mind. Still, he was disappointed and disheartened. It might be that after all he had no gift for writing. Somehow, the fact that he had always been so determined to write had seemed to him to imply a gift; but it struck him now that this view was optimistic. Determination was all very well, but it couldn't work miracles. Nor could the School of Journalism—an institution with which he had begun to feel completely disenchanted. There, on the table, lay a whole portfolio of stuff produced under its auspices. Brian pulled it towards him and wrote in large letters on the pale buff cover, 'Some Specimens of Tripe, by B.W.'

This action made him feel slightly better, nevertheless the sound of the tea-bell came as a welcome relief. He rose with alacrity and replaced the cover on his typewriter, while Claire and his mother closed their books.

"You look quite inspired, dear!" Mrs Westby murmured, gazing at him with a little smile. "Or is it only that you've been ruffling your hair and it's standing on end?"

Brian was annoyed. He made no answer, but in the privacy of his bedroom he stared at himself in the looking-glass and decided to have his hair cut on Monday morning. He put water on it now and plastered it down with a brush—the immediate result being to transform him outwardly from Micky's spirit of the winds and the sea into an efficient young man, the peer of Derek Graham and Jimmy Garratt.

Strangely enough, he approved of this change. It did not strike him as depressing; it actually helped to disperse the clouds. "Still raining," he announced cheerfully, when a minute or two later he joined the others at the tea-table. "And the glass is going down steadily."

"Not steadily," Claire yawned. "It goes either up or down according to the side on which you happen to hit it."

"Well, it went down an inch for me," Brian replied, pulling out his chair.

He said grace—his duty at all meals—and he had no sooner finished than his mother began to talk about Mr Martin. She had already talked about Mr Martin at dinner, but he had become a favourite topic of late, and now she wanted to know if Brian would be going out with him to-morrow—a question which instantly put him on the alert.

"Why?" he answered guardedly.

He had a very genuine reason for wanting to know why, if his mother had only been aware of it; but she wasn't, and merely said that she wished he would get out of the habit of replying to one question by asking another. At the same time she handed him his tea.

Brian received the cup with a murmured thanks.

But that was all; he appeared to have nothing further to say; and his mother, after waiting a moment, had to speak again. "You haven't answered my question yet," she told him.

He started, or pretended to, for he hadn't really been absent-minded. "I don't know," he said. "It all depends."

"Depends on what?" Mrs Westby asked.

Brian thought it best to assume a mild jocularity. "On the weather for one thing; on whether I'm still alive for another; on whether he's still alive; on whether there *is* any to-morrow."

But nobody was amused, and his mother said, "I've asked you before not to talk in that way."

"In what way?" Brian murmured innocently.

"I've asked you not to make fun of serious things. You know I don't like it."

"But it does depend on those things," Brian argued. "You're always saying yourself that the end of the world may come at any moment."

"Will you be going out for a walk with Mr Martin to-morrow afternoon?" Mrs Westby asked once more, and this time her tone necessitated an answer.

Brian looked down at his plate and mumbled, "I suppose so."

Yet he was not trying to conceal his plans (for that matter she knew quite well he would be going out with Mr Martin), it was only that he had a sharp premonition of what was coming next, and had been expecting it, indeed, for several days.

It came—leaving no loophole for evasion. "Then you'd better

bring him back with you to tea. It would be only common politeness to show him some little civility after all the interest he has taken in you. I intended to remind you this morning to ask him, but you ran out in such a hurry."

Brian could not think of anything to say. He racked his brains for an objection, but the only one which occurred to him was feeble in the extreme, and he produced it with a total lack of conviction. "He has dinner in the evening," he said.

Mrs Westby dismissed it at once. "We can have tea early—at five o'clock—ordinary afternoon tea. It's only a matter of letting Mrs Belford know beforehand." Then, since Brian made no further protest, she went on as if the matter were quite settled. "Ask him properly," she said, "I mean, give him the invitation from me. Tell him that I'll be very glad if he can come."

Brian, with his head bent obstinately, continued to eat in silence.

"Do you hear me, Brian?"

"Yes," he replied.

"Then why are you behaving like this?"

"Like what?" he muttered.

"Why don't you want to have him?" Claire suddenly put in, penetrating, as usual, to the true difficulty, which her mother had missed. "If you're such friends with him, I suppose he's at least presentable. He must think we're frightfully inhospitable—especially when he knows we know that he's there all by himself."

Brian forced himself to an effort. He wanted to tell Claire to mind her own business, but this impulse he repressed. He saw the line he ought to have taken from the beginning and took it now. "He's not very well," he explained, looking at his mother and deliberately ignoring Claire. "He had to have an operation before he came down here, and he hasn't properly got over it yet."

Mrs Westby gazed at him in unfeigned astonishment. "And you've known this all along, I suppose! And never breathed a word about it till now! Really, Brian! When he's been so friendly with you too! I should have thought you'd have *wanted* to show him some little kindness!"

"It's because I know it *wouldn't* be a kindness," cried Brian in exasperation. "Heavens! you'd think it was some priceless treasure

you were offering him, instead of a wretched cup of afternoon tea!
He doesn't *like* meeting strange people. Nobody does when they're
not well."

"He's met much the strangest member of the family already,"
Claire pointed out. "And he can't be so ill as all that or he wouldn't
be able to go for long walks with you."

Brian glared at her. "We don't go for long walks. We only potter
about, and then sit down somewhere."

"At least you can give him my message," Mrs Westby interposed,
"and allow him to decide for himself. Perhaps you've no objection
to doing that—unless you think it's too much trouble. If he refuses,
well and good—that will be the end of it."

"He won't refuse," Claire pronounced confidently. "I've met him
on the golf-links when he was by himself, and he looked as lonely
as anybody *could* look. Brian only sees him when he's with him,
and of course he's different then."

"Naturally he must be lonely," Mrs Westby said, with a reproach-
ful glance at her son. "And when you're ill it's just the very time
you appreciate a little attention." Then, after thinking a moment,
she added in a gentler voice, "Hasn't he *anybody* belonging to him,
Brian?"

"I never asked him," Brian replied.

"No, of course you wouldn't," Mrs Westby returned, vexed
anew by his manner. "I suppose you only want to talk to him of
what concerns yourself—about your writings. I don't believe you've
a spark of real affection for anybody."

Brian did not contradict her.

"If you *don't* ask him," said his mother, "I shall write him a note
myself."

And he knew she would, for she always kept her word; so he decided that he must deliver her message. Mr Martin wouldn't come,
but that was his mother's affair: if she insisted on being snubbed,
he couldn't help it. He wouldn't soften it down either. The whole
thing was too silly! As if either she or Claire really cared a straw!

Perhaps it was this fuss about Mr Martin, perhaps it was merely
dissatisfaction with his afternoon's work, which upset him; but

whatever the cause, Brian's moods all that evening were singularly unstable. He set out with Claire to go to the pictures, determined to enjoy himself; they called for the Grahams and the Garratt boy, and before they reached the hall he had begun to feel bored. Then had come the actual show—commencing with a knockabout farce at which he had laughed. Yet the next picture had hardly started before he realized that he loathed it. How could anybody enjoy such stuff? It was moist with soulfulness, though its attraction was precisely that of a bedroom keyhole; and he watched the carefully exploited sexuality with a growing disgust of human nature, his own included. Suddenly a more than usually repulsive 'close-up' made him shut his eyes....

The atmosphere was now dense with smoke, and he felt the beginnings of a headache. The ugly vulgar jazz rhythms, thumped out interminably on a piano by a vigorous young woman in evening dress, did not improve it. He would have left the hall had they not been so tightly wedged in the middle of a row that to have moved would have meant disturbing everybody. And when at last the performance ended, and they had pushed their way out into the street, he determined never to go to a picture-house again.

The rain was over and a soft pleasant wind was blowing. Brian drew the fresh pure air deep down into his lungs. His headache already felt better, and deliberately he loitered behind the others with the intention of losing them. As it turned out, this was not difficult, for they never even glanced round, and when he reached the sea-front they were no longer in sight.

He stopped walking, and stood looking out over the dark water, and listening to the waves. In five minutes he had forgotten he had ever been to the pictures and also that he was on his way home. Something seemed to be speaking to him in the voice of the sea, but though he listened and tried hard to understand he could not understand. Perhaps it was not really speaking to him—for presently he felt that whatever meaning it might hold had nothing to do with human hopes or desires, loves or sorrows....

He went down to the water's edge and sat there in the darkness and solitude. The revolving lamp of Rathlin lighthouse flashed its signal across the water, but he turned his back on it and fixed his gaze on a star. In the night sky above him shone a crowd of stars, and a thin crescent moon hovered there like a wraith; but Brian looked only at this particular star which had first attracted his notice, and seemed nearer and brighter than the rest. And presently he began to weave the dreamlike pattern of a story. It was the kind of story Mr Martin wanted him to write: it was about the birth of a star—*this* star. It began with a boy leaning out of his bedroom window and looking into the darkness. Brian seemed to know this boy: he was lonely and sad—and perhaps it had been his own fault, but he could not mend that now.... And he watched the star being born.... It was wonderful and lovely: it was *his* star. All his happiness was there—all the happiness he had missed because he had let it go by him—and in the end he too would go there and find his lost happiness....

Brian sat on in a kind of trance, his mind filled with happiness and sadness. He did not want to return to ordinary life: if he had been able to, like the boy in his story, he would have gone to a star. All the emotional side of his nature, the very existence of which he was loth to allow anyone to suspect, had risen to the surface. And he dreamed on, and in that hour was the kind of boy he always was, or nearly always, when Linton thought of him.

At last he got up from his sandy shelter, and immediately the yellow lights of the hotel sprang into view. His friend would still be up, perhaps, and Brian knew that if he were to ask him to, he would go for a walk with him along the beach or over the golf-links, and talk about his star. And he knew he would like to be asked.... But Brian wanted to be alone—and—anyhow he must go home. He returned to the road, scrambling over black slippery rocks—once or twice nearly falling. He passed the hotel and began to climb the hill. There was a light in the sitting-room of his own house, and the outer door was still open. He turned the handle of the inner glass-door and hung his waterproof up on the hatstand. Then he went upstairs.

Chapter XII

BRIAN

As he entered the room his mother closed and put down a book.

"You're very late, Brian," she said. "It's long after eleven. Where have you been?"

He looked at her absently; fragments of his story were still floating in his mind, and it was in an abstracted remote voice that he answered:—"Only sitting on the shore. I forgot the time, and I hadn't my watch with me, and I was thinking about a story."

It would have been pleasant if she had let it go at that. Then he would have sat down and talked to her for a little and perhaps told her about his story, and they would have been friends. But he knew from the expression on her face that something was amiss, and half bored, half resigned, he waited for her to tell him so.

"Why didn't you come back with the others?" she asked. "Claire came home nearly two hours ago, and she didn't know where you were."

Brian stood by the table in the lamplight. He again explained what he had been doing. "I went down to the sea. I wanted to get some fresh air. The atmosphere in the hall was poisonous and there were no windows open. The show was poisonous too," he added, stifling a yawn, for he had suddenly begun to feel sleepy.

His mother noticed the yawn, and told him to get his supper.

"I don't want any, thanks," he answered. "At least, I only want a drink."

Still standing there, and still thinking of his story, he poured himself out a glass of milk, and began to drink it slowly, sip by sip. He had finished, and was on the point of wishing her good-night, when she spoke again. "I have something to say to you before you go to bed. Please sit down."

Brian glanced at her, vaguely startled, though he had no idea what was coming. Nothing cheerful at any rate—her gravity and the sound of her voice indicated that.

"Please sit down," she repeated, and he left the table and came over to the fireplace. But he did not sit down; he stood leaning against the chimney-piece, waiting to hear what was wrong.

His mother looked up at him and their eyes met. In this mutual silence his uneasiness increased, though he did not withdraw his gaze, and still could not imagine what he had done.

"I went to your room this evening," she began in a low voice. "I wanted to see if any of your clothes needed mending, and in a drawer, under your shirts, I found this book—which you must have been hiding."

As she spoke the last words she lifted the book up and held it out to him, but he had no need to take it, he had already recognized it. "I didn't hide it," he answered without thinking. "I put it there to be out of the way—that was all."

His mother laid the book down. "I don't think there is much difference," she said.

Nor was there—though he had not meant it quite in the way she thought—so he remained dumb.

"You certainly took care that I shouldn't see you reading it," she went on. "I don't know whether you call that hiding it or not."

"Yes, I did hide it," Brian admitted abruptly. "I kept it locked up in my suit-case. But it was only because I thought you wouldn't like it."

It was the truth, though as a justification perhaps somewhat obscure. She merely answered, "I don't see how that makes it any better. Who gave it to you?"

"My housemaster. At least he lent it to me: I've got to return it.... He thinks father's books are all right," Brian added impulsively. "He thinks a lot of them: he talked to me about them."

His mother's head was bent so that he could not see her face. She appeared to be thinking:—perhaps after all it was only because of the concealment, because he had kept the matter secret, that she was annoyed. "I don't say that the books aren't well-written," she answered at last. "I know very little about that side of it, and have been told, and have read myself in reviews, that your father writes well. But it is not of that I am thinking; it is of the contents of his books—of their whole tone and influence—which seems to me—objectionable."

Brian felt himself colouring—he did not know why. "What do you object to?" he asked.

It was perhaps a latent hostility in his voice, rather than the actual question, which caused Mrs Westby to look up at him quickly. "You must know very well, Brian, what I object to," she said. "You can only be pretending not to. You must know that everything your father writes is definitely and aggressively anti-Christian."

"Oh, he's not aggressive," Brian returned. "If he was I'd dislike him."

All the same, that she should have spoken in such a way gave him the measure of her own dislike, and he knew it would be hopeless to try to remove it. "Well—perhaps 'aggressive' is the wrong word," she conceded after a pause. "But that makes him all the more dangerous to a boy of your age—naturally impressionable—whose mind is more or less unsettled—especially on these subjects."

"You usually tell me I'm not impressionable enough," Brian retorted. "You complain that I'm cold: at least that's what you've always said until now."

"I don't think I said quite that. I may have said you were cold when *I* tried to influence you, and in your attitude to religion—for so you are. But this is different. I don't pretend to have any gift of persuasion, such as your father has. It is really because these books seek to cover their true teaching under a kind of beauty that their influence is so dangerous—their wickedness——"

"Wickedness!" Brian interrupted, half aghast.

For just a few seconds his mother wavered: then she repeated the accusation firmly. "Yes, wickedness. It is not as if he knew no better, as if he had not been brought up as a Christian, as if he had not been given a choice. He has made his choice deliberately, with open eyes, and the whole aim and purpose of his writings is to extol and inculcate a kind of paganism. Pantheism, he would call it, I dare say, but the name does not matter, and the more attractive he makes it the more harm it must do." Suddenly she put out her hand and took one of Brian's, which she held closely, though it remained limp and unresponsive in her clasp. "You would have seen this for yourself, Brian," she went on urgently, with a kind of passionate gentleness, "if you had not been blinded by superficial qualities which appealed to you and which you admired. But you *must* see it now—now that it has been pointed out to you. You can't help seeing it. All you have to do is to think quietly for a moment."

"I *have* thought," Brian answered, "and for a good deal more than a moment.... You don't understand," he added, while half unconsciously he drew his hand away. "You look at it only from *your* point of view, which of course is different from his. But a writer has to express his own point of view. Otherwise everything he said would be dishonest: it would be the same as if he were telling lies.... Besides, if it comes to that, I don't suppose I'm any more a Christian than he is—really."

"How many of these books have you read?" his mother asked.

Brian hesitated, while a succession of unspoken thoughts passed across his face. "Only three," he said at last. "But I want to read the others.... I don't think you ought to forbid me.... Apart from their not being Christian, there's nothing in them you could possibly object to, and they can't do me any harm in *that* way. I mean, I don't believe what you believe, and I had stopped believing in it long before I ever saw father's books."

His mother was silent, but she looked so unhappy that he turned away and stared hard at the lamp. He felt himself weakening, and he mustn't, he wouldn't. If he did, it would all only come up again in some other form, and he had a right to his own opinions, his own views. Anyhow, he couldn't help having them.

He heard his mother saying, "I want you to promise me one thing, Brian—that you won't read any more of your father's writings at present—not till you are older—not till you are twenty-one."

He knew just how she was looking at him, for more than in her words, there was a definite appeal in her voice, and in his determination not to hear it his face became stony. "I'm afraid I can't promise you that," he began—and then stopped.

It wasn't so much that he cared especially about the books (he was interested, of course, but he had read other books he liked better), it was the whole attitude—of not allowing him to think for himself, judge for himself—that he rebelled against. He could not help looking at her. The distress in her face had deepened, and to escape from it he turned his back and walked to the door. He reached it; he grasped the handle; and still she said nothing to keep him. "Oh, well," he jerked out over his shoulder, "I promise.... And I think I'd better go to bed now. Good-night."

Without giving her time to speak he left the room.

Chapter XIII

LINTON

'Ask, and it shall be given you; seek, and ye shall find....' The words—perhaps they were not quite the right words, for it was long since he had heard them—were suddenly present in Martin Linton's mind, as he walked leisurely along on this peaceful Sunday morning.

He wondered what had suggested them, for certainly he had not been pondering the Scriptures. What *had* he been thinking about? He could not remember: very likely he had not been thinking at all. But he had stopped for a while to look at a crowd of scarlet poppies growing in a cornfield, and then, when he had begun to walk on again, suddenly the words were there....

It was blissfully, exquisitely still, with only the faint far-off whisper of the waves to deepen his sense of rest and solitude. Presently he stopped once more, but this time it was because he had reached the small grey church whose distant bell it must have been he had heard half an hour ago. Now it was almost noon....

They would be well on with the service, Linton thought—somewhere about the psalms—and the ghost of a smile passed across his face. How many years was it since he had last been to church? Twenty-five at least—a quarter of a century. No—it must be more than that. At any rate it did not matter, for abruptly he decided that he was going to church to-day.

Yet still he lingered by the open wooden gate. What *was* this unknown church—right out here in the heart of the country—several miles from Ballycastle? Had he ever visited it before, or did he only fancy he remembered it? There were no houses near; no cottages even. Who could be its rector and why had it been built in this spot?

A sparrow flew out of the ivy, a low droning of bumble-bees came from a patch of red clover beyond the porch. It was all strangely familiar, and memory droned in Linton's ears an ancient tune of a poet beloved in his boyhood.

> *I have been here before,*
> *But when or how I cannot tell.*
> *I know the grass beyond the door,*
> *The sweet keen smell,*
> *The sighing sound, the lights around the shore....*

He was on the point of sinking into a dream, but recollected his purpose in time to resist the temptation. He cast just one friendly glance at the dark, green churchyard with its old gravestones warming in the sun, and then banished that allurement too from his mind. "Vade retro, Satana," he murmured amicably, as he walked up the trim, shadowed path....

Now was his time—while they were singing: he could slip in without attracting anybody's attention. The door, in fact, stood slightly ajar, as if to make it easier for him, as if he were expected. "There's a fatality in all this!" Linton mused, half seriously, half whimsically.... "If it wasn't so like the last scene in *Through the Looking-Glass*.... Put cats in the coffee, and mice in the tea—and welcome Queen Alice with thirty-times-three!" But he pushed the door wider—though only wide enough to admit him—and on tiptoe entered.

He stood still on the threshold; but it was all right; every back was turned to him and nobody looked round.

There weren't a great many *to* look. Perhaps it was because of the exceptionally fine morning that the church, small though it was, was not more than three-quarters full. All the pews near the door were unoccupied, and Linton, entering one of these, stood at the end of it, listening to the familiar hymn. It was not till half way through the next verse that his gaze began to wander. Then instantly he caught sight of Brian and Claire.

It was the last thing he had expected; they must have come simply for the sake of the walk; but there they were—just four pews in front, though at the side, under one of the windows.

Following immediately on Linton's surprise came an instinct to conceal himself. So far, he felt sure, his presence had been undetected; but if Brian looked round, or even half round, he could not fail to see him, for most of the space between them was vacant. Linton moved cautiously along so as to get more out of the line of the boy's vision if he did turn. He chose his position carefully. Then the hymn ended, and with the rest of the congregation he sat down.

It was very strange, but as the service continued it seemed to him somehow—prayers, lessons, and even the text of the sermon—to fit in miraculously with his mood and the train of his thoughts. He liked the service; he even found it oddly touching; but he knew nevertheless that the real source of its attraction was not in its freshness and simplicity and comparative novelty, but in the presence of Brian. Without him all would have been different. Linton was watching him in new surroundings, and these surroundings, like the old ones, took their charm and their beauty from him.

Brian, all unconscious of the late arrival, was listening to the sermon, and Linton watched him listening. A thin arrow of sunlight touched the boy's loose fair hair, which was fine, like spun flax, with threads of gold or sunshine in it. And perhaps it was this, perhaps it was the story of Jacob's vision, or perhaps it was everything combined, which coloured Linton's imagination, so that presently it seemed to him that he was looking at an angel.

The impression grew stronger, and though it was half dream, it was not, in a sense, fantastic. For if it was not an angel, it was at any rate an ideal Linton saw. He felt a quiet happiness, as of one who has found at last his longing fulfilled, his quest accomplished. Here where he sat he was more or less safe from observation, and he could look at his picture to his heart's content, and nobody, except the parson perhaps, be any the wiser. His thoughts slid into a reverie that was half mystical and half pure dreaming. And out of his reverie something lovely emerged—and he saw the boy, he saw everything, as a kind of answer to a prayer—even if it was a prayer that had never consciously been prayed. Looking back along the years of his life, they seemed to him now like a long probation, a preparation for what at last had happened. 'Ask, and it shall be given you; seek, and ye shall find.' He had asked, and it had been given. For an ideal in itself is a prayer, and to remain constant to it is a faith, and a faith kept for years, kept for half a lifetime— kept sacred, kept unspoiled—in the end perhaps *is* rewarded.

Linton believed this, and because he believed it he was happy and all his anxieties were at rest. It was the kind of happiness, too, which awakens gratitude, and the desire to express that gratitude. Therefore, for the first time since his boyhood, he said his prayers —and just in the old ingenuous fashion, though he was praying to the unknown God.

In the midst of the quiet congregation, in the small sober church, in the corner of his straight-backed pew, Linton prayed for Brian—and then prayed a little for himself. It did not in that hour even occur to him that his happiness was precarious, that nearly everything in the world threatened it. The accumulated affection of years had found at last an outlet, and in this passion of protec- tive tenderness which filled him, his life acquired a new meaning and usefulness. Had there not been, in the very fact of their meet- ing, something which suggested intention, beneficence, a con- scious providence? It so easily might not have happened, and that it should have happened made so wonderful a difference! Surely if there were any spiritual reality at all, an emotion which aroused and encouraged all that was best and least selfish in him could not be wasted? And it would be wasted if, to the object of it, it might as well never have been; if it awakened no response, if it did no good, if it lived and died only in itself. For it was primarily an impulse to give, an impulse to share—not only material things, but the beauty of this summer day for instance—the beauty that has been achieved by the spirit and genius of mankind working on, age by age, in poetry and stone and music—the beauty that is goodness. And it was an impulse to protect—to protect from what is hurtful and unclean and evil. And it was an impulse to strengthen and encourage and arm, to implant wisdom and independence, to quicken generosity, admiration, and compassion....

"Just one thing more——" The words reached Linton's ears, and he realized that he had better go now if he did not wish to be discovered. Nobody except the parson had seen him enter, and nobody, he felt pretty sure when he had stolen quietly out into the vestibule, had seen him depart.

Part Third

THE CHOICE

★ ★ ★

Speak!—though this soft warm heart, once free to hold
A thousand tender pleasures, thine and mine,
Be left more desolate, more dreary cold
Than a forsaken bird's-nest....
Speak, that my torturing doubts their end may know!
                                                    Wordsworth.

Chapter XIV

BRIAN AND LINTON

B rian called for him in the afternoon and they walked along the shore. "Before I forget, I've got a message for you," he said.

"And I've a confession to make to you," Linton replied.

Brian turned to him quickly. He was much too inquisitive about what this might portend to proceed further with his mother's invitation. That could wait—particularly since there wasn't the least chance of his forgetting it. "What?" he asked curiously, but Linton was not to be hurried.

Brian suppressed his eagerness. "Let's sit down," he proposed, as being the shortest way to get Linton to talk: then, as soon as he looked comfortably settled, "What?" he repeated more peremptorily.

"It's nothing alarming," Linton pronounced, with irritating deliberation. "At least, most people wouldn't think so."

"That means I will," Brian answered. "You'd better tell me quickly for I know it has something to do with me and I'd rather hear the worst at once."

"There isn't any 'worst'," Linton replied, casting a placid glance around him. "It happens to be a confession of excellence—many persons would regard it as a sign of grace."

"What is this sign of grace?" Brian demanded; but immediately added with less dignity, "You always take such hours to tell anything!" His gaze was fixed on Linton's face, and suddenly he burst out, "I know what it is: you've got me all those books!" But as Linton merely shook his head, he felt somewhat abashed. "It's the kind of thing you *would* do," he justified himself, "and anyway there can't be much excellence or grace about it or you wouldn't be so frightened to tell me."

"I'm not frightened," Linton said. "I'm not even nervous. I'm only preparing an effect."

Brian sat still for a minute or two watching the sea. Then he said abruptly, "If you don't tell me before I count fifty I'll go away and leave you."

"Oh no you won't," Linton contradicted. "You're much too curious to do anything like that."

For all answer Brian sprang to his feet and began to count aloud —"One, two, three, four, five, six, seven, eight, nine.... Honestly, I will," he paused to give warning. "Ten, eleven, twelve, thirteen, fourteen——"

"You're counting too quickly," Linton objected.

"I'll count quicker as I go on. Fifteen, sixteen, seventeen, eighteen, nineteen——"

"I was at church this morning," Linton said, and Brian's counting ceased.

His face at the same time expressed a half-indignant disappointment. "Is that all!" he exclaimed. "I might have known!" And he stretched himself out again on the grass and pretended to go to sleep.

But this did not last long. He suddenly opened his eyes. "That was a trick!" he said. "I don't know that I oughtn't to go after all— as a punishment." And he got up once more, but rather slowly, so that Linton had plenty of time to pull him back by his jacket.

"I was sitting three or four pews behind you," Linton said. "I came in late and went away early."

Brian bent forward a little and sat with his hands clasped round his knees. By and by he asked, "Did you come because you knew I would be there?"

"How could I know you'd be there?" Linton replied.

"You might have seen me starting and guessed."

"Well, I didn't. I didn't even know the church was there."

Brian accepted his word: and of course, if it was only an accident, it didn't matter.

"Why didn't you wait and walk home with us?" he asked—"I mean, when you *were* there? Claire wants to meet you.... However, she'll do that this afternoon, because mother says I'm to bring you back with me to tea. That was my message. She told me to be sure to bring you: in fact she told me about sixty times."

Linton stared into the sunshine and for a while neither accepted nor refused. "Brian, I can't," he said at last. "I dare say you'll think I'm being pig-headed and disagreeable, but it's not that: I can't come."

Brian had expected a refusal—or at any rate had almost expected one—yet somehow now that he had got it he felt none the less annoyed. It *was* 'pig-headed', he told himself: it was also rude —just as if Mr Martin was afraid of being bored. "I explained that you had been ill before you came down here," he grumbled, plucking at the grass and frowning, "and that you didn't like meeting people. Nobody believed the last bit—naturally."

He waited for Mr Martin to defend himself, or at least to produce some conventional explanation or apology, but nothing of the kind happened: Mr Martin sat there like a stone.

Brian's annoyance increased. "I must say it looks pretty queer!" he went on discontentedly. "It makes it a good deal more difficult for us to be friends, too, when you won't come to the house. I think you ought to. I don't think you should allow anything my father may have told you to prejudice you—at least, not to that extent. I know you're his friend, but after all you're my friend too."

The silence which followed this reproof was protracted, because Linton couldn't think of anything to say. Brian's remarks seemed to him perfectly sound, and the only thing to do, since he couldn't answer them, was to ignore them. "Will you come with me for a picnic tomorrow morning?" he asked, changing the subject not very happily. "All day, I mean. We'll drive to the top of Fair Head and spend the day there."

Brian did not reply.

"*Will* you come?" Linton repeated, looking at him; but Brian's face was cold and unresponsive.

"I don't know," he answered stiffly.

It was not encouraging: it sounded as if he really were offended—which indeed, in the circumstances, was not unnatural. Still, Linton was determined to persevere. "Why don't you know?" he said. "Is it because I refused to go back with you this afternoon?"

Brian remained unmollified. "It may be partly that," he answered in the same wooden fashion.

"But you *will* come, won't you?" Linton coaxed.

"I don't know."

It left Linton at a loss how to proceed. This picnic was not a sudden inspiration; he had thought of it all the way home from church; and to have his plan upset just because of Stella's wretched invitation was singularly aggravating. He wished that Brian was alone in the world:—or at least alone at Ballycastle. "You'd rather wait till to-morrow morning before you decide?" he suggested for want of anything better.

"Yes: there's no harm in that, is there?"

Linton shrugged his shoulders. He felt the spirit of opposition behind the question, and he could hear it in Brian's voice. He heard it again when the boy went on, "I suppose you think there is."

"I think it a one-sided arrangement—yes," Linton admitted.

Brian sat dumb, frowning deeply. "But if I don't ask you to bind yourself either?" he presently and very characteristically produced.

"It still doesn't seem to me satisfactory. For one thing, you know I *will* bind myself."

"I can't help that, of course," Brian retorted. Then, as Linton said nothing, he brought out the real grievance. "You didn't take *me* into consideration very much when I gave you mother's invitation. You didn't even tell me your reason for refusing it." He had no sooner uttered this speech, however, than he glanced at his companion—made a little unconscious movement with his hand—and then glanced at him again. "Did you?" he added more pacifically.

"Yes," Linton answered. "I didn't tell you my reason, but I took you into consideration."

Brian instantly believed him.

The belief, moreover, brought him a surprising feeling of gladness. "Of course, very likely I *will* come," he said, with a quick little smile. "Only it may be wet."

"Yes, it may be wet," Linton agreed.

Brian once more looked at him. "Do you want me to tell you definitely now?" he asked.

"It would be more convenient," Linton returned quietly. "I'll have to tell them at the hotel to pack a lunch-basket for us, and I'll have to hire a car."

"Will it do if I let you know to-night?" Brian compromised. "I can't very well let you know sooner. I must say something about it at home first, and see what the others are doing."

Linton was gazing at the waves. Brian's sudden thoughtfulness for the others left him unimpressed. It wasn't his habit to be so considerate of them. "All right," he answered dryly, and presently added in a voice carefully devoid of expression, "Perhaps you could let me know now whether you *want* to come or not? That really is the chief point, and the one you usually make so doubtful."

Brian was taken aback. "I don't think so," he said. "I mean, I don't intend to make it doubtful."

"I'm doubtful at present," Linton told him.

Brian was silent. Then he asked, "Is that my fault?"

"You think it's mine?" Linton said.

"I think you're very much inclined to read imaginary meanings into things."

"Things that don't matter to you?" Linton suggested.

"And that oughtn't to matter to you."

"How can you tell what ought to matter to me?" Linton asked. "You can't, merely by referring to your own feelings. It's a question of understanding—of trying, or not trying, to enter into another person's state of mind."

"I don't think you always enter into mine, you know," Brian said simply.

"I dare say not; but isn't that partly because you won't allow me to, and partly because it varies so much from day to day? I've seen you reacting in totally opposite ways to precisely the same sugges-tion—and that within twenty-four hours."

"I don't think so," Brian repeated. "At least—not really."

"Not really?"

"No.... I mean—the first time I probably wasn't expressing my real feeling. I don't always, you know."

Linton received a shock. Such a thing had never occurred to him, and he looked at Brian, at first in astonishment, and then in growing consternation. "What do you mean?" he stammered. And immediately afterwards, "Why don't you?"

But Brian seemed unable or loth to say why. In the end he

murmured tentatively, "It's partly, I suppose, because I sometimes express yours."

Linton frowned. "You mean you don't want to disappoint me?" he questioned.

"Yes—something like that.... Though it's not altogether that...." After which he seemed to think there was no more to be said, and relapsed into silence.

But Linton, who knew his capacity in this direction, was now determined to get to the bottom of the matter. "What is it then— you must know?" he persisted grimly.

Brian returned his scrutiny with thoughtful though untroubled eyes. He could see, however, that Linton was worried, and after further self-communing made a second attempt to answer him. "I suppose I feel it at the time," he brought out slowly—"when I'm with you. And then afterwards, when I'm alone, it's different, and I go back to my own feeling."

"But how do you expect me to know which from which?" Linton asked helplessly. "How am I to know when you're being sincere and when you're only trying to please me?"

"I am being sincere," Brian said.

"Not if you make me think you feel something you don't feel."

Brian hesitated. "I know it's complicated," he murmured half apologetically, "but I'm afraid I can't make it any clearer.... I expect I don't always know myself what I really feel. I mean, how long I'm going to feel it."

Linton sat mute, trying to extract comfort from this explanation. Only what did it amount to—what did it really tell him? Suddenly he broke out, "Do you *like* mystifying me? Do you *like* me not to understand you?"

"No," Brian replied.

"But it doesn't trouble you?"

"No."

Linton gazed at him in discouragement. "Sometimes I think I understand you," he began dubiously. "And then, just as I'm gaining a little confidence, you say or do something to upset it. And you won't help me. I know you pretend you can't, but you could— if there wasn't so much that you're determined to keep to yourself. It makes it very hard—hard for me to know what I can count on."

"You'd better not count on anything," Brian recommended.

"But I must," cried Linton in indignation. "You've no right to say a thing like that—not now at all events. If it's true, you should have said it at the beginning; but it isn't true; and if you really meant it, it would be horribly cynical."

"It's only that I don't want you to form too high an opinion of me, and then be disappointed," Brian explained patiently. "It would really be better the other way round, because then, when you did get a surprise, it might occasionally be a pleasant one.... All the rest I can't help."

Still Linton did not look convinced. "I wonder!" he said. "I think you could at least help it more than you do. If you allow me to think the wrong thing about you, that comes to pretty much the same as telling me the wrong thing.... After all, I've helped it," he continued. "It's a matter of trust—of not having reserves and secrets. You'd know exactly in any given circumstances what I'd want, what I'd do—wouldn't you?"

"Yes," Brian admitted at once, "I think so."

Linton felt defeated. He had hoped Brian would deny having any such reserves, but he didn't:—didn't deny it, didn't admit it—and Linton was left knowing no more than before whether he really had the boy's confidence or not.

And then, as he sat brooding, it suddenly occurred to him that, in spite of his criticism of Brian, he hadn't himself been so wonderfully candid. Instantly he made up his mind that he would be— that he would tell him the whole truth—not here, not now, but to-morrow on Fair Head, when they were alone, with plenty of time, with no danger of interruption.

"You see," Brian was explaining carefully, "you're easy to know because you *want* things so much, and cry out for what you want— really very like a small boy. I don't want *anything*, I think, so much as you want some things. And when you don't get what you want you're disappointed and show your disappointment. Everybody knows exactly what's going on inside you: when you're pleased and when you're not pleased. If what pleases you doesn't happen to please the other person you're frightfully worried about it, and think there must be something wrong with him, and make all kinds of trouble for yourself—and incidentally for the other person too. I know you imagine you're very calm and reasonable and philosophic and all the rest of it, but you aren't. You don't mind my telling you this, do you?"

"Some of it I expect is true," Linton replied. "Only, I'm sure I can always be brought to reason."

Brian left him in his belief. "Let's talk of something else," he proposed. "This doesn't seem to be leading to much, and it's making you melancholy; whereas there's really nothing to be melancholy about.... Is there now?" he went on coaxingly. "After all—even if you don't know quite everything about me, you know a good deal—more than anyone else does. It's extremely likely, too, that I'm coming for a picnic with you to-morrow. You'll have about seven hours of my company, absolutely unbroken—and I suppose that's what you want."

Linton smiled: he was suddenly happy—conscious only of the extraordinary charm the boy's voice had for him when he spoke like that. "I'm not melancholy," he declared.

"Well, worried then—disturbed—as if you'd just received a telegram with the worst possible news."

Linton made a feeble attempt not to surrender completely. "That's all very fine," he objected, "but it was you who sent the telegram, and whatever news was in it was the news you put there."

"What I put there was—Coming Fair Head to-morrow if possible, Brian. That was the entire message."

"You really think so? It may have been the final one, but it certainly wasn't the first."

"Nor was it the final: I've another still undelivered. Do you want to hear it?"

"Yes," said Linton, though with a shade of returning anxiety.

"It's all right," Brian assured him, "it's quite pleasant: it's only that I got an idea for a short story last night—about a star—the birth of a star. Do you think it sounds promising—or possible?"

"Both," said Linton. "What put it into your head?"

"It came from the star itself. I was sitting on the shore, listening to the waves, and feeling rather fed-up:—and then I saw the star."

"But why were you feeling fed-up?" Linton asked him.

"I don't know. I just felt that everything had gone wrong somehow. I expect it was partly the result of a visit to the pictures."

"Were you all alone?"

"Yes—then."

"Why didn't you call for me?" Linton asked.

Brian was silent. If he told him why, probably he wouldn't like it. "I did think of it," he said.

"Why didn't you do it then?" Linton persisted.

That was so like him!—and Brian resigned himself to the inevitable. "Well, for one thing, it was very late," he said.

"Did you think I'd mind that?"

"No: I knew you wouldn't. But it *was* late."

"So you've said:—the real reason, I suppose, being that you didn't want to.... Well, did you get your story?"

"Not all of it last night. I only got one scene then—not what led up to it, nor what followed it. But I went over it in church this morning, and I think I've very *nearly* got it."

Linton recalled the picture he had sat watching: he could see it almost as clearly now as he had seen it then. "*I* thought you were listening to the sermon," he said.

"I'm afraid I wasn't. Was it good?"

Linton wondered if it had been good. "Yes," he decided.

"You don't seem very sure about it."

"Well," Linton admitted, "actually I was so busy observing its effect upon you that I didn't hear much more than the text."

"Oh, I heard that myself!" Brian exclaimed. Then another thought struck him, arousing his curiosity. "What made you go to church?" he asked. "You don't often go, do you?"

"Why should you imagine that?"

"I don't know. I've really no reason—except that I wouldn't go myself if I didn't have to."

Linton wondered how far the compulsion actually went, and had a vision of Stella exercising it—of Stella standing in the hall, dressed and waiting, overruling excuses, deaf to grumblings, quiet but firm. It revived memories of similar happenings in his own boyhood. "You say your prayers, don't you?" he questioned.

Brian shook his head. "Not now: not for the last year or two. You can't go on after you've stopped believing in it. You do believe in it, I suppose."

"Not very much," Linton confessed. "Not at all in the way I expect you mean. Still—if there's anything there—it can do no harm to say your prayers. And this morning—you see—I almost felt there was."

"Only not quite?"

"I don't know.... Yes, at the time, I think, quite."

He was silent for a little, and Brian too was silent:—Linton could see that he was dreaming.

"I think you'd better write your star story," he told him, "and drop the other one—ours. You'd like to do that, wouldn't you?"

Brian abruptly came back to earth. "Yes," he said.... "Though we may as well compare what we've each done—as we arranged. At least, I want to see what *you've* done: what I've done is rotten.... And by the way, you mustn't give me that book."

Linton's face clouded. "Why?" he asked, for he knew the book referred to.

"It would be better not. There was a row when I got home last night. At least—not a row," Brian corrected himself. "But mother had discovered the other book—the one you saw me reading—and she was rather peeved about it."

Linton flushed. "I don't think——" he began, but Brian didn't allow him to finish.

"It wouldn't do," he said quietly. "There's no use making matters worse. Anyway, I've promised not to read any more of father's books until I'm twenty-one."

"Oh," Linton said, and Brian caught the disappointment in his voice. He turned to him in some surprise. He couldn't see why he should mind—after all they weren't *his* books—and yet he looked as if he did. "You see, she was really upset," he went on in explanation—"genuinely—she wasn't pretending. I know it was quite unreasonable, but still—— Anyhow, I'd rather you didn't give me the book. You understand, don't you? It's not because I wouldn't like to have it. But if you did give it to me I'd have to tell her about it or else hide it—and I don't want to do either. You can give it to me when I'm twenty-one."

He smiled—a little uncertainly—and Linton waited until an elderly couple had passed before he spoke. Then he said, "It doesn't matter. I'll get you something else instead."

"Yes," Brian murmured, "but I think you'd rather have given me that. I'm sorry. Only I really couldn't help it."

"No," Linton agreed.

Brian looked at him doubtfully. "I don't believe you mean 'no'," he said. "Do you think I oughtn't to have promised?"

Linton did not reply: he did not want to discuss the matter.

"*Do* you think I was wrong," Brian pressed him, and Linton still refused to speak.

But at last he said, "I can't answer, Brian. In the particular circumstances I dare say you were right: at any rate I'm not surprised."

Something in his tone aroused Brian's inquisitiveness. "Why can't you answer?" he asked. "I think myself I was right. After all— it would have been rather rotten of me to have refused—wouldn't it? It only means waiting another two years. But I wish you'd tell me what you really think about it. I won't be offended."

"It isn't that——" Linton began. "I'm not afraid of offending you." Then abruptly he made up his mind. "It's because I'm not disinterested."

He was conscious, though he kept his own eyes lowered, that Brian's gaze was now fixed upon him intently. "I want you to be reconciled to your father," he went on. "I mean, I want you to be friends with him. It is the thing I want most in the world."

Brian was surprised and puzzled; and immediately afterwards he realized that for some reason, in spite of their kindness, Mr Martin's words had not given him as much pleasure as they ought to have given him. On the contrary, they gave him no pleasure at all. "I thought what you wanted most was for me to be friends with you," he said ingenuously.

"You are—aren't you?" Linton hastily asked, and Brian laughed. "Yes," he said.

Both felt relieved, and Linton began to straighten out the brim of his hat and to brush imaginary dust from it. He laid it on the grass beside him, and when he looked up the boy was still watching him steadfastly. "What is it?" Linton murmured. "Why are you looking at me like that? What are you thinking about?"

"I don't know," Brian answered.

"You must know what you're thinking."

"I don't. It's just that sometimes you give me a queer kind of feeling."

"What kind of feeling?"

But Brian was wondering and frowning, and presently he began to bite the side of his hand. "As if there was something behind all this," he produced at last. "Is there? Does my father know you're here?"

"Yes," Linton said.

"Though of course that doesn't mean anything," Brian continued, half to himself——"because he can't know I'm here.... Unless you've told him." He turned quickly to Linton, suddenly eager and excited. "Unless you've written to him! Have you?"

Linton shook his head.

"You're sure? No; I shouldn't have said that: I'm sorry."

"It's all right," Linton answered, and for a minute or two said nothing else. But it was his opportunity, and he knew it, and in the end took it. "There's something, Brian, that I've been meaning to tell you for a long while. I've kept putting it off and off, with one excuse and another, but it has always weighed on my conscience, and I know I ought to have told you much sooner.... It's about your father and about me.... I don't want to say more than this at present. I'd rather wait till we have plenty of time:—perhaps to-morrow."

Brian's face was now alive with curiosity, but he was never importunate, and he only said, though a little regretfully, "You'll promise to tell me to-morrow? You won't change your mind?"

"No. That was my reason for mentioning it:—to burn my boats, so to speak."

"Thanks," Brian replied: and feeling there was nothing further to say he rose to his feet.

Linton also got up, and they stood for a minute or two before starting on the homeward walk. "You *have* got yourself into a mess!"

Brian suddenly laughed. "You've even got straws in your hair—like Ophelia—and quite a lot of the golf-links on your clothes." He began to brush the back of Linton's jacket with vigorous thumps suggestive of the beating of carpets.

Linton stood submissively till his grooming was completed. "It's well you've got me to look after you," Brian told him.

"Yes," Linton answered gently; and they began to walk slowly back across the links.

It was at this point that Mr Martin abruptly and surprisingly said, "Don't talk to me for a minute or two: I want to think."

Brian obediently remained dumb. But he began to think himself; and one of his thoughts was that if they continued at this snail's crawl it would take them about an hour to reach home and he would be even later than usual. He did not want to be late—to-day especially—because, with the expected visitor, he knew they would not begin tea without him. So by a series of small pushes, administered in silence since words were denied him, he gently impelled his companion forward.

He was extremely inquisitive as to what Mr Martin had to tell him; but only inquisitive—not at all uneasy. His father was too remote from him to arouse anxiety. No matter what the news might be, it couldn't, as things were, really affect him deeply. Not emotionally, at any rate. After all, it was news of a stranger.

Into the calm pool of these reflections Mr Martin suddenly dropped a stone, and a big one. "Look here," he announced brusquely; "what I'm going to tell you may make a difference. I don't say that it will; but it may.... A difference to *us*, I mean. Mightn't it be better to let things go on as they are?"

"You've told me too much," Brian answered at once. "You shouldn't have told me anything if you were going to draw back."

"I haven't told you anything."

"You've told me that there *is* something; and I must know what it is.... Besides," he added with complete confidence, "it can't make any difference. At least I can't imagine anything that could."

"Do you really mean that?" Linton asked, his face brightening. "But you don't know yet," he added next moment, the words tailing off below his breath. "There's no use talking about it."

"I know already that you'd rather not meet my mother," Brian said. "And I expect I more or less understand why. But you've only heard one side—my father's side—you haven't heard hers."

"I've heard yours," Linton reminded him.

"Yes," Brian answered. "That was just what I was thinking. I'm afraid I've given you a wrong impression. I didn't mean to, but I know I have."

"In what way wrong?" Linton asked quickly, and with a vague foreboding in his voice.

Brian noticed it, but it only impelled him to go on. "I've grumbled and groused far too much, for one thing. It was partly because you were the only person I had to talk to, and I usually talked when there had been a fuss, or I was feeling fed-up about something. That's always the way: at other times there doesn't seem to be anything to talk *about*. Anyhow, I know I've exaggerated—unintentionally. Mother has always been very decent to me. She's really very fond of me, and I'm very fond of her."

Linton made no answer.

"I'm not sure that you'd get on awfully well with her," Brian continued. "You're too different in most things. But I don't know either that you wouldn't. In fact I think you might, because she already thinks you've been very kind to me—and that goes a long way. Part of the trouble has always been that she's too anxious about me; and in your way, you know, you're much the same. It's a different way, of course, and more convenient to me personally; but it's only different because your ideas are different—your object is the same."

"What is my object?" Linton asked.

"Oh, well—you *know*," Brian mumbled awkwardly.

"I don't know: tell me."

Brian wished now that he hadn't mentioned it, but he had to go on. "Well—— Oh, I hate talking about these things, but I think you want me to—— Well, you want everything to be all right for me."

"Yes, naturally," Linton exclaimed in some surprise.

"And so does she: that's all," Brian finished with relief.

Linton pondered a moment before he asked, "Do you think I'm *too* anxious?"

"Yes—a little. I mean—I don't see why you shouldn't treat me in the same way as you would treat anybody else."

"How do you know I don't?" Linton said.

"*You* know you don't," Brian answered.

"You think I shouldn't be so friendly with you—is that what you mean?"

"No, of course not: I'm friends with *you*."

"Then I'm afraid I *don't* understand," Linton confessed.

"You want me to have special privileges," Brian explained. "You want to make everything easy for me. And I don't see why I *should* have special privileges. If I'm any good I oughtn't to need them, and if I'm not I oughtn't to get them."

"What special privileges do you refer to?" Linton asked, with perfect sincerity. "Really I haven't the faintest notion of what you're trying to get at."

Brian kicked the grass as if it had annoyed him. "It's not so much what you've done," he murmured deprecatingly, "though perhaps——"

"You mean it's a kind of favouritism?" Linton suggested.

"Yes."

Yet still Linton could not quite see the difficulty. "Everybody has favourites," he pointed out, "if by a favourite you mean a person for whom you have a special liking. Sokrates had, and I should think he was as just as it is humanly possible to be. Your idea seems to be that it is *unjust*."

"Well—in a way it *is*," Brian declared. "No, I don't mean that either, for I know it's nonsense.... It isn't that I don't like it," he hurriedly added. "In fact, I think we'd better decide that I don't know what I mean."

"Jesus had a favourite," Linton went on thoughtfully: "and even God had one: the little boy Samuel was his favourite. What are you laughing at?"

"Nothing.... Only at the examples you're choosing."

"I'm choosing examples you won't be able to take exception to—that's all."

"But I do: at any rate to the infant Samuel."

"It's in the Bible," Linton said. "There's no doubt whatever that

God felt a special affection for Samuel.... And it makes the whole
story rather lovely."

"To you," Brian qualified. "Because it happens to appeal to you.
But you're not supposed to get that kind of story out of it at all."

"Why not? It's there."

"For you," Brian qualified again. "Anyhow, I know you're not.
In fact," he went on, half laughing, "I expect what you're saying
would be considered frightfully profane—possibly blasphemous.
You like it, because you can turn it into a quite human story—about
God and a little boy. And you make God feel exactly the way you
would have felt yourself. Really it's just father's story of the old
alchemist and his grandson over again."

"But supposing you're right—even granting all that," Linton
persisted, "doesn't it merely prove how universal such a feeling
is? You can see for yourself that it existed in ancient times, and yet
your father still can use it in a modern novel."

"Yes," said Brian, his amusement deepening:—"if you call father
modern."

"So there you are!"

"There I am."

"At all events," Linton retorted, "you'll never succeed in arguing
anybody out of such feelings. They're not based on logic and no
reasoning can alter them."

"I don't want to alter them," Brian assured him, "but I don't
want to be regarded as an infant Samuel either, because I'm not
one."

"I never thought you were."

"You think I'm a good deal more like him than I am. You seem
to forget that I've been through a public school, and that leaves you
fairly tough, if nothing else. I've seen and heard what other boys
see and hear."

"That," Linton returned, "is based on an absolute fallacy. I don't
say that you mayn't have come up against unpleasant things. It
would be rather remarkable if you hadn't. Nevertheless your generalization is false."

"What generalization?" Brian asked him.

"Your implication then. You imply that in the same surroundings everybody sees and hears the same things. They don't. To a very large extent you only see and hear what you're looking for."

It flashed upon Brian that this was eminently true of his companion, but he did not tell him so. "How do you know what I was looking for?" he asked.

"I don't know—I can't know—naturally. At least I can't be sure. But I can give a pretty good guess from what I see now."

Brian glanced at him obliquely and the corners of his mouth twitched. "I think you'd be the easiest person in the world to take in, you know. I mean, by anybody who had an object in doing so. Haven't you guessed that too?"

"I never thought about it," Linton answered innocently. "Besides —I know you don't want to take me in."

"Yes—that's just it: you can't possibly know.... Well, I'll admit I haven't *tried* to do so," he went on. "Trying wasn't necessary."

He looked to see what effect this last remark would have, but none was visible on Linton's face: he rather astonishingly did not even appear to be listening. He had stopped, and now he laid a hand on the boy's arm. "I don't think I'll come any further, Brian," he said. "There's your house, and I can't very well go right up to the door."

Brian's face fell. He had forgotten all about the difficulty that still awaited him, and Linton's words switched his mind unpleasantly back to it. He looked at him in reproach. "What am I to say?" he asked ruefully.

"I'm afraid I must leave that to your tact," Linton answered. "You can say I'm very sorry, but that I didn't feel up to it. You told me you'd already prepared the ground in that direction."

"I can say that you've made it a rule never to do anything you don't want to do," Brian grumbled.

"If you like: if you think that would be best."

"It would at least be the truth," Brian declared: and then added— "in this particular case."

"Well, good-bye," Linton said. "And you'll let me know, won't you, as soon as you can about to-morrow?"

"Yes—though you don't deserve it. Either to-night or first thing in the morning."

Chapter XV

LINTON AND BRIAN

A tiny field-mouse crept out from beneath the grey rock, had a peep at Linton with bright black beads of eyes, and then sat down on the sleeve of Brian's jacket, which he had thrown on the heather. Brian himself was not there, he was scrambling down the Grey Man's Path, a narrow cleft in the face of the cliff. Linton could hear him, or rather hear the showers of stones and sand he was dislodging. Brian had said he would climb down to the sea and up again.

Linton altered his position. The movement he made was ever so slight, yet the field-mouse instantly vanished. He hoped it had not taken refuge in one of Brian's pockets or up his sleeve, but when he shook the jacket no mouse appeared.

He could no longer hear the climber—nothing but a faint murmur of water which came whispering up the grey steep walls of rock. The whole climb would take Brian three quarters of an hour perhaps: it was now nearly three: the car was to return to the cottage for them at half-past five: that left them more than two hours before they need start.

Linton ran his fingers through the warm crisp scented heather. A deep blue sky arched over him, and down below was the sea—a broken, streaked green, except where the powerful current which ran round the headland was marked by a long smooth paler band, like a river. The silence lasted for another twenty minutes; then the showers of loosened stones recommenced: Brian would soon be back.

Three and a half hours had gone by very quickly. Brian had bathed in one of the fresh-water lakes on the top of the headland; they had walked round to Murlough Bay, but had not gone down to it; they had found several fly-catching plants; they had eaten their lunch—that seemed to be all; and yet more than half the day was over.

It had been a strange day, very happy, though for Linton haunted all the time by the promise he had still to keep. His promise had hovered there, not distracting his thoughts exactly, but never really absent from them, producing a restless excitement, now hopeful, now filled with apprehension. Only nothing had worked out as he had expected.... He had expected Brian to remind him of his promise, and Brian had not done so: indeed, it looked now as if he did not intend to do so.

He had been in an unusually talkative mood, and had chattered away about things which gave Linton himself no opportunity to introduce the subject. "I'll tell him when we reach that lake," Linton had said to himself, but when they reached the lake Brian had instantly wanted to bathe in it, though there had been no previous idea of bathing and he had not brought a towel. It didn't seem the right moment, while he was dancing about naked on the grass, plunging in and out of the water, laughing and singing:— better let him get his bathe over first, Linton had thought.

But when the bathe was over it didn't seem the right moment either, for Brian had found the water unexpectedly cold, had stayed in too long, and had begun to run up and down to warm himself. "I'll tell him when we reach Murlough Bay," was Linton's next decision, and when they reached Murlough Bay, Brian was in the middle of a description of a school story he was reading, and from that he passed to reminiscences of his own school. Then he had wanted to light a fire, and by the time the fire was lit he was hungry and wanted to have lunch.... Afterwards—while they were walking back along the edge of the cliff—it had seemed to Linton better to wait until they sat down somewhere. He had found the place, and they had sat down, but just as he had screwed himself up to the point of beginning, Brian had announced that he was going down the Grey Man's Path.

Of course Linton really knew that these were the excuses of timidity. With a little more courage he could have told him hours ago. All he had had to do was to say a word, and Brian would immediately have given him his whole attention. "I'll tell him when he comes back," he determined finally.

And he knew that if he were going to tell him at all, it must be soon. Quite apart from his promise, he realized that it would not do to wait. It was even lucky that Brian had not found out the truth a week ago for himself. They had been coming out of the post-office one afternoon when he had suddenly grabbed Linton by the arm. "There's mother," he had said—"in that car"; and Linton had only just had time to draw back.... It had been a narrow escape: if his business in the post-office had ended five seconds earlier, if they had actually reached the street instead of only the door, recognition would have been inevitable. Since then he had kept a sharper look-out and had avoided main roads as far as possible.

But it had brought home to him the risk he was running. With the inauguration of Stella's daily drives discovery became only a matter of time. She must be curious about her son's friend, and nothing was more probable than that she too was keeping a look-out. He wished he had told Brian at the beginning, and yet here he was, still shilly-shallying, though now there was nothing in the wide world to fear. If anything, their friendship could only become closer when Brian learned the truth. There might be a slight embarrassment at first, a mutual shyness, but that would quickly pass.

This was not the psychology Linton would have put into a novel had he been treating the subject, and he knew it wasn't—knew that it tallied neither with his intuition nor with his experience. It was the psychology he *wanted*—the good old Christmas-story psychology, invented to set an example to human nature, but which hitherto had failed signally to alter it. Yet Linton clung to it—blood was thicker than water—all the old comfortable clichés....

Brian's face, looking very hot, but also very pleased, at that moment appeared above the edge of the cliff. His shoulders followed; then his whole body; till, with a last heave and scramble, he flung himself down on the heather beside Linton, and lay panting rather ostentatiously.

He turned over and buried his face between his hands. "Have you ever been down?" he asked, and Linton replied, "Yes; it's quite easy, or I shouldn't have allowed you to go."

Abruptly Brian jerked himself round. "I say! I like that!" he exclaimed: then thought better of it, or was too lazy, and lay back again.

Linton, as a matter of fact, regretted his own words: they were the kind of thing he never could resist saying to the boy, but they weren't at all the right introduction to what he had on his mind. And when Brian suddenly sat up and said, "I wonder if I could cross that rock—the one stretching over the gap," he knew he had only himself to blame.

Brian made a movement to rise, but Linton caught him by the arm. "No," he said.

The boy struggled free. "Why? If the other's so easy, I'll see if I can't do something that isn't." He sprang to his feet.

"You're not to, Brian," Linton called out excitedly. "I mean that: I'm not making fun."

But Brian only partially yielded. "Why?" he repeated. "I bet you've done it yourself."

"I haven't."

"Well, I don't see why I shouldn't: that is, if I can." He looked at the narrow stone spanning the break in the cliff's edge, took a step towards it, and then paused to glance back at Linton, who had made no reply. "Oh, very well," he grumbled, re-seating himself. "But you've no right to dare me to do things and then not let me do them."

Linton breathed a sigh of relief. "Feel in the pockets of your jacket," he said. "I don't think there is, but there may be a mouse in one of them."

Brian snatched up his coat. "Goodness!" he cried. "You actually allow mice to attack my clothes!" Gingerly he tucked in the flaps of the side-pockets and held the jacket upside down before giving it a vigorous shaking. No mice fell out: only several pencils, a fountain-pen, a few lumps of sugar, a notebook, and a roll of paper. "That's the short story," Brian cried, pouncing on it. "I'd forgotten all about it. Did you bring yours?"

"Yes," Linton admitted reluctantly.

Brian had already begun to straighten out the leaves of his manuscript. "Then we may as well read them," he announced:— and Linton's confession seemed as far away as ever.

"'Clayton awoke with a slight shiver,'" Brian began. "But here—you'd better read it for yourself, while I read yours…. I say: you've written quite a lot!"

Linton submissively had handed him a bundle of small square sheets. "Not really very much," he said. "And I don't know whether you'll be able to make out my writing."

"I can make out to begin with that you've pinched the hotel note-paper," Brian told him gaily. "And I *can* make it out: it's as plain as print."

He began to read, and for several minutes there was no sound except the turning of a page, and from far below, the faint whisper of the waves. Linton made no pretence even to glance at the manuscript he held, but sat watching Brian, and waiting…. Would he recognize it? It all depended. Depended on how far he had a sense for such things—an ear—a *flair*. At all events he seemed to be reading with unusual attention, and his face was very grave. Sometimes he would turn back and read half a page over again: now and then Linton could see his lips moving; now and then he appeared to stop reading altogether:—only he never once looked up….

He had reached the last page, and still without a word or a glance at Linton, he turned back to the beginning. But at this Linton leaned forward and took the manuscript from his unresisting grasp. Brian said nothing. He sat motionless, with his head lowered, and Linton knew that it was not of Clayton's adventure he was thinking. The boy's face was troubled, but it was—even more—deeply, painfully shy. As if conscious that Linton was watching him he drooped his head still lower, and then turned away so that Linton could not see his face at all.

The minutes of suspense which followed were the most poignant Linton had ever known. He had an intense desire to speak, but was as tongue-tied as Brian himself. He could not speak: he leaned forward instead and touched the boy's shoulder. Brian neither drew away from the touch nor responded to it; he remained absolutely still, as if he had not felt it, and Linton removed his hand.

Yet they could not go on like this: he must break the silence or it would never be broken. "Have you guessed?" he asked; and the answer came at once, but in an oddly husky voice, "Yes, I think so."

Linton's heart sank. It looked very much as if what Brian had guessed were painful, at any rate distasteful, to him. Presently he was sure it was; and as he sat there, he saw his dream fading, dying, and a grey desolation stretching out in its place. The sudden collapse of what had been more than hope brought with it a kind of physical sickness, as if all that was vital in him had been drained away, leaving a feeling of emptiness, weakness, and exhaustion. "I'm sorry," he muttered.

Brian stirred nervously, and his shoulders moved with a movement of incipient impatience. "It's all right," he answered without looking round. "I'm trying to get used to it: I want to think."

Linton let him be. He did not even try to imagine what he might be thinking. Another five minutes passed, and then Brian turned round abruptly. "It's awful!" he said.

Not a comforting remark—yet for some strange reason it brought Linton a measure of comfort. "What is awful?" he asked.

"I don't mean 'awful': I mean I won't know what to do.... I won't even know what to call you.... I won't know how to behave to you.... It makes it all so different."

"Why need it be different?" Linton said softly. "It won't make any difference to me. Why can't we just go on being friends the way we have been.... And for the present you needn't call me anything."

"I *can't*," Brian said frankly. "You'll have to give me time."

"Yes," said Linton, "I'll give you all the time you want." Then, as the boy made no response, he asked, "Would you rather I hadn't told you?"

Brian shook his head. "Of course you had to tell me. I can see that. What I can't see is why you didn't tell me long ago—at the very beginning."

"I didn't know who you were at the beginning," Linton reminded him. "And I came here wanting to be alone: I didn't wish to be recognized by anybody who might have known me in the past—or who might know my name.... Not that I don't admit I was wrong," he added immediately. "At any rate wrong not to have told you sooner than I did."

"You didn't even tell me after you *did* know who I was," Brian answered reproachfully.

"I know…. I was afraid your mother wouldn't allow you to be friends with me."

The explanation, he saw, was unsuccessful: Brian's face did not clear, and all he said was, "How could she prevent me from being friends with you?"

"Still—if she had been against it——" Linton argued gently. "You only knew me very slightly then; we were only beginning to be friends; you might easily have thought that, just to please her, you ought to drop me."

Brian frowned. "I wouldn't have dropped you," he said. "And I'm not so fond of pleasing people as you imagine."

Then once more he began to think, and the result was the question Linton had been both dreading and expecting. "Couldn't you come back with me this evening and clear it all up—explain how everything happened? I'm sure if you did come you could make it all right even now."

"I don't think so," Linton answered colourlessly. "You don't understand."

"But why?" Brian persisted. It seemed to him that he did understand—or, if he didn't, that he ought to be told. "Is there anything that makes it impossible?" he asked.

Linton met the deeper interrogation in his eyes, but did not answer it. "You know what there is," was all he said.

"I don't. I know nothing. And anyhow, whatever there may have been, it's all over now."

"It isn't over," Linton replied. "It will never be over so far as your mother is concerned."

"But don't you see, she'd *have* to accept it now," Brian urged with a repressed impatience. "I've got to know you, and we've been seeing a lot of each other—nothing can undo that. I mean, it has *happened*; so, even if she wanted to, it would be too late for her to object."

Linton gave up the dispute, but in the silence he felt Brian's gaze becoming more and more insistent. "*Is* there a reason why she wouldn't want us to be friends?" the boy asked. "I mean a genuine reason—not just a personal prejudice?"

The question sounded oddly in Linton's ears, coming from

this source, and he had a sudden feeling of bitterness against the woman who had made it possible, who had made it indeed inevitable. "You know the reason already," he said. "It's in what you've read—in what I've written—in my opinions—in my way of looking at things—in myself. There isn't any other reason and there never was."

He stopped short: he could not tell whether Brian believed him or not. The boy must know enough about life to have attached in his own mind a meaning to the hard ugly fact that his parents were divorced. He must at one time or another have come across newspaper reports of such cases. Heaven knew, they were made prominent enough, with all their details presented in the fiercest light sensational journalism could throw upon them! "Your mother will do her best to prevent you from seeing me again," he pronounced stonily.

"I don't think so," Brian was beginning, but at sight of Linton's face he checked himself. He sat silent, while gradually his expression softened and cleared. At last he said, "I'll not tell her if you don't want me to."—And he dropped again into a reverie, which this time Linton did not interrupt.

It was Brian who spoke first. "I don't suppose it matters very much whether I tell mother or not," he began innocently. "I mean, I won't be seeing you anyhow after this month, and there's only about another week to go."

Linton made no answer, but his hands gripped tightly on the heather on either side of him. Yet it was not so much the boy's words as the tone of complete acceptance behind them which hurt him. If he took it like that, what was the use of further struggle? Better to have said nothing at all.

Next moment, however, he realized that he must speak. And speak as quietly and dispassionately as he could. It took him a minute or two to be sure of himself: then he said, "Why shouldn't I see you? There's no reason why I shouldn't."

"But you don't live in this country," Brian pointed out, in a slightly surprised voice. "We've known all along that I couldn't go on seeing you after this month. For one thing, I hope I'll soon be getting a job."

"I *could* live in this country," Linton answered. "I've no ties—
there's nothing to prevent me from living anywhere I choose. And
even if I didn't, you could come and stay with me." Then, when
Brian merely gazed at him with rather wondering eyes, he could
not help adding in a tone that was far from dispassionate, "You
surely don't *want* everything to end when we say good-bye at the
railway station!"

Brian looked away. "I don't want it to end," he said, "but naturally I thought it *would* end—after we went home.... I mean, so far
as seeing you is concerned:—of course, I'd write to you."

"And writing would do as well?"

Brian's face had clouded. "I don't think you ought to say that.
I didn't even think of it like that. I hadn't thought of the future at
all."

Linton checked himself. He *must* get this other point of view.
If he didn't, everything he said would be disastrous. With an effort
he tried to dismiss his own interests and to put himself in Brian's
place. Only, even *in* Brian's place, he knew it would not be the
same, because he himself was not the same.

"You mean you would come with us?" Brian asked, after a slight
hesitation. "Take a house somewhere near us?"

"Yes," Linton replied.

There followed a silence, which was broken by the boy's falter-
ing objection, "You couldn't do that, of course, without mother
knowing. And if she would object to you now, wouldn't she object
still more then?"

"Yes," Linton agreed gloomily. "You'd better tell her. I can see
now that she'll have to be told."

But having gained his point, Brian felt that it did not help him
much. He walked on, and once or twice seemed on the verge of
speaking, but did not speak. Linton knew his difficulty, and left him
to it. He could not help him: whatever eventually emerged must
now come from Brian's own unprompted wish.

"If you couldn't see me often," the boy began, "would you mind?
. . . . I know you would mind," he hurried on, "but I mean, would
you mind very much, would it make you unhappy?"

Linton did not answer, and Brian sighed.

"Suppose you are forbidden to see me," Linton asked, "what will you do?"

"I don't know. I'll kick up a row for one thing."

"And then?"

There was no reply, and after waiting a little while, Linton spoke. "I don't think you understand your mother. She is very determined, very thorough, very sure she is right. Can't you guess what her views are when she wouldn't even allow you to keep my name—*your* name? That was going pretty far. I hadn't disgraced it. Did you think I had?"

"No," Brian murmured. "I don't now, anyway."

The answer decided Linton: he would finish what he had begun. "It was like this," he said. "Your mother and I separated. Our marriage had proved a failure, and we were both unhappy. I dare say if we had been people of a different kind, leading a social life, out a great deal, wealthy, living in a big house run by servants, it wouldn't have been very hard to carry on a divided existence. But we weren't of that kind: nor were our circumstances. An ordinary business or professional man goes every day to his work and his club—there are at least those hours of escape—but with us there was no escape, and the strain, once it had begun, grew quickly until it became intolerable. The solution we reached was not a matter of choice; it was the only one. Your mother went back to Ireland, and for a year and a half I heard nothing of her. But in the meantime, I suppose, she had met your step-father, for when at last I had a letter, it was to tell me that she wanted to marry again. I was very much surprised, though perhaps there was no reason why I should have been, since the thing was quite natural. It was only that I imagined her views would have prevented it, and also that I thought she wouldn't have had the courage to face the inevitable unpleasantness—the legal proceedings, the publicity, the gossip.... This latter, I now see, was a stupid view, for she would have the courage to do anything, once she made up her mind that it was right. And if it was a matter of their mutual happiness I agree that it *was* right. Only, to bring it about, there was no other way than the way we took. You understand that? Without a divorce she couldn't have married again, and while there was every reasonable, every spiritual and temperamental ground for a divorce, there was no more legal ground than there had been before: *that* had to be manufactured. Mind you, I still believe your mother was perfectly justified in all this: in fact I would go so far as to say that if she had done anything else it would have been wrong—a mere cowardly submission to convention. I never knew your step-father, but I am quite sure that a very deep attachment must have existed between them. That is obvious. Also I don't want you to imagine that I acted the part of a martyr. I didn't: I was completely indifferent. Of course, if I had known about you—then it would have been another matter; but the first news I ever had of your existence was from your own lips.... That is where the real wrong came in. You believed, I suppose, that I knew about you and took no interest in you. I didn't know about you. I was far away; I saw no English papers—very few English people—and your mother decided to keep me in ignorance. I can guess her motives, but I think they are indefensible. At all events, what I have told you now is the whole truth."

"I'm glad you told me," Brian replied, and for a long time said no more, and neither did Linton.

It was Brian in the end who broke the silence. "You've crumpled your manuscript," he half whispered.

Linton smiled. It was a queer little remark to make, but somehow it touched him. The words did not matter; he heard only their friendliness. He smoothed out the pages he had been holding all the time clutched in his hand, and put them back in his pocket. "We can't very well discuss the story now—can we?" he said. "I haven't even read your share of it, and our car will be here very soon."

Chapter XVI

LINTON

The boots was locking the front door when Linton came downstairs and took his hat and coat from the rack. "Going out, sir?" he asked, in accents that managed to combine discouragement with surprise.

"If it's not too late," Linton said politely. "Aren't you closing up earlier than usual?"

The boots admitted that he *was* closing up earlier than usual, though only a few minutes earlier. "It's nearly eleven o'clock, sir," he mentioned, just in case Linton should have mistaken eleven for ten. "And being such a wet night——"

But Linton had not mistaken the hour. "If you leave the side-door on the latch," he said, "I'll lock it when I come in. I'll not forget, and I don't want to keep anybody up."

This idea of going for a walk had been a sudden impulse, but he was tired of reading, and knew that if he went to bed now he would not sleep. So, under the still only half-reconciled eyes of the boots, he buttoned up the collar of his coat and sallied forth.

It was anything but an attractive night. True, it was not at the moment raining heavily, but a thick persistent drizzle was falling and there was no wind to disperse the clouds. It was a night for keeping to the main road, Linton decided, not for wandering over the golf-links; and turning his back to them he began to climb the hill. He had the world to himself, but that was what he wanted; and he tramped on, splashing through the puddles. Along the sea-front most of the houses were in darkness, though here and there a light shone, and presently he saw that there was a light shining from an upper window in the house of which he was thinking. As he approached it his pace slackened, and when he came opposite it he retreated into the shadow of the bank and stood still. He wondered whose the lighted room was; and in the end his question was answered. The blind was pulled aside; a figure stood there looking out into the rain; and the figure was Brian. He seemed to be looking straight at Linton (perhaps he had heard footsteps approaching and stopping), but evidently he could not see him, for he made no sign. Then, after standing motionless for a while, he turned back into the room, the blind fell once more into its place—he was gone.

The light remained, however, and Linton continued to watch it. This was not the walk he had promised himself; moreover the rain was growing heavier; but an emotion he was powerless to beat down held him rooted to the spot, and he leaned back against the loose stone wall that topped the bank, his gaze immovably fixed on the window.

Brian ought at this hour to be in bed and asleep: all the other windows in the house were dark: why was he sitting up? Was he reading or writing, Linton asked himself? But if he had been doing either it was not likely he would have come to the window to look out. Perhaps he was only sitting up because, like Linton, he felt restless and wakeful: perhaps he was thinking things over and thinking of the future. Linton wondered what he had said to his mother—how much he had told her—what attitude he had taken up—and what had been the end of it? Whatever he had told her, Stella would not have made it easy for him; and for that matter he had not made it easy for him himself. Between them they had created a situation which must be more than unpleasant, and from which there was no escape. It was not fair, Linton thought: he was too young to have that kind of responsibility thrust upon him—too young to be forced to make a decision which he could not help knowing, however he decided, must make somebody unhappy. "I should have gone away," he mused sombrely. "To stay on when my staying was bound to lead to this, was pure selfishness." And he remembered that there had been a moment when he very nearly *had* gone. Even now it was not too late. He could pack up his things to-night, and leave to-morrow morning by the first train. Brian might wonder; might be hurt, disappointed, perhaps; might miss him for a little; but very soon he would get over it....

And yet Linton could not believe that to go like this really would be best. It would entail an unqualified, an absolute self-sacrifice, but that didn't necessarily make it right. On the contrary, wasn't it a direct denial of all that had come to him only yesterday morning in that quiet country church—a denial of his faith? If he gave up, if he went away, he would be turning his back on what had seemed to him then a kind of revelation. There could be no doubt that it would make things easier for Brian. It would solve his problem for him at a stroke; or rather there would be no problem left to solve. But would it ultimately be better for him? On Linton's view, it would not ultimately be so good. On the other hand, he knew that, try how he might, where his own feelings were so inextricably entangled his view could not be dispassionate. It was as instinctive in a human soul to reach after happiness as it was in a plant to turn to the sun, and it would be the veriest hypocrisy to pretend that the knowledge that Brian was happy would in itself be sufficient, should he never see him again, to make *him* happy. It wouldn't. Nor could he now, he thought, find courage to face the existence which had been tolerable a few weeks ago, because, even to reach *that* apathetic state, he would first have to become indifferent, have to forget. And in a sudden final flash of self-knowledge he spoke aloud the truth: "I cannot live without him."

His eyes were still fixed on the lighted window, and as he gazed the light beat down upon him; it glowed and shone, till he saw nothing else. He was like a man who watches a vision, and it absorbed him utterly, leaving him insensible to the time and place—to the mist and the darkness and the rain. All physical conditions were outside the rim of his consciousness. It was as if a magic circle had been drawn on the night, and he stood within it—alone with a lighted window. He did not feel the rain, though his hat was now soaked through and the water was running down his face. For the light flashed its continuous message—it held him, it filled his mind—and in it he saw things, heard things, remembered things....

They were small things; there seemed to be no particular reason why they should come back to him rather than others—certainly no reason why they should have an emotional significance so out of all proportion to their superficial aspect. He remembered a question—repeated on several occasions in the earliest days of their friendship, when he still did not know Brian's name, when all was still strange and untried. It used to come in the brief pause just before saying good-bye. There would be a momentary silence, and Linton would wait expectantly. Then the question would come— half shyly, half confidently—"When do you want me again?" It was extraordinary how those simple words could give him so much pleasure—so much pleasure at the time, so much pleasure after- wards in recollection. A word, an intonation, a passing change of expression, a sudden smile—what was there in things like these which seemed to twine them around one's very heart, so that never afterwards could they be forgotten?... Fragments of talk—scenes— pictures—arose before Linton in the golden light:—all the hours that had been happiest and pleasantest.... And it seemed to him now, that in comparison, nothing else in his life had ever been worth while....

He could not let him go.... Why should he? Why should all this be sacrificed for nothing—absolutely nothing? The only thing that could make him give it up would be Brian's own desire that it should end, and so far he had expressed no such desire....

Still, it was not enough to say this: he must *do* something; and the only thing he could do was to do what Brian himself wanted—go to Stella and try to patch up some kind of reconciliation. Perhaps she would listen to him. After all, she owed him something, if only because he had not stood in the way of *her* happiness. And maybe the years had altered her—made her more tolerant, more yielding. There had been a time when she had liked him—though perhaps a liking based on misunderstanding does not count for much. But his affection for Brian ought to count—Brian himself had said so. Besides, it was not as if he wanted to take the boy away from her: he wanted no more than to be free to see him....

And there was Brian's affection for him—a boy's unspoken affection—all freshness and brightness and delicacy—half-hidden and half-revealed, like the first spring buds softly unfolding on trees and hedges. He knew it was there: he had seen it in his expres- sion—had heard it in his voice—had been given countless small proofs of it from day to day. How could she be insensible to that? No—he could not give him up....

Suddenly, without even a warning flicker, the light upon which Linton's eyes were fixed went out, and he found himself alone in the darkness. So abruptly it happened that he had the sense of a physical shock, violent and brutal. Instantly the empty dreary night was there, and he became conscious of the rain and the cold—and of his own body chilled and cramped and wet, while far down below, on the desolate shore at the cliff's edge, he heard the remote, unresting crying of the sea. Yet the shock was less physical than spiritual. It was like a callous and cruel awakening. Until now, through all his long vigil, he had had the feeling that Brian was with him. The river of light flowing between them had been a bond. Now this bond was broken, and in the darkness Linton knew he was alone. And his loneliness aroused in him an intense desire to attract the boy's attention—to call to him, to throw a handful of gravel at his window—a desire none the less acute because he never for a moment dreamed of yielding to it. If he could see him and speak to him, only to say good-night—that would be sufficient, that was all he needed, and he could go home in peace. But it was as if Brian by turning out his light had deserted him, had left him alone in the rain and darkness—alone, and infinitely unwanted. He knew it was useless to wait, yet still he could not go. He watched and waited—waited absurdly, unreasonably—for the light to come again. It might: he knew it would not, but it might: and in the grip of a blinding emotion he felt he could not go while there was even that remote chance.

Chapter XVII

BRIAN

At tea Brian was in one of his more trying moods. That is to say, instead of telling them all about his day's outing the way any other boy would have done, it had to be dragged out of him bit by bit—like drawing teeth, as his mother sighed wearily, when in the end she relinquished the attempt from sheer exhaustion. All she had learned, as the result of a prolonged cross-examination, was not much more than that he had enjoyed himself, and that Mr Martin had enjoyed himself, and that everything had been highly successful. Why, in that case, he should have returned looking as if all the cares of the world were on his shoulders, was a mystery she had not energy left to fathom.

Upstairs in the sitting-room it suddenly occurred to her that he had not told her the truth. He had told her part of it perhaps—the unimportant part—it was always the unimportant part he preferred to tell. She looked at him across the room. She could not think why he should be so secretive, so different from Claire, who told her everything. It certainly was not a reassuring trait. And he had been like that even when he was a little boy—a very good little boy on the whole—but always living in a private world of his own, never very responsive, never wanting to be petted, in fact evincing a strange dislike for anything of that kind. And there he was now—not even reading—but sitting wrapped in meditations which appeared to be gloomy in the extreme. Why was he so uncommunicative, she wondered? She didn't believe he had enjoyed himself. She believed that something was weighing on his mind. She believed something must have happened—that he had quarrelled with Mr Martin or else offended him—something of a disturbing nature at all events. And of course, if it was that, it would be just like him to say nothing about it, but to brood over it in silence, when probably a word or two would make it all right. She was sure, if he told her, she could help him: she was equally sure that without her advice he would make matters worse. He blundered so where other people's feelings were concerned; and he was so dreadfully obstinate and self-willed —always certain he was right. Mrs Westby was by this time convinced that he *had* offended Mr Martin. He had so frequently and unconsciously hurt her own feelings that it seemed but too likely he would hurt those of other people as well—anybody who happened to be fond of him, that is to say, as this Mr Martin must be.

But there was no use questioning him: she knew from past experience that he would keep his own counsel, and even feared that if she pressed him he might tell her an untruth. Perhaps that was wrong of her; perhaps she was being unjust to him; it was very hard to know really what one ought to do....

She looked out at the weather, which had changed with the capricious suddenness that had characterized the whole summer, and was now as dismal as Brian himself. But it was one of Mrs Westby's principles that the weather under no circumstances ought to be condemned. It was sent to us; therefore it was either what was best for us, or else what we deserved. At the present moment it was singularly what we deserved, so that it became almost a duty to view it from a cheerful angle. "You were very lucky," she pointed out to Brian. "If you had been caught in all this rain at the top of Fair Head you would have been drenched to the skin in a few minutes, and I'm sure a wetting would be the worst possible thing for Mr Martin. Had he a waterproof with him?"

She had a faint hope that the renewed mention of Mr Martin's name might elicit a ray of information, but it didn't. "No," was all Brian replied.

"You see," Mrs Westby continued, "it *was* providential!"

"That he hadn't a waterproof?" Brian answered.

"No, but—since he hadn't one—that the weather kept up till you got home."

"Do you really think it kept fine specially for us?" Brian asked; but his mother was not going to argue with him in his present mood, and took up a magazine.

She turned the pages, looking for something to read, though she didn't want to read, she would much rather have shared Brian's troubles, whatever they were. Claire, in the window-seat, was working at a crossword puzzle; Brian had sunk back again into the abstraction from which his mother's words had briefly aroused him. When once more he awoke to his surroundings, it was to find her gazing at him in earnest solicitude. "Aren't you feeling well, Brian?" she asked.

He repressed his impatience, but he wished she would leave him alone. She might see that he wanted to be left alone. "Yes, thanks," he said, "I'm all right." Then, to avoid further questioning; "I've got a bit of a headache: it came on before tea."

His mother, whether she believed in the headache or not, accepted it—at least to the extent of telling him that he had better go to bed early. He hadn't the least intention of going to bed early:

nor had he really a headache—at least it was barely perceptible. If
that beastly rain would only slacken off a little he would go out.
He had half a mind to go without waiting for it to clear—go for a
walk—not down to the hotel....

He got up and stood beside Claire at the window, with his
hands in his pockets: then he began to move aimlessly about the
room. He opened the door of an ornamental cabinet, and took out
and put back again several large pink-and-white shells. The shells
bored him, but so did everything else, and he wandered over to the
chimney-piece where he stared at his own image in the gilt-edged
mirror. It struck him that he looked wild, white, and scared—just
as if he had seen a ghost. Why should he look like that when he
was only worried? And to escape the unpleasing presentment he
turned to an imitation Japanese bowl, and took from it the key of
the clock. He glanced round at his mother. She was now really
reading her magazine, so he began to wind up the clock. This was
a typically Victorian object—large, gilt, and ornamental—and
he wound and wound, without thinking of what he was doing,
until suddenly there was a sharp snap. Brian hastily drew out the
key, but the expression of guilt on his face was unmistakable, and
Mrs Westby immediately saw what had happened. "I suppose it's
broken!" she said. "I must say it's too bad of you!"

"Sorry," he apologized. "I was thinking of something else." But
he was angry with himself; he didn't know why he had wound up
the clock; and he continued to stand there, looking half dismayed
and half astonished.

"What's he done now?" Claire inquired absently, as she sucked
the point of her pencil.

"You may speak to Mrs Belford yourself," his mother told him.
"*I'm* not going to. And you can tell her that you'll take the clock to-
morrow morning to be mended. That is, if there's anybody here
who *can* mend it."

"I think there is," Brian murmured in a conciliatory voice. "I
think I saw a shop with clocks and things in the window." He was
silent for a few moments, at the end of which he asked, "Do you
suppose it's going to cost much? Because I've practically no money
left."

"Then I don't know why you haven't," Mrs Westby answered. "I don't see what you can possibly have found to spend it on in a place like this.... At any rate, if I've got to give you the money, I shall deduct it from your next month's allowance. That may teach you to be more careful."

"I know. I'd rather pay for it," Brian assured her.

"So you always say," returned Mrs Westby, unimpressed. "It's extremely easy to talk like that."

Brian flared up at once. "I say it because I mean it. I'm *going* to pay for it." After which demonstration he sat down at the table and spread out his manuscript.

He did so from mere force of habit, however, and straightway the inevitable words caught his eye: 'Clayton awoke with a slight shiver.' Brian crumpled up the manuscript and flung it into the waste-paper basket. He had suddenly conceived a violent dislike for Clayton and the tale of his misfortunes. He wished he had never begun it; it was mixed up with everything that had happened; and certainly he would never finish it. He would begin his star story; and he wrote the title, *The Birth of a Star*, and for a while sat staring at it. Then he scored this out and wrote instead, *The Story of a Star*. There was a further interval before he added, 'by Brian Linton.'

He glanced quickly across at his mother, as if the very movement of his pencil might have betrayed him, and hastily turned the sheet over, but almost immediately turned it back again. Why shouldn't it be by Brian Linton? After all, he *was* Brian Linton. Brian Westby wasn't his name, and he was going to write under his true name. But presently, as he sat there, his face began to change. It became more dreamy, less overshadowed, and all its lines were softened. He was not thinking now of his story. Perhaps he *would* go down to the hotel: perhaps it would be rotten of him not to.... Yes, he would go.

It would be a surprise visit, for their appointment was for to-morrow morning; but he knew it would be a pleasant surprise. He had seen, too, that Mr Martin was very much worried, and probably he would become more so when he was alone. Brian did not want him to lie awake half the night brooding over difficulties and troubles which might never come to pass. The only objection to

going was that the hotel would be full of people, and Mr Martin
mightn't care to go out for a walk in such a downpour, or might be
tired. Still, if he didn't wish to go out, they could always sit upstairs
in his bedroom: he would suggest that....

"Here's Derek!" cried Claire from the window-seat, "looking
like a drowned rat."

Brian frowned. "What does he want!" he muttered angrily.

"Come right in, stranger," Claire screamed down through the
window, in an American 'talkie' accent; and the voice of an invisible Derek replied, "O.K. chief."

They heard the inside glass-door opening and slamming. "Why
can't he stay in his own house?" Brian continued to grumble, though
nobody took any notice of him.

Derek charged up the stairs and entered boisterously. "Poisonous weather! Don't believe it's been fine for three days running since
last January."

The rain, for all that, evidently had not damped his spirits, and
Claire, who had been languid enough before, suddenly became
equally cheerful. She asked why he hadn't brought Eva with him,
but Derek had turned to Brian. "Saw your pal just now, mooching
about the door. Looked a bit lost, I thought."

This startling intelligence brought Brian with a jump to his feet.
"What door?" he gasped, almost knocking over the chair in his
alarm.

"Oh, not yours: the door of the hotel. I very nearly brought him
along."

Brian sat down again. He felt annoyed at having betrayed himself unnecessarily, and still more annoyed with Derek for frighten-
ing him. Therefore it was in his most distant tone that he inquired,
"Why?"

But Derek was not easily snubbed. "Because I thought you'd like
to see him," he answered promptly.

"Brian was out with him all day," Mrs Westby interposed. "They
went to Fair Head together."

"Yes, I know," Derek replied. "I saw them starting off, though
they wouldn't look at me. Mr Martin nodded to me this evening,
all the same, and told me it had turned out wet."

Brian in silence had begun to tidy up his papers. He continued to do so, while Claire said, "He wouldn't have come even if you *had* asked him. We've invited him several times."

"Once," Brian corrected.

"Grumpy old bachelor and all that kind of thing!" Derek commented lightly. "That is, if he *is* an old bachelor. I must have a chat with him now the ice is broken."

Again Mrs Westby intervened. She had recently decided that she liked Mr Martin, and that if he hadn't, so far, responded to her invitation, it was probably because Brian had managed to bungle things in some way. "I don't think for a moment he wishes to be unsociable," she declared. "It is only that he happens to be very shy and isn't in particularly good health just now. At any rate he has been extremely kind to Brian."

Brian, for no reason whatever, suddenly found himself blushing. He frowned and looked still more severe.

"Two high-brows, you know!" Derek pointed out. "He looks as if he might be literary or something."

"He *is* literary," Mrs Westby said. "He gave Brian a little book of verses he wrote when he was a quite young man—at Oxford, I think."

Derek began to chuckle. "And nobody told the pater! That's hardly fair, you know. I must give the glad tidings when I get home."

"You needn't," Brian said quickly, and then bit his lip in vexation.

But it was too late; Derek had understood; and was gazing at him with an irritating blandness. "Why not?" he asked. "It's just what the old man would like—somebody to gas to about poetry. I bet he calls on Mr Martin to-morrow—complete with sonnets."

"Derek, you mustn't talk that way about your father," Mrs Westby was beginning, but Claire, who had been growing more and more bored by the turn the conversation had taken, now decided to end it. "Let's have a game of Rummy," she proposed. "It's better than doing nothing, and there's no use asking Brian to play Bridge."

Brian looked at her coldly. "Why?" he demanded, and Derek laughed.

"Not that there's much use asking him to play anything when

he's in this mood," Claire went on, with a shrug of her shoulders.

Brian had been on the point of saying he had to go out, but now immediately he went to get the cards. He was perfectly aware himself that he was not in a genial mood, but Derek and Claire annoyed him and he wasn't going to do anything they expected. Having produced the cards, he seated himself at the table, with an expression of glacial reserve upon his face. He saw Derek winking at Claire, but it was impossible for him to freeze more than he had already frozen. So, while the others drew in their chairs, he proceeded to deal, and even played the first round or two in a normal if austere fashion. But this was only because he had determined to do so, and the moment his will relaxed so did his attention. He drew cards and discarded cards at random, without even bothering to arrange his hand. It was his turn to draw now, but he made no movement, because suddenly he was back on Fair Head, sitting just above the Grey Man's Path, and reading Mr Martin's manuscript.... "Have you guessed, Brian?...." Yes, he had guessed—he knew....

"Brian! It's your turn! If he's going to keep on like this we may as well stop playing!"

He started, and found that he was being slowly shaken to and fro by Derek, though it was Claire's shrill voice which had awakened him. Mechanically he laid down his hand face upward on the table.

"What are you *doing*?" cried Claire in exasperation. "You haven't got anything! What are you putting down your cards for?"

"Suspended animation," Derek suggested good-humouredly. "There was a young man of Penzance—who sat all day long in a trance.... I forget the rest."

"I'm going out," Brian announced abruptly, pushing back his chair and getting up.

"You're not to go out again to-night," his mother told him, while Derek grinned, and Claire, with an expressively expressionless face, silently gathered up the cards.

"Why?" he asked.

"Because it's still pouring, and if you have a headache you'd be much better in bed. You *look* tired. I can always tell when you've been taking too much out of yourself."

"I haven't taken anything out of myself," Brian said. "I've done nothing all day but loaf about on Fair Head. I drove there, and I drove back."

"Well, you're not to go out." And Mrs Westby appealed to the visitor. "He does look white, Derek, don't you think?"

"White as a ghost," Derek agreed cheerfully. "Noticed it the minute I came into the room."

"That's a lie," said Brian.

There was no getting over it: the words had had an emphasis which made it impossible to pass them off as a joke.

"Brian!" Mrs Westby exclaimed, genuinely shocked.

For that matter, he was a little shocked himself, though he wasn't going to admit it. "Well, so it was," he repeated, and then stood still. Nobody else spoke, and presently he muttered, "Perhaps I *will* go to bed.... Good-night."

There was no attempt to dissuade him: the others seemed to think it decidedly the best place for him; and he left the room, feeling ashamed, angry, and unhappy.

He wasn't going to bed, however; and while he paused on the landing after closing the door behind him, he even considered the plan of slipping quietly downstairs, putting on his hat and water-proof, and going out by the back-door. Only it would mean defi-nitely disobeying his mother, and after a brief self-communion he gave up the idea.

He went instead to his room, lit the lamp, and drew down the blinds. There was no comfortable chair, so he made a kind of couch on the bed, as they had sometimes done at school, by arranging the bolster and the pillow, though that wasn't comfortable either. It was the best he could do, however, and better than sitting down-stairs. He opened a cheap edition of *The Fortunes of Nigel* and tried to read.

After a while he heard Derek going away. He *had* treated him rather rudely, he supposed, but it couldn't be helped now. There were times when Derek jarred on him, and he had jarred par-ticularly to-night. It was usually when he was with Claire that this happened, for he wasn't half bad—in fact he was really quite decent—when you got him alone. But to-night, Brian knew, nearly anything would have irritated him; he had been in the kind of mood when what you secretly want is a pretext to be disagreeable.

There came a knock at his door, followed by his mother's voice saying, "We're going to bed, Brian: are you all right? is there anything you would like? will you take an aspirin if I bring you one?"

"No, thanks," he answered drowsily.

There was a pause before the voice, now faintly discouraged, spoke again. "Then good-night. I hope you'll be better in the morning."

"Good-night," Brian answered; and after an interval, in which his mother had had more than time to reach her own room, he added, "Thanks."

But he wasn't in the least drowsy—that had merely been a ruse to avoid further conversation and to keep her from coming in. Even his incipient headache had vanished. He sat up and appeared to be listening. It was only a little after ten: they were certainly early enough!

He took off his jacket, and stretching himself at full length on his back, stared for a long time up at the ceiling.... He had decided nothing, and again he wished that Derek had not come in. If he hadn't, Brian was sure he himself would have gone down to the hotel, and he felt that if he had seen Mr Martin again it would have been much easier now to make up his mind as to what he ought to do. Only he must get out of this habit of thinking of him as Mr Martin. He wasn't Mr Martin: there was no such person as Mr Martin.

It was difficult, nevertheless, to think of him as anything else, no matter by what name he called him. Brian still felt towards him very much as he had felt before, and not a bit in the way he felt towards his mother, which perhaps was how he would eventually feel. Or how he would have to try to feel. He supposed it was because of the way they had met, and of all the days they had spent together—just as friends. It could never really be like that again. It was all very well for Mr Martin to say he wanted it to be, but it couldn't be, it was impossible. Your father wasn't the same as a friend: you couldn't talk to him in the same way—nor with the same freedom. And then—it was different in other ways too.

For one thing, he had an authority, whether he exercised it or not: if he told you you weren't to do a certain thing you couldn't very well go and do it. Perhaps it would work out all right in the long run, but at present the position seemed to be that the old relation was ended and the new one hadn't begun. Would it, could it—the new one—ever be so intimate? Brian didn't know, but he knew that if it wasn't it wouldn't be what Mr Martin wanted. Not that, he thought, in any relation could he ever quite be what Mr Martin wanted. It was a pity—but he couldn't help it. It wasn't that he was indifferent: he liked Mr Martin probably more than the latter guessed: only he couldn't express his liking; he didn't want to; it wasn't his nature to. On the other hand he wanted to please him. But how? The answer came immediately that the only thing Mr Martin really desired was his affection, and this did not advance matters much. Of course it was all nonsense—the idea that he might drop him at his mother's bidding. Still, if she *did* act as Mr Martin was so sure she would, he could quite see how there might be trouble. It might even be serious trouble. It might even reach a point when he would have to act in open defiance of his mother's wishes. Suppose, for instance, she positively forbade him to see Mr Martin again....

Brian's mood grew darker and darker, and in it not only his present doubts increased, but old unhappinesses that belonged to the past returned like ghosts to haunt his mind. Why should he remember them now? Yet he did remember them—remember everything he most wanted to forget—darker hours, imaginations, thoughts, temptations, failures—hours in which life had seemed a hopeless mess and muddle—when, in a kind of sickness of it all, he had wished it were ended....

It seemed to him that things which have actually happened never really are over, but live on under the surface, like the broken roots of garden weeds, which you forget, or do not think of, because you no longer see them, until one day two or three new green shoots thrust their way above the soil....

And then once more he began to think of the scene on Fair Head. The whole day had been so pleasant up till that moment when he had read Mr Martin's manuscript. And looking back at their friendship, it seemed to Brian now that from the first it had been singularly pleasant. In spite of differences and misunderstandings, they had understood each other so well—even though Mr Martin in some ways had a wrong idea of him. He knew pretty well what Mr Martin thought of him and it wasn't quite true. At least it was true perhaps—only he wasn't like that always....

He longed for the morning. In the morning he would be able to do something, but till then there were all these hours in which he could do nothing. He would have put out his light, only he felt quite sure that he would not be able to go to sleep. Why hadn't he allowed his mother to come in? It was too late now to go to her room, but it would have been far better to have talked to her to-night—to have told her about his father, and then, at any rate, he would have known how she was going to take it....

It was queer that she should seem to have formed a liking for Mr Martin! It didn't mean very much, doubtless, since it was only imaginary—but still—— Of one thing he was certain:—all this long concealment had been a mistake. In spite of what Mr Martin said, concealment was the worst course he could have chosen—and even the reasons he had given for choosing it were based entirely on things which had happened years and years ago. It must be different now, because the whole situation was different, and in the past there probably had been faults on both sides. How could there not have been, Brian thought—especially with two people who didn't understand each other, and who both were, though they didn't realize it, so exacting? For they *were* exacting—Mr Martin perhaps even more than his mother—though it was in a different way and about different things. He knew that Mr Martin had tried to be scrupulously fair and had believed every word he had said, but he knew also that he had expressed only part of the truth—had seen only part of it—for his mother was not really like that. There was another side, another aspect. All the past suddenly rose before him in witness of it. She might be as strict and resolute as Mr Martin believed, but beneath this there was something else, something very human. He remembered the time he had been ill—the only occasion when he had ever been seriously ill—and how she had watched over him then. It had happened five or six years ago, but it came back to him now with the clearness and vividness of yesterday—her untiring gentleness and care. There was no use pretending that she didn't love him: and he hadn't given a great deal in return—had he?—ever. It wasn't even as if he didn't know: he had always known, but had pursued his own path. It suddenly seemed to Brian that if he could be granted a single wish, his wish would be that he might never make anyone who cared for him unhappy....

As for himself, happiness—lasting happiness—he thought was impossible. He didn't feel that there was anything to be happy about—either in the past, the present, or the future. You were happy in the beginning perhaps, as a puppy or a kitten is happy, but once that brief period was ended, once you came in contact with reality and began to think, the world grew steadily darker.... He remembered a remark Mr Martin had once made, that life, even at its worst, will always seem to be worth living if there is some-body for whom you care sufficiently. Some one—or some thing.... But suppose there wasn't? All that remained then was the feeling that there are certain duties which you must do your best to fulfil, though even where *that* feeling came from, or why you had it, you did not know. Only there was nothing else—and the sooner you had done your task the better....

He got up and walked over to the window, where he pulled aside the blind and stood gazing out into the night. Nothing but rain—rain and mist—and the salt smell of the sea, and the sound of the tumbling waves. He looked for his star, but no star could be visible through that heavy murky atmosphere, and no star was shining in Brian's spirit. It seemed the kind of rain that might go on for ever, and the kind of night that could have no morning. He saw what looked like a deeper shadow in the darkness, and for a moment thought it was a human figure:—he had heard the sound of footsteps some time ago he now remembered. But the shadow never moved; it was only a shadow. Besides, who would be such a fool as to stand out there alone in rain like this? Despondently he let the blind drop back into its place and began to undress. It was a very long and dilatory process, interrupted by protracted periods during which he sat on the side of his bed brooding; but at last it was accomplished. Then, not even bothering to turn it down, with a single sharp puff he blew out the lamp.

Chapter XVIII

LINTON

From his bedroom window next morning Linton saw Brian passing below. He had not expected him so soon, and hurried out into the passage and downstairs, but Brian was not there, he must have gone on to the town. Instantly it occurred to Linton that this would be a good opportunity to visit Stella.

True, it was early to pay a call—barely ten o'clock—but now that he had made up his mind to it, the sooner he learned his fate the better. He left a message for Brian with Susan, and also scribbled a note to him, saying where he was going and that probably he would be back in an hour. The note he placed in a conspicuous position on the hall-table.

He put on his hat and went out into the fresh morning air. All trace of last night's rain had disappeared, except that the sun was shining on a wet and glittering earth. Linton began to climb the hill to the house, and about half way up met Claire who was descending it, carrying her golf-clubs. As they passed each other she glanced at him with a little smile, to which he responded, raising his hat. The smile answered one question at all events: it was clearly only for her brother's friend Mr Martin.

On reaching the house he had to knock three times before Mrs Belford heard him. Evidently he had disturbed her in the very thick of matutinal labours, for her head was wreathed in a turban arrangement of blue, spotted dusters, and she held an empty bowl in her hands, which she pushed impulsively into the pit of his stomach. Linton recoiled, and Mrs Belford apologized—she had thought he was the milk—she hadn't looked. Yes, Mrs Westby was at home. She retired, and presently came back with an invitation for him to step upstairs. Outwardly calm, but inwardly in a state of acute nervous anxiety, Linton followed her.

Stella was on her feet when he entered the room, standing between the door and the windows, with her back to the light; and almost his first thought was how little she had changed. She had not refused to receive him, but she confronted him now without a word, without a smile, without a movement of welcome of any sort, so that after taking two steps forward he stood still. Between them, in the centre of the room, was a table with a typewriter and a litter of papers on it, and across this she looked at him and then looked away, her face whiter than he remembered it perhaps, and a little strained, in the effort to betray no emotion. And actually she did betray none, unless it were a slight shrinking from an ordeal she nevertheless had nerved herself to meet. Linton's hands dropped to his sides. "I'm afraid you're not very glad to see me, Stella," he said.

She did not contradict him, but pulling a chair out from the table, sat down on it. It struck him as a sign of momentary physical weakness—though he could not tell; nor could he tell anything from the low voice in which she answered, "You must forgive me.... I could hardly believe—even when Mrs Belford said—— How did you know I was here?"

Immediately he perceived that Brian had told her nothing; and, which was more astonishing, that even now it did not dawn upon her to connect him with the Mr Martin who was her son's friend. Evidently she took it for granted that he had arrived only last night or yesterday, and might be moving on again to-day.

"May I sit down?" he asked. "I feel that you think I ought not to have called—or at any rate not without writing to you first. But I had a reason. In fact I have an explanation to make."

Still she did not seem to guess the truth. Very slightly she inclined her head, and Linton took the nearest chair and stared down at the carpet. When suddenly he looked up her eyes were fixed on him, but the instant she encountered his glance her own was averted. Not quickly enough, however: for just a second she had been off her guard: and in that second he had seen her watching him intently, with held breath, as if out of an almost unbearable suspense. Good heavens! what was she frightened of? She had never been frightened in the old days. Was she afraid he might stumble on the secret she had kept so closely and for so long? Or did she suspect he had already stumbled on it? In either case, he knew, her one object would be to get rid of him before Brian or Claire returned.

"I want to assure you that the whole thing was accidental," he began. "You may find some excuse in that—at least I hope you will. Naturally I should not have come to Ballycastle if I had thought there was the least likelihood of our meeting."

He paused, but she still only made a faint noncommittal sound, from which he might infer anything or nothing: she was not going to help him, he could see.

"I came here quite by chance," Linton went on. "During all the years since I last saw you I have never been in Ireland, and it would be hard to say what put it into my head a few weeks ago to come back. I simply thought of this place and for some reason felt a desire to revisit it.... It was equally by chance that I met Brian. And it was not till the third time I met him that I learned his name."

Again he paused, and again she said nothing, though he saw from the barely perceptible twitching of her lips, and the nervous movement of her hands, that at last she had begun to take it in.

And suddenly she spoke, with a kind of quiet unhappiness, and in a voice that was almost a whisper. "So you are his friend!—the Mr Martin he has been talking about!"

"Yes," Linton answered half sadly.

She would not even now look at him, but sat with her eyes lowered, and the long slender fingers of her hands closely interlocked. He knew that sign of old—knew what it meant, and that she was exercising a strong self-control, though nothing of the struggle was visible except in this unconscious and tell-tale clasping of her hands. "I suppose you will think I deceived you," he continued, "and of course afterwards—after I had learned the facts, I mean—I did deceive you."

"Yes," she answered, without raising her head.

"It was most unwillingly," Linton said slowly, "and you must remember *I* had been deceived.... You even changed his name."

"Yes," she answered once more; and then added quietly, "I am not blaming you."

Linton shrugged his shoulders. But it was because he suddenly felt sorry for her. He would not, must not weaken, however, or the whole battle would be lost. "I felt that the only way I could get to know him was by deceiving you," he went on. "I thought that if you knew, you would try to keep him from me. Perhaps I was wrong."

"No," she answered scrupulously, "you weren't wrong: I would have done that."

It was honest at any rate, and after all only what he had expected. He received it without surprise and without comment. "That is why I came to see you. I wanted to give you this explanation and to try if we couldn't reach some kind of agreement, some kind of understanding."

She appeared to weigh the idea for a minute or two, and he had a sudden flash of hope, but in the end she only said, "We were never very good at understanding each other. I don't think you'll find me very good at it now."

It was the attitude, gently and patiently immovable, which in the past had always most exasperated Linton, but he was resolved not to let it exasperate him to-day. "At least you might make an effort."

At this, as if catching the strained note in his voice, for the first time since he had entered the room she raised her head and looked him steadily in the face. "I *am* making an effort," she told him; "but I think you have taken an unfair advantage. There have been all these days and weeks when you could have warned me, and when you kept me in ignorance. Of course, I see it now—why you took a false name—why you pretended to be too ill to come to the house.... And then—after everything had happened—when, you thought it was too late for me to interfere—you decided to tell me."

Sheer amazement held Linton for a moment dumb: then amazement and indignation combined, found vent in words which broke from him impulsively. "What are my days and weeks to your *years!*" he exclaimed. "What have I done that you didn't do infinitely more —and I suppose think it right to do!"

She allowed the outburst to pass. "You said something about wishing to reach an understanding," she reminded him—"that that was what brought you here. Perhaps it will be better if you tell me plainly what you want."

"I'm very fond of him," Linton answered simply, and said no more.

He sat watching her—watching for a sign. Yet when at last one came, it took the form merely of a slow silent headshake, and he felt himself flushing. "Don't you believe me?" he said.

She turned away. "It's not that," she answered, with a simplicity that matched his own. "I can quite believe you're fond of him. I know you're naturally impulsive and quick to form attachments. But it isn't of you I am thinking at present—it is of Brian—of what will be best for him. Does he know?"

"Know what?" Linton asked gloomily.

"Know who you are."

"Yes, he knows: I told him yesterday."

Then, as she sat there, so strangely and utterly remote from him, he could not help realizing that any further words would be wasted. His whole cause must have been tried and judgment passed on it years ago: otherwise she never would have acted as she had done. She had made up her mind: she had no doubts, no misgivings: even if he could gain her sympathy she would still believe it her duty to harden her heart against him.

"It upset him very much," she said presently, always in the same gentle voice.

"What upset him?" Linton asked. "Did he tell you he was upset?"

"No, but I saw he was. He told me nothing—whether at your desire or not I can't say. I thought he was only tired and not feeling very well, and I persuaded him to go to bed early: but I can see now that it was this."

"He said he was going to tell you," Linton answered gruffly. "He intends to.... And if he was upset it was because of you."

She did not deny it. From the beginning, indeed, she had made no attempt to justify herself, as if realizing that he could never comprehend her motives, and that anything she might say in explanation of them would only irritate him more. "What do you wish me to do?" she asked. "I still think it is strange that you should come now when you didn't come before, but I suppose you have a purpose."

"I've already told you my purpose," Linton answered. "I only want you to allow him to be friends with me—to let us go on being friends as we have been. That surely isn't a great deal to ask."

"His holidays are nearly over."

"I know." Linton's voice had momentarily dropped, but with his next words he began to speak eagerly and rapidly. "I don't want this to end with his holidays. I thought of taking a house—not too far away from yours for him to come to see me. I can easily do that. But I'd much rather do it with your permission.... After all, isn't it natural that I should want to see him? I am getting older, and he is all I have."

"Yes," she admitted, "I dare say it is natural."

"Then?"

But he saw that he had gained nothing—that he might extract yet further admissions and still it would make no difference.

"I have devoted my whole life to Brian and Claire," she told him quietly. "You have known Brian for a few weeks. I even doubt if you *do* know him, for he isn't easy to know, and I doubt if anybody knows him. At any rate, how can you think that a few weeks' acquaintance justifies you in trying to take him away from me?"

"I never thought of taking him away from you," Linton interrupted.

"Perhaps you didn't. But whether you thought it or not means nothing. He can't belong to both of us. Every idea he picks up from you will remove him further from me and from what I wish him to become. He is very young—even for his age—and he can talk to you of the things he is most interested in. You must have seen for yourself that he is excitable and impressionable. I see it, at all events, and I know that the influence you would have——"

"But I don't *want* to influence him," Linton broke in impatiently. "Least of all in the way you mean. I have no objection to his being a Christian, to his going to church, to anything of that sort. I believe in allowing people to develop along their own lines. All I want to do is to help him, and I *can* help him."

"Not in that way. In his career, perhaps; but there are more

important things than his career.... Don't mistake me," she continued, as if trying to put it as kindly as she could: "I believe you when
you say you would not deliberately try to influence him. But that
makes no difference. If he is in sympathy with you—if he likes
you—whether you try to or not, you can't *help* influencing him. He
could not be with you without that happening. It is not as if you
did not feel strongly about things. You do. And you know yourself
you would not want him unless you believed there was this sympathy between you."

"But if I promise never to mention religion?" Linton urged.
"Can't you trust me? I don't think I ever *have* mentioned it—except
once—and then it certainly was not to discourage any faith he may
have."

She did not answer, and he could find nothing further to say.

"You won't let him see me?" he asked after a silence.

She shut her eyes, and for a few tense seconds it seemed to him
that everything hung in the balance. Then, quickly as it had arisen,
the crisis, if there had ever been a crisis, passed. "I shall ask him not
to," she said. "I am very sorry, for your sake, that it should be like
this; but I can't help it; it is not my fault. I know you don't understand; I know you think it is because I am hard and narrow and
inhuman—but it isn't that."

"I think your creed is inhuman," Linton answered harshly, "if
this is in accordance with it. I think it is uncharitable, stupid, and
cruel."

She looked at him with a strange bright light in her eyes, and
yet with something tragic in them too. "I know—I know.... And
perhaps it *is* inhuman, if by that you mean that it does not put
human wishes first. But I am not asking you to do anything for
my sake, or to make a sacrifice I should not be prepared to make
myself. If I thought by so doing I could bring Brian to believe, to
see, the truth, I would promise this very moment never to set eyes
on him again."

"I don't doubt it," Linton returned savagely. "Martyrdoms and
self-torturings and human sacrifices are the very breath——" But
he checked himself, and asked instead, grimly and brusquely, "What
will you do if he refuses: if he doesn't promise to give me up?"

"There is only one thing I can do—take him away. I have no right to ask *you* to go—particularly when you came here for your health.... I am sorry you have been ill."

Linton rose from his chair and she too rose. He had not answered her last speech; but as he reached the door and opened it he turned round. "I'm not going to make the sacrifice," he said. "I'm not going to do what you want. And I think if you try to force Brian to obey you, even if you succeed, it will be at the cost of alienating him for ever from the very thing you desire."

Chapter XIX

BRIAN

Brian entered the shop, unwrapped Mrs Belford's clock (quite small it turned out to be when denuded of its splendid case, which had been left at home on the mantelpiece), set it down, and scribbled a figure in his notebook. The little gnome-like man behind the counter watched this performance with interest—particularly its conclusion.

Brian put away his notebook, glanced up, and pushed the clock towards the expert. "I'm afraid something's gone wrong," he said, "but I hope it only needs cleaning. Perhaps you'd have a look at it."

The little man, disappointed to find that this was after all a more or less ordinary customer, turned his attention to the object thrust at him. He screwed a magnifying-glass into his eye, carried the clock over to the window, opened it, and made a prolonged investigation punctuated by 'hums' of dubious significance. He was like a surgeon examining a sick but reticent patient, and his 'hums' grew more and more ominous, filling Brian with alarm. "The mainspring is broken," he finally announced; and then added more sternly, "This clock has been overwound. Carelessness!" The last word was practically an accusation, for he looked very hard at Brian, as if he had no doubt at all as to the identity of the over-winder. "You'll have to leave it with me.... What name, please?"

"Linton.... No, I mean Westby. We're staying at Mrs Belford's."

The little man gave him a still more searching look. "Mr Westby,"
he repeated slowly and as if he didn't half believe it. He wrote the
improbable name on a ticket, however, with a stump of pencil.
"Staying at Mrs Belford's."

Brian said good-morning, and left the shop.

The moment he was outside he began to count:—"One, two,
three, four, five, six, seven——" and it was not until he had reached
the eight-hundreds that he suddenly remembered he hadn't asked
either how long it would take to mend the clock or how much
a new mainspring would cost. This was annoying—the more so
because it wasn't at all like him to forget such details. It just showed
how much he had to think of at present! He stood in the middle of
the road, debating whether he ought to return to the shop at once,
or if it would do to call later in the day. In the end he decided on
the latter course. It would be a nuisance to have to begin counting all over again—especially when he had so nearly finished—and
he proceeded methodically with his task:—"ninety-seven, ninety-
eight, ninety-nine, nine hundred."

This rather peculiar, yet highly characteristic industriousness,
was the outcome of an argument which had taken place that morning at breakfast. He had maintained—against both Claire and his
mother—that the back road into the town was shorter than the
sea-road. On his way to the clockmaker's he had paced the distance going by the sea; now he was pacing the inland route, and
the result was so satisfactory that, though he had intended to go
straight on to the hotel after concluding his test, the desire for an
immediate triumph was irresistible, and he decided that it wouldn't
take half a jiff to run upstairs and let his mother know.

It didn't really take much longer—he raced up, three steps at a
time—but when he flung open the sitting-room door, the cry of
victory died upon his lips, and with a sudden jerk he stopped dead
just inside the threshold. The door was still wide behind him; his
breath was exhaled in a mute gasp; his blue eyes grew round as
saucers; his whole face became the picture of astonishment and
dismay. For his mother was on her knees, praying.

Brian's first impulse was to retreat before she had seen him, but
thanks to his explosive entrance this already was impossible. Mrs

Westby had looked round: she seemed in the same instant to have divined his intention, for even before rising from her knees she said, "Don't go away, Brian; I want to speak to you."

Brian closed the door behind him with a sinking heart; and then, still staring at her, advanced slowly, step by step, as far as the table, while his mother got up and seated herself on the sofa. *Something had happened!*—and that it was something pretty awful he could tell from her countenance. There were the marks of recent tears upon it, though her eyes were now dry and her expression resolute. The sound of her voice interrupted his uneasy apprehensions.

"Sit down," she murmured, and he sat down, choosing the chair Linton had chosen, which meant that the whole width of the room remained between them. Still he did not venture to speak; but he knew one thing at least—that whatever her prayer had been, it had been answered; she had got the guidance she had sought for, and was utterly purposed to follow it without flinching and without compromise.

His mother was in no hurry to speak either. She was not even looking at him, and, in the silence of suspense, gradually the dark cloud of last night, which sleep and the morning had lifted, began to creep back again into his mind. Once she raised her eyes and gazed at him as if searching for something in his face—some sign of guilt it must be, since it could hardly be a sign of innocence—but, whether she found it or not, she said nothing.

And all he knew was that she must have seen his father and that the meeting could not have brought about a reconciliation. Why had he allowed it to take place? What had possessed him to go to that wretched shop instead of straight down to the hotel? Even if he had spoken last night—even if he had spoken this morning! But this morning everything had appeared so much brighter and more hopeful, and he had wanted to have one more talk with his father first, had even thought that they might come back to the house together and tell her. He had been nearly quite happy about it this morning—a little nervous of course, but sure that the only real difficulty would be the first breaking of the news, and that afterwards it would be all right. It did not look all right now....

"Your father has been here," she said, without any preliminary speech or question. "He left only a few minutes ago. Did you meet him?"

"No," Brian answered.

Her manner and the tone of her voice increased his misgiving: it had been a strange way to tell him, he thought—almost as she might have told him that Mr Graham or the vicar had called. No, not like that—but as if she were speaking to someone she barely knew.

"I came by the back road," he went on nervously, in explanation. Then he sat still, and gazed at her with troubled eyes.

"For how long have you been hiding this from me?" she asked.

Brian faltered. "About—father?"

"Yes."

Brian hung his head. "He only told me yesterday."

His distress was visible, but his mother ignored it, and he saw that she felt he had failed her, had possibly been conspiring against her. "Why then did you say nothing about it yesterday," she continued in the same tone—"*or* this morning? I asked you: I gave you plenty of opportunities: I even came to your room last night, and you pretended to be sleepy: I knew from the beginning you had something on your mind."

Brian's voice sank to a mumble. "I wanted to think it over first. I intended to tell you."

"When?"

"I don't know.... Sometime.... After I had talked to him again."

He looked up and saw that his mother was watching him closely, with an expression in her eyes he did not understand. Then he realized that she didn't believe him—or at least had very little confidence in him. "I suppose I must accept your word," she said at last; "only I cannot help thinking that in all these weeks of close intimacy you must have learned something, guessed something, which you concealed from me. I find it hard to feel the same trust in you I once felt. There seems to be something in your nature which I am only beginning to see. I always thought it was merely that you were reserved and disinclined to take anybody into your confidence, but now it looks as if there were more than that—a lack of straightforwardness, which comes to the surface when you wish to avoid anything unpleasant. There was first that book you hid from me, and now there is this: it seems unlikely that there should not be other things too."

Brian listened in silence. He did not know why she should speak to him like this, but the hardness and coldness of her attitude removed any inclination he might have had to defend himself. It did not occur to him that this attitude might owe something to an earlier encounter which had left her nerves on edge; he only felt that for some reason she was determined to place what he had done in the worst possible light. "I'm sorry you have such a poor opinion of me," he said.

It somehow did not sound propitiatory: it would have been better if he had not spoken at all. "You are not sorry," his mother told him. "If you were, you would not speak in that tone. You are only obstinate and resentful because your self-esteem is hurt. If you were really sorry you would admit you had done wrong."

"I don't feel I have done wrong," Brian answered. "I haven't had much *time* to tell you. I told you I was going to, and I can't see that I injured you in any way by wanting to think it over first."

"No, you never feel you are wrong," his mother said. "Whatever your behaviour may be, you always manage to justify it in your own eyes."

"I don't see why I shouldn't justify it," Brian retorted. "I don't see what you have to complain about, except that you think I'm not straightforward—which of course I can't help. I mean, I can't help your thinking it. I don't see why I should say I am wrong when I don't believe it. I think what I did was right."

"And in the same circumstances you would do it over again—I suppose that is what I am to understand?"

"Yes," he said. Only he knew he wouldn't—knew that she was forcing all this upon him, and exaggerating everything.

"Why then do you say you are sorry?" she persisted. "Isn't it rather unnecessary—except that I've noticed you always do say so when you intend to be more stubborn and disrespectful than usual."

"I didn't say I was sorry for what I had done," Brian answered. "I said I was sorry you had such a poor opinion of me."

A long silence followed this speech, and he did not know whether to go or to remain, for she seemed to have nothing further to say to him, and he could not, after this, ask what had happened or was going to happen. But he had an intuition—a foreboding—that his father had been right after all, and that the optimism and confidence with which he had at the time opposed him had been shallow and not really founded on anything more genuine than an unwillingness to accept what threatened his own peace of mind. He had willed himself into believing it, and that was all.

In spite of this, he was completely unprepared for her next words, which were spoken gently, almost appealingly, and with no trace of the bitterness that had underlain everything she had hitherto said. "I want you to promise me not to see your father again, Brian. Perhaps I have misjudged you: at any rate I ought to have made more allowance than I did for the position in which you were placed. I know that was not your fault, and I am sorry.... But of this I am sure: a further meeting between you can do no good. It will be easier for him—and easier for you—if you simply write to him. I have spoken to him already and he will understand."

Brian sat momentarily dumb. Then, as the full meaning of her words dawned upon him, a hot wave of indignation surged up within him. He controlled it, however, and his mother, who had turned away, was not at once aware of the effect her words had produced. "You mean I'm not even to see him to say good-bye?" he asked.

"Yes.... It would be painful for both of you and could do no good."

"I see.... You think it will be less painful for him to get a note saying I have done with him. I shouldn't like to get a note of that sort myself."

His mother glanced up, struck perhaps by something in his voice. "It will be less painful for you at any rate," she replied.

"I see."

"Oh, don't keep on saying 'I see' to everything," she broke in with sudden exasperation, as she read the suppressed hostility in his eyes. "You don't see. You don't want to see. You are merely doing everything in your power to resist and defy me. I never suggested that you should tell him you had done with him."

But her words left him unmoved: they were only words. "What else will it be—what else will it come to—no matter how I put it?" he said.

"You can tell him the exact truth—which will place the whole responsibility with me. At any rate *he* will do so—you may be quite sure of that—whatever explanation you give him."

"I see." He had said it again, but he didn't care: he did see. "So you think that if I can let him down without the discomfort of an interview I will be quite happy about it—that nothing else matters?"

"You don't care for displays of emotion," his mother told him, "and I am trying to save you one."

"Perhaps I don't dislike them quite as much as that," Brian returned. "What do you suppose he would think of me?"

"He will think you are obeying my wishes." Then, as he merely looked at her fixedly, she drew a sharp breath. "I don't understand what you mean, Brian. I am not asking you to do anything dishonourable. You have only known him a short time, and it was he who sought you out—deliberately deceiving you—telling you a lie—giving you a false name—giving you that book simply to support his lie—and keeping up the deception as long as he possibly could. Do you think *that* was honourable!"

"It was because he knew this would happen if he didn't," Brian answered. "I didn't believe him when he said so, but apparently he was right....

"What am I to do when I meet him?" he went on, as she made no reply. "Look the other way? There's no use telling me I *won't* meet him, because I'm bound to, if I go out at all."

It was not intended as a signal of surrender—nothing could have been further from his thought than that—yet astonishingly his mother appeared to take it for one, and immediately answered, "I don't think you will meet him. Not, at any rate, after to-day."

To Brian the words were startling. They suggested a possibility which, in spite of all that had passed, until this instant had not occurred to him. "Why?" he questioned; and as she did not tell him why, a second question broke from him quickly. "Did you ask him to go away?"

She showed no embarrassment: it was as if she were completely unconscious that his father possessed the slightest claim upon either of them. "I asked him to, and he refused," she said quietly. "So I told him I would take you away unless you gave me your promise not to see him.... But I don't think it will come to that. I feel sure— if you write him a letter such as I suggest—he will go himself. He knows your holidays aren't over, and it can make very little difference to him whether he goes or stays. I mean, little difference so far as what he originally came here for is concerned. There must be plenty of other places just as good for that."

"For what?" Brian asked.

"For what he wanted, what he was looking for—rest and sea-air.... You are taking this interest he has shown in you too seriously: he has other interests, other friends. You forget how short a time you have known him, and that his work has always been the chief thing in his life.... Besides, you must not think he is ungenerous— or likely to be where you are concerned at all events. He will think it over, and the last thing he will wish to do is to spoil your holidays."

Brian, motionless as a statue, slowly took it all in: and while he did so he gazed at his mother with the strangest look. Possibly she meant what she said: possibly she *couldn't* understand, and it did appear to her like that! Finally he spoke. "So what it amounts to is that you first tried to drive him away, and then threatened that unless he went I would have to!"

He saw that he had wounded her profoundly, for the look she turned on him was filled with pain and reproach. "I think you forget you are speaking to your mother!" she said.

"I don't forget," he answered. More than anything else that remark about his father's not being ungenerous had stirred him dangerously. They were first to disown him, and then to accept a favour from him! "Nobody else would have treated him like that," he added.

"If you really mean what you say," she answered slowly—"then perhaps you will be sorry some day."

He shook his head: "I don't think so." But further talk he knew was useless, and could only lead to a deeper dissension between them. He got up and walked to the door.

Instantly his mother called him back. Her manner had suddenly changed. "Where are you going?" she demanded peremptorily, but he did not tell her.

"Are you going to your father?"

Still he refused to speak.

"If you go to him now," she said, fixing her eyes on his, "you will be deliberately doing the thing that will hurt me most. I made an appeal to you and you rejected it. What I am going to say now, you force me to say. You are *not* to go down to the hotel: you are *not* to go to your father."

He turned in silence to the door, and this time his mother rose to her feet. "Brian!" she cried sharply, "come back!"

But he had opened the door, and now he pulled it behind him and ran down the stairs.

Chapter XX

LINTON AND BRIAN

L inton found the note where he had left it, and tore it up. So Brian had not called! But he knew he *would* call—sooner or later—and he sat down in the empty smoking-room to wait for him, attended by the faithful Micky.

To sit still like this was difficult, and after a very brief trial of it he began to pace up and down. For the first few turns he was accompanied by Micky; but since Linton invariably came back to the hearthrug, Micky, who was a labour-saving dog, presently decided to watch him from there. Linton's restlessness he found unusual and distracting—it wasn't what Micky associated him with—and he wished he would settle down so that he might do the same. This prowling about made it quite impossible—or nearly impossible—impossible——

Micky's head had begun to nod when all at once, with a start, he found himself lifted from the floor. Linton had unexpectedly sat down again, and Micky in a dazed fashion realized that he was on his knee and being held tightly. He gave an odd little wheeze;

but that was because he had not been on a knee for years. He felt surprised, though only for a moment; he had always known he was an attractive dog. He wriggled his body into a better position, and had just got it nearly right when he was set down once more on the rug. Micky was surprised again. He had been planning that henceforth he would always sit on Linton's knee, and now here he was back on the floor. He lay down, turned over, and waved his four paws in the air. Then, this mute invitation likewise failing, he closed his eyes....

Linton had recommenced his restless prowl—to and fro, to and fro—between the door and the fireplace.... Nearly an hour went by in this fashion, and Micky had long since dropped asleep, when suddenly Brian passed the window, walking very rapidly—and Linton stood still. He listened; he heard the sound of footsteps in the passage; and next moment Brian entered the room. In his spirit Linton held out his arms to welcome him, but in his body he remained motionless.

"I've come to you," Brian said at once. "What do you want me to do?"

Linton did not answer. One cannot answer a question like that as quickly as it is asked, even if the answer is "I want to keep you, I want you to stay with me always, and I want you to want it and be happy." Brian's words may have justified such an answer, but his voice did not. Linton knew there must have been an interview with Stella—a scene—almost certainly a quarrel—and the temptation to profit by the boy's immediate and violent reaction from it was acute; nevertheless he resisted it.

In the silence Brian looked at him, and Linton saw that he was in a state of extreme nervous and emotional excitement. Again temptation overswept him. All he longed for seemed to be there: he had only to make a gesture, only to say a word, and Brian would come away with him. Yet what good was this? None, unless the boy really wished to come. He had not wished it yesterday. Might he not now be speaking merely out of a mood of temporary exaltation? No happy, no permanent future could be built on that.

Yet—with all his heart's desire hovering like a beckoning spirit before him—it was hard to see anything else, hard even to speak calmly, and only by exerting his whole strength of will did he succeed in doing so. "Let us go out," he said. "We can talk it over better outside."

Brian without a word accompanied him; but they did not go far—only down to the sea—to a spot below the hotel and close to that from which the boy had watched his star. It would do for their purpose, however; they would be as free from intrusion here as anywhere else.

Linton sat down on the rocks and Brian sat close beside him, actually touching him—yet still it was not easy to begin. It was not that he felt uncertain; his thought was definite enough, and very simple. He could have put it nakedly in half-a-dozen words quite impossible to be misunderstood; the whole thing could be settled in three minutes if he were really sure that Brian knew his own mind. It was his doubt of this which held him back. He knew that the boy was powerfully moved, was at this moment not really himself, was feeling, expressing, obeying an impulse too purely emotional to last. What he could not tell was whether below this impulse there existed another feeling, deeper and more reliable—one which had nothing to do with his present wrought-up state of mind, his quarrel with his mother. He could not tell, and the very fact that he longed to trust him, to take him at his word, was in itself a danger. At least he must get this clear: there must be no ambiguity, no loophole left for misunderstanding; Brian's decision must be made with open eyes, with a full realization of what it meant to both of them, a full sense of responsibility. "Tell me what you mean!" he said, and Brian replied at once, "I mean that I'm ready to go away with you—any time—anywhere.... What you said yesterday was true. If I don't go, I won't be allowed to see you. I was forbidden to come this morning. Mother knows I've come: she knows I'm here now, and she'll ask me about it as soon as I get back. That is, if I ever do go back. Whether I do or not depends on you. It might be safer not to. I don't know. I suppose if I don't go back she'll come to the hotel. But I'll stay with you if you tell me to."

All this he poured out in one impetuous stream, and with bright, shining eyes that watched Linton's face closely, as if trying to read an answer there before one could be spoken.

No doubt he did read it, for it was impossible that it should be hidden, though Linton only said, "You can't take such a step as this without thinking it over carefully, and you haven't had time yet to think it over."

Brian's gaze did not waver. "Tell me, do you *want* me?" he asked.

Linton turned away. He could not look at him. He had a strange, weak feeling that he mustn't look at him or he would give in at once, without seeking further, without further question. "You know I want you," he muttered. "You've always known it. But that isn't enough." Then, in the tensity of his feeling, his voice acquired a sudden harshness. "In itself it isn't enough. Your mother wants you too."

The words, or possibly their tone, seemed to sober Brian, to restore his self-control; for when he spoke again it was with a good deal less excitement. "She has Claire," he pointed out. "Besides— she says she doesn't trust me: she told me so this morning."

"Still, that isn't enough," Linton repeated.

"I don't know why it isn't," Brian answered in discouragement. "I don't know what more you want—what more there *can* be."

"There can be the other half," Linton said. "What you have mentioned is only my half of it.... I mean, it isn't enough for *me* to want it: you must want it too."

"But I do," Brian urged him. "And I *have* thought it over. I've thought of very little else ever since I left you yesterday."

There was so much sincerity in his voice that Linton's doubts began to waver, and when he turned to him, and met the steadfast assurance in his face, they almost disappeared. "I'm going to be completely frank with you, Brian," he said; "and to begin with I'm going to ask you to think of me as well as of yourself."

"I *am* thinking of you," Brian told him. "It's of you I'm thinking chiefly."

"Yes, I know that: and I know you want to come with me— now.... But this moment won't last, and later on it may be different. Don't you see that if it *should* be different then:—for me that would be worst of all."

Brian made no reply, and after a minute or two Linton continued. "That is why I am asking you to be so careful. I want you to think not only of the present, but also of the past and future.

You must do nothing unless you feel certain of yourself—certain that you aren't just acting upon impulse. You must think of all you will be leaving behind you, because you will be bound to think of it later. Suppose you were to find out that you had made a mistake: suppose you wanted to go back. It wouldn't be easy to tell me—would it? And it wouldn't be easy to hide it either. I know it is impossible to be absolutely sure in such matters, but it is at least possible not to act lightly and without consideration."

"I'm not acting lightly, and I have considered," Brian said.

Linton was silent, and in the silence there floated before him a vision infinitely alluring. It took shape and colour in his imagination—a dream of renewed life and happiness. It grew brighter and brighter, more and more tempting—a dream of their life together—of work and of leisure, of sympathy and friendship, of shared thoughts and feelings and plans, of the long intimacy of firelit winter evenings, of summer holidays, of watching Brian's career, of helping in it, of being present when he had his first success. The dream rose before his inward gaze, like a summer-morning sun over a lonely world, filling the sky and drenching the earth with its light and warmth and blessing. And from a dream it could so easily pass into reality! There would be plenty of time later to discuss details—to plan and to settle. Plenty of time—an enchanted river, cool and fresh and clear, flowing on and on to an unknown sea....

All this, or much of it, must have been reflected in his face when he next turned to the boy, for Brian smiled. "I'm glad it's all right," he said, and his voice was so confident that Linton felt confident too. He even felt confident that they had found a perfect solution: by which he meant that, after everything was fixed up, there would be nothing to prevent Stella from seeing her son as often as she desired—from having him to stay with her. He had no wish to separate them: he was prepared even now to fall back on the plan he had originally suggested—the plan of taking a house near hers, so that she could have Brian with her just as before, the only difference being that he would see him too.

"What are we going to do?" Brian questioned, breaking into these eager imaginations. "Because, whatever it is, I think it ought to be done at once. After the way things have gone, mother very likely will make arrangements to go home to-morrow or next day."

"You mean that you could come to-day?" Linton asked; and Brian answered, "Yes: I'll come any time."

Linton thought rapidly, and in the midst of his thought Brian said, "There is a train at three-forty-five. That's the one we'd have to catch."

Linton suddenly made up his mind. "I don't think we'll go by train," he answered. "It would be safer to go by car. Could you meet me just beyond the town—opposite the school, say—at five o'clock? You know the school?"

"Yes."

"Even if we have a break-down, that will leave us lots of time—too much time: the boat doesn't sail till nine. Still, it's better to be early. We can go on board and wait there."

Having decided to act, he had suddenly become full of energy; but Brian saw a difficulty. "Y–es," he hesitated. "The only thing is —how am I to get my suitcase along? Mother may be in the house: in fact, she's pretty nearly sure to be. Even if she goes out for a drive—and I don't believe she will—she's certain to come back about four or half-past. If she *isn't* there, of course, I can manage. I'll go by the inland road, and you never meet a soul on it except a few farm-labourers and children."

"You're not to bring a suitcase," Linton told him. "That's the very last thing to do. You must come just as you are—without any luggage whatever. I can lend you all you need for to-night, and to-morrow we'll be in London."

"But that will cost a lot," Brian murmured reluctantly—"if I've to buy everything."

The objection struck Linton as odd in the face of what they were contemplating, but all he said was, "It will only be a temporary extravagance. Your own things won't be lost. Don't bring anything—except perhaps your overcoat."

"At least I'd better put on my good suit," Brian said, and Linton demurred again.

"I shouldn't—unless you particularly want to. I think it would be much better to wear nothing likely to attract notice if anyone does happen to see you. I'm even doubtful about your overcoat. You can change your shirt and collar and socks if you like, but I'd let that do."

"I must bring my shaving-things and pyjamas," Brian declared. "I can stuff them into my coat pockets."

"You can get all those in London," Linton persisted. "There's no use making yourself uncomfortable and conspicuous—and, as I've told you, I can lend you everything you need on board the boat."

Brian gave in, and Linton breathed a sigh of relief. "Then I'll pick you up just outside the town," he said, "at the school-gate, at five o'clock:—is that clear?"

"Yes," Brian answered.

Linton looked at him for a moment, gravely and steadily. "You're sure you'll be able to manage it, Brian," he said slowly, "and that nothing or nobody will stop you?"

"There won't be anybody," Brian answered. "And even if there was, how could they stop me; what could they do?"

Linton did not know: he did not see himself how anyone could stop him. "Well," he murmured; "I shan't see you between this and five o'clock:—I think it would be better not to." He looked at him again, and this time he smiled. "It will be all right," he said softly. "At least, I'll do everything in my power to make it all right. You believe that, don't you? You can trust me?"

"Yes, of course," Brian replied. "It's much more the other way. I mean, it's you who'll have to trust me."

Chapter XXI

LINTON

It was twenty minutes to five, and Linton stood at the window looking out. He had paid his bill, his luggage had been brought downstairs, and the boots was now mounting guard over it in the hall. He had tipped the servants, had said good-bye to Miss O'Casey, had put on his coat, was ready to start. And suddenly he felt that his whole body was shaking with nervous excitement.

This was stupid; he must control himself; there was no reason to be so agitated....

But the car was late.... Well—no, it wasn't, for he heard it at that moment at the door. Linton left the room and walked quickly down the passage.

His baggage was already being stowed away, and while this was proceeding he told the driver what he wanted him to do. He had told him before, but he told him again. He was the same man who had driven them to Fair Head and he assured Linton that he understood:—they were to pick up the young gentleman—young Mr Westby—at the school.... The boots was holding the door open, and Linton took his seat in the car.

Once they were started he felt better. It had been the interval between packing up and the arrival of the car which had proved so trying. He had found it impossible to do anything except watch the hands of the clock; but now, with the journey actually begun, though his excitement and anxiety had not decreased, he felt the relief that comes from action. He leaned back, not looking out of the window as they drove past the post-office, past the turning down to the railway-station, past the shops in the main street, and so on to the end of the town. There, close to the side of the road and immediately opposite the school, the car drew up, and Linton looked out eagerly. But nobody was waiting.

Of course nobody *would* be waiting, he told himself: he was much too early. His hand was trembling as he unbuttoned his overcoat and fumbled for his watch, getting it out with some difficulty. Yes, he was eight minutes before his time. Once more he leaned back, and tried to drain his mind of all thought. He would not look out again until he heard footsteps. But almost immediately he did hear footsteps, and started up.

It was only an old man carrying a spade over his shoulder. Linton leaned out of the window and gazed back along the straight dusty stretch of road. It was empty and bathed in sunlight. He sat now with his watch before him, his eyes fixed on the tiny hand that marked the seconds and was the only one which appeared to be moving. And then suddenly it seemed to be moving very fast indeed, and he watched it completing circle after circle. Somewhere behind him he heard a clock striking the hour, and directly afterwards the rumble and rattle of an approaching cart. The cart lumbered by. It was carrying a load of wet brown seaweed, and a man was walking at the horse's head, holding the bridle. Two girls passed on bicycles, and after that nothing till a yellow cat appeared at the entrance of the school, pausing cautiously for a few seconds before gliding on round the side of the house.... Linton put away his watch and shut his eyes.... Brian was late....

A long time seemed to elapse before he felt a kind of faintness, and struggled against it. He must not—he must not.... Two or three drops of sweat trickled down his forehead. He took off his hat and wiped his forehead with his handkerchief....

The driver had got out some time ago, and now he approached Linton's door. "How long am I to wait, sir?" he asked. "It's nearly twenty-past."

"How long *can* you wait?" Linton said, conscious that the man was looking at him strangely.

"Well—better not cut it *too* fine, sir. Say, a quarter to six at the latest." But he still lingered by the door, and next moment he added awkwardly, "What about getting out, sir, while we're waiting? You're looking kind of—not too well; and you'd maybe find it fresher outside. You could sit there on that wall."

Linton followed his advice, though he did not sit down. He stood by the wall, resting his hand on it; and the driver stood by the door of the car and presently lit a cigarette. The clock chimed the half hour.

There was still plenty of time, Linton told himself. After all, even if they missed the boat——

Brian had said he would come by the inland road. Should he go back to meet him? It would be easier than waiting like this. But suppose he missed him!—suppose he came by another way! No, it would be safer to wait on here.... Only, why *didn't* he come? Surely he must know that this kind of thing was an agony....

Again he shut his eyes, but opened them, almost at once, at the sound of an approaching car. It was climbing the long straight hill, and as it drew rapidly nearer both its shape and colour were vaguely familiar to Linton. "Mr Graham's car, sir," the driver mentioned, as if reading his thought.

The car was almost abreast of them now. Now it *was* abreast:
and now it had gone by—leaving a falling cloud of dust behind it.
Linton stood gazing after it, though presently only at the empty
road and through a kind of mist. What was he waiting for? There
was no longer any need to wait. Yet still he stood there until the
driver spoke.

"Wasn't the young gentleman *in* the car, sir?" he said; and
Linton's lips moved though no sound issued from them.

"And he never looked out," the driver muttered half to himself.
"The young lady—she looked out; but *he* kept his head down....
Well, I suppose we needn't wait any longer."

Linton took a step forward. "No," he said. "We can go now."

"You're not well, sir," the man exclaimed, catching him by the
arm, and speaking with a rough friendliness. "If you ask me, I don't
think you're fit for this drive. Best let me take you back to the hotel,
and put it off till to-morrow."

"Yes, I'll go back," Linton murmured. "Perhaps—to-morrow
morning."

He got into the car, stumbling clumsily over the step, and the
driver followed him. But while they were turning, Linton leaned
forward. "Take me to Mrs Belford's," he said, "not to the hotel."

"All right, sir." And they started.

At the post-office they branched off, going by the inland road,
and when they stopped at Mrs Belford's door Linton got out.
"Perhaps you would take my things on to the hotel for me," he
said, "and perhaps you would explain to them."

"Hadn't I better wait for you, sir?" the man asked doubtfully.

"No, thanks; I'll be all right now." He stood motionless till the
car had started: then he walked up to the house and knocked at the
door.

Again it was Mrs Belford who answered it, though this time
she was prepared for visitors and immediately recognized Linton.
"They've gone, Mr Linton," she said brightly: "the whole family's
gone. It's too bad you're missing them, for it's hardly a quarter of
an hour since they left, with young Mr Graham, who's going to
drive them home."

"Yes—I thought I saw them: I just wanted to know——"

Mrs Belford's face had suddenly altered: she was looking at him now the way the driver had looked. Why should they look at him like this? "Mr Brian——" he said. "I called in case he might have left a note for me—a message perhaps——"

He broke off as he saw there was no note, no message. Mrs Belford, indeed, appeared to have been struck dumb. But presently she answered, "No, Mr Linton. No; he left no message."

Linton felt himself flushing violently. "Perhaps—at the hotel—" he stammered.

"Well, perhaps," Mrs Belford agreed. But he could see, he could hear, that she was only trying to be kind, and in fact almost immediately she contradicted herself. "Mr Brian wasn't out all afternoon," she said, "and they didn't drive that way." Next moment, however, she looked at him with an increased uneasiness, as if conscious that for her hearer these words must hold some deeper and more painful significance than any she could find in them. "Mr Brian wanted to," she went on—"he did his best to persuade them to go home by the coast, but Mr Graham had some reason for taking the back road, and the others wished to go that way too. I'm just telling you in case you'd be thinking maybe they stopped to leave word for you in passing, and be disappointed. It's more likely you'll get a letter in the morning."

Linton said nothing; but neither did he move; and Mrs Belford, not caring to close the door while he still remained there, after waiting a little while was obliged to speak again. "Mrs Westby didn't make up her mind to go until after two o'clock. Both she and Mr Brian seemed very much upset, and though she didn't say so, I'm sure something unexpected must have happened. She only told me it would be necessary for them to get home to-day. Maybe it was young Mr Graham who brought a message, for he was the only one who called, and I know there was no telegrams or letters. It was decided all in a hurry, you might say; and I don't think they can have been expecting you."

"Thank you," Linton murmured.

The sun was hurting his eyes, and he pulled his hat lower. For a few seconds he shut his eyes. It was this glare, this heat…. Then he turned again to the house, but Mrs Belford was gone and the door

closed: the house itself, in fact, was several yards away. He didn't
remember her shutting the door.... Perhaps——Anyhow he must
not stand here, and he began to descend the hill.

When he reached the hotel he turned to the left and went down
to the shore. He found the place where they had sat that morning
making their plans. But the tide was farther out now: there was a
broad strip of uncovered yellow sand between the rocks and the
sea.

January 1932.
September 1933.

Appendix I

Letter from Forrest Reid to Stephen Gilbert.[1]

1/2/32
9.45 P.M.

Stephen dear,

I've just finished the outline of our tale, under the preliminary title of

Sea Magic:
an episode

and there I shall leave it until the light of your intelligence may be thrown upon it. There are fifteen chapters and the scene remains unchanged. At present I can't see any other chapters. You can condense a story easily enough, but it's a perilous business trying to expand one, and this seems to be all there now. But you mayn't like it, & if you like it you mayn't approve of it, so I'm not going any further till I know. Even my own feelings are divided. I believe it might be made rather lovely in a melancholy way. The great pitfall is that while it must be emotional it must *not* be sentimental, and this is a pit into which I shall be only too likely to fall. It is only the brevity of the synopsis that has prevented me from falling already.

I've an idea of making the first two chapters overlap, using the same incidents & parts of the same dialogue, but telling it first from Henry Linton—the father's point of view, & secondly through Gilbert Westby. It's only a technical trick of course, but if workable it might be rather good.

It would strengthen the whole thing & certainly expand it if I

1 Special Collections, Queen's University Belfast, MS45/1/14/5.

set the two influences side by side, but I can't do this without presenting the religious side and this would be dangerous & probably create ill-feeling, which I don't want to do.

Remember, if you don't like the thing I won't go on with it.

Ever your

F. R.

And meanwhile if any bright ideas occur to you put them down in shorthand. I mean, if you *are* being absent-minded you might as well be absent-minded about this. Mrs. Westby might be keeping her second husband with a few hymn-books in a suitcase for instance. Anything cheery of that sort.

Appendix II

'Nature Suppressed' by Stephen Gilbert, incomplete typescript draft with handwritten corrections by the author, c. 1931. 'Stephen's novel' is written at the top of the first page in Forrest Reid's hand.[1]

Chapter 1.

Broken Bliss.

Edna Kearney had been out to the post and as she neared her father's office her steps insensibly grew slower. She was feeling very pleased with the world and she did not wish to return to the dust and grime of the little rooms.

Life was really rather good and she hoped that soon it would be better. She wondered if Eric Best would ask her to marry him to-night. She knew that he wanted to but she decided that he would need encouragement. He was awfully slow and shy, and she laughed to herself as she remembered his heavy manner. Then she grew serious. Should one laugh at the man one loved? For she did love Eric Best. She smiled again. "Love Eric Best." It sounded as if he was one of many admirers, whereas he was the only one.

For the last few minutes she had been climbing stairs and now she arrived at the door of her father's office. It was at the top of a large building and looked out at the back. He was an agent and both she and her brother Harry, worked for him. Her brother did the travelling and she stayed inside and did the typing for her father. She envied her brother his job. It kept him out, while she had to sit in a dirty office all day. That would all be over soon when she married Eric.

She hung up her coat and hat and walked into the office. Her father was there and seemed annoyed at the time she had taken.

He dictated two letters to her and lost his temper when she asked him to repeat some names.

At last she got them all down and sat down happilly [sic] enough to type them. She had bought the evening paper when she was out and as she typed her father picked it up and began to look at it. Suddenly he began to swear. She heard him repeat the name, "Batry", several times. She asked him what was wrong but an uncivil growl was the only reply.

Soon he retired into the inner office, taking the paper with him. She heard him start to use the telephone and immediately picked up her vanity bag. Her father did not approve of powdering in the office and she was careful to do it only when his back was turned.

She had the mirror up to her face and was engaged in rubbing the powder off with her hankerchief [sic] when she noticed that the door of the private office was begining [sic] to open slowly. The slow manner in which the door was opening compelled her attention and she kept the mirror close to her face.

At first there seemed to be no reason for the opening of the door. Thinking that the wind had blown it open she was about to get up and shut it. Suddenly she noticed that her father was creeping across the floor behind her on his hands and knees. In one hand he held the poker.

She dropped the mirror and jumped aside with a scream. At the same moment he sprang and brought the poker down with a crash on the spot where she had been a moment before.

The next five minutes was a nightmare. She scrambled round the office, dodging round tables and chairs in a frantic effort to escape him. All the time he was shouting, "Batry, Batry," and aiming blows at her with the poker.

At last she managed to slip inside the door of the inner office and slam it in his face. As she turned the key in the lock she heard him panting outside and then there was a crash as he flung himself against the closed door.

Quickly she ran to her father's desk and gasping with effort and with fear she dragged it across the door. As she did so crash after crash shook the little room. Time after time she heard the running footsteps of her father as he hurled himself at the door.

Again came the running footsteps and she felt that this time the door must surely break. Instead she heard him slip and there was a heavy thump and a groan as his body hit the floor.

Edna waited a while. Then, as all was silent, she moved back the furniture and opened the door slightly. Her father was lying motionless on the floor and a pool of blood was gradually spreading round his head. She opened the door fully and came out. Then completely conquering her fear she knelt down and felt his pulse; it had stopped beating.

Her first thought was to telephone for a doctor. Suddenly she remembered Eric Best and her love affair.

Her father had died in a fit of madness. There must be madness in her family. People who had madness in the family had no right to marry. Even as she was thinking it she blamed herself for the selfishness of the thought; but she decided instantly that she would try and hide the fact of her father's insanity; and she invented a hundred and one reasons to excuse her conduct.

Quickly she replaced the furniture and generally tidied both rooms. Then she surveyed herself critically in the mirror of her bag. Then, and only then, did she go into the inner office and telephone for the doctor.

Trying to control the fear in her voice she said, "Oh Doctor, a dreadful thing has happened. Father fell when he was going into the inner office, and he hit his head on a table leg, and I think he's dead." She ended with a gasp which the kindly doctor interpreted as a sob.

At first she had determined that she would remain in the private office until the doctor's arrival, but a morbid curiosity overcame her. She went out to have another look at the body. She was glad she had done so. She would have had difficulty in explaining away the poker.

Suppressing a shudder, she ungrasped his hand from the poker, and carrying it into the cloak room she washed it carefully. When she had assured herself that all the blood was removed she dried it and washed the basin. Then she returned it to its proper place.

She took a last look round the room and noticed the grasping position of her father's hand. She picked up the paper and placed it in it. She was becoming quite an accomplished criminal.

It suddenly occurred to her that the first action of a loving daughter, would be to bathe her father's wounds. It was too late. The bell rang at the outer door and she hurried out to meet the doctor.

She explained her story further to the doctor. She was thankful when he told her that her father was really dead and had been killed instantaneously. Her manner was frightened and she was afraid that he would notice it. He did notice it, but thought it natural enough under the circumstances.

He told her that there would have to be an inquest and arranged for the body to be taken to a mortuary. Then he did all the other things that a good doctor can do, making frequent use of the telephone. After that he tried to comfort her and she broke down completely. She nearly told him what had really happened, but just prevented herself.

Soon after this her brother arrived in and they told him all about it. He showed a foolish inclination to giggle as he always did when anything serious had happened. She felt rather sorry for him, but the doctor who knew them well gave him a long lecture on respect for one's parents.

Their mother still had to be told of the accident. They had a long discussion as to who should do it. At last Edna volunteered. So the doctor took them both home in his car. When they got home their mother was out. They had to sit down in the drawing room and wait for her and they did not know what to talk about. It was about six o'clock by this time and nearly the time at which they usually arrived home.

About a quarter of an hour later Mrs Kearney did arrive in. She was so full of some story that she had heard that they had great difficulty in making her realise that Edna wished to speak to her privately. Then Harry and the Doctor retired leaving them alone.

"Mother dear," said Edna, "Father is very happy now." It ought to have been plain enough, though of course Mrs Kearney was quite unprepared and unfortunately rather stupid. Instead of understanding she burst into a rapid flow of invective.

"That always is his way going off and enjoying himself and leaving me at home to do all the work," she screamed.

"I mean father's dead," said Edna bluntly. Mrs Kearney burst into tears and through her grief she could be heard sobbing fragments; "What a good man, ... never a cross word .... always thinking of other people." It was a strange contrast.

When Edna at last opened the evening paper she saw the news of another misfortune that touched the Kearney family closely. She read the first particulars of the arrest of Batry and his confedrates [sic] and realised what had sent her father mad.

They had had all their money in one of the Batry companies and she could realise from this first news that they had lost it irretrievably.

As she lay in bed that night whe [sic] wondered what would become of her family. She did not think that she and her brother could make enough, from the business, to keep themselves. They had not liked to tell their mother about the Batry crash. Her hysteria about her husband's death had been bad enough.

The inquest of the next morning was [a] short affair. The jury brought in a verdict of accidental death and the coroner sympathised with the family of the deceased.

Edna went home with a somewhat easier heart. When she got home, however, her high spirits were brought down again with a crash. Her mother was still making the most of her grief. She sat in the drawing room receiving the condolences of the numerous callers and bursting into a fresh ecstasy of grief for the benefit of each individual.

The whole of Harry's time was occupied with business arrangements. The maid had gone away to see her sister who was sailing for Canada, after the invariable fashion of maid's sisters in times of trouble.

This laid the whole burden of the house work on Edna's shoulders[.] In addition to making the beds, the ordinary meals, and dusting the rooms (work which was usually shared between Mrs Kearney and the maid) she made to make fresh tea for each batch of visitors. Also Mrs Kearney had to be comforted from time to time by her daughter. All this on top of the night-marish experience of the day before was a heavy load for anyone to bear. When we remember that she could unburden herself to nobody, we find it difficult to understand how she kept herself from breaking down. Probably she was too busy to break down.

The next day Edna and Harry went to see their family lawyer, a dry little man named White. Though their affairs were in a very bad way they were not quite as bad as Edna had imagined. It is true they had lost about six thousand pounds in the Batry smash. There still remained the business which, if they worked it themselves, would bring them about four hundred a year. In addition Mrs Kearney was left an annuity of a hundred a year, to be paid by an insurance company.

Edna was anxious that she and her brother should could [sic] continue to work the business together. Harry had been offered a post by his uncle in Canada, who had a fairly prosperous business there. It offered him a good chance of rapid promotion, as his uncle was anxious to retire at the end of a year or two.

After very little hesitation Harry decided to accept his uncle's offer. Mrs Kearney was going to live with some relatives in Ballymena. This left Edna alone unprovided for. To give Harry his share of the estate it was neccessary [sic] to sell the business. Harry was anxious for this and did not seem to feel that he ought to assist his sister in any way.

Having come so suddenly upon the present crisis of the Kearney it may be interesting to consider their past history. Mr Kearney had been the son of the cashier in a large Belfast firm of wholesale druggists and Grocers. Charles Kearney, the son, was possessed of good deal of push and through his father's influence he obtained a junior clerkship in McKenzies his father's firm. Being clever and extremely hard working he rose by rapid steps until he too became head cashier.

If he had been connected to the business by family ties he would at this point in his carreer [sic] been made a junior partner. As an outsider he would in the ordinary way have had to wait some years longer before he got the position. As it happened the business was formed into a company about this time. McKenzie promised to give him the managership of the firm when he had seen it into a sound position after its reorganisation. This would he considered be in about five years time when he himself would retire.

Five years passed; they were years in which the Firm of McKenzie went from strength to strength and for this Charles Kearney was chiefly responsible. McKenzie senior, however, showed no inclination to retire. He was not an old man, he told himself. Kearney was still quite young and it would not make any real difference to him waiting another year or two.

So it was not until eight years after the company was formed that McKenzie really made arrangements for giving Kearney the management and retiring himself. One day he called Kearney into his office. He had drawn up a form giving Kearney the management. All that was now neccessary [sic] was Kearney's signature. He read through the terms of the agreement and was about to sign, when McKenzie stopped him.

"Take till to-morrow to think it over," he said. "It doesn't do to make sudden decisions. You may regret them later." Kearney acquiesced reluctantly. He believed in, "Do it now."

McKenzie died that night in his sleep.

The shares in the business were all left to MacKenzie [sic] relations and Kearney was painfully aware that he was not popular with the McKenzie connection. He was not very surprised, therefore, when he was not given the appointment, but instead had his salary reduced. The managership was given to a brother of old McKenzie's who had been in a similar business all his life.

It was made obvious to Charles Kearney that he was no longer wanted in the firm of McKenzie and that he would never be given the management. So he decided to set up business on his own account. He had not the money to start a firm on the same line as McKenzies [sic] and he had not the influence to obtain an appointment in any firm where he would have the chance of making good.

That was why there was started, high up at the rear of a dark and dusty building in Donegal Square the firm business of Charles Kearney, Commission agent.

The working of agencies is on the whole a some what precarious way of making a living. Yet by dint of working late hours Kearney not only managed to live, but also to save and to marry. In fact he was able to keep himself in a comfortable position in the middle grade of the middles [sic] classes.

The middles [sic] classes are composed of two kinds of people. The people who rose from, what is called, the working class, and those who sank from the class above. The Kearneys properly came under the former class, but the neccessary [sic] middle-class grievance was supplied by the fact that Mr Kearney might have risen higher but for the ill-will of his employers.

This type of middle-class people, who have risen from below, are very much influenced by advertisements and it was this tendency that lead [sic] to Charles KearneyMs [sic] downfall. He was taken in by the promoters of the much pushed and much advertised Batry shares. The results have already been seen.

For the rest, it is enough to say that Kearney was slightly fanatical as regards religion. He attended a gospel hall and preached both there and in the streets. He was a pacifist and had there been conscription in Ireland during the war, he would have been a conscientious objector. We will see later what points of character Edna inherited from him.

In many ways Mrs Kearney made an ideal wife for her slightly over-religious husband. In most things she was placid and easy going. Her opinion was that of the person she had last spoken to, but she never tended to defend that opinion. She automatically changed sides with the first words of opposition. In one thing only she resolutely went her own way ----- her reading. She had a low taste in literature and, to the despair of her husband, she could never be persuaded to take any interest in the "Life of Faith." What she did read lead [sic] her to imagine that her husband, and husbands generally, were invariably unfaithful. He was watched over and at the end of the day was expected to account for every minute of it. Mrs Kearney suspicions were easily aroused, as when Edna tried to break the news of her father's death.

Harry inherited his Mother's selfishness and part of his Father's ambition. He wore pointed shoes and greased his hair copiously. He had plenty of friends and little soul; though like all the Kearney family he had been saved in his youth. His ambition was to have good time, a comfortable life, and safe old age; nothing would tempt him higher and he made sure that nothing would come between him and its fulfilment. How small! Yet these are the people who enjoy life most. They have no worries in this life and they imagine that they have a safe place booked in the next.

As for Edna we will leave our readers to judge her. May they look kindly on her faults.

Chapter 2.

Eric Best.

A short, dark haired, sallow faced young man, with rather serious black eyes was standing on the Newtownards Road and gazing down the Beersbridge Road in the direction of Bloomfield. Every time a tram passed going out of town he cast a rather angry look down the road and then signed resignedly. The trams going towards Belfast did not appear to interest him in the slightest.

An intelligent observer might have surmised that he was awaiting the arrival of a companion with whom he intended to board an outward bound tram. The observer would have been right. The young man was Eric Best and he was awaiting the arrival of Edna Kearney, who had agreed to accompany him to the Dundonald cemetry [sic] to view her father's grave.

Of course he had no particular desire to see her father's grave. This was just the first means that suggested itself to him of getting into contact with Edna after the temporary break caused by her father's death. He wished to get to some quiet place where he could tell her that he loved her and ask her to marry him. It did not occur to him that a cemetry [sic] was not a suitable place to make proposals. His mind was far above such trivialities.

Presently Edna appeared. She came form [sic] the far side of Bloomfield station. From the fact that she had been hurrying and that she had had to cross the footbridge as a train was in the station, she was rather out of breath. She did not like to be late for appointments though she frequently was so.

"I've been waiting fifteen minutes," said Eric. Edna knew that this was declaration of devotion rather than a reprimand. She glowed gratefully as she apologised.

They were both rather silent during the tram journey, Edna because she was thinking over her guilty secret, and Eric because he was saving his conversation until they were alone.

Dundonald cemetry [sic] lies on the road that runs from Belfast to Newtownards. It is at the end of the tram lines, and not very far from the village of Dundonald whose name it takes. It is one of the largest, if not the largest, cemetry [sic] in Belfast. It is as pleasant as it is possible for a cemetry [sic] to be and has a beautiful view of the Castlereagh hills.

Both Eric and Edna had imagined that the cemetry [sic] would be quiet and peaceful and they were surprised to find that all their fellow passengers were also going into the graveyard. They were even more surprised when they got inside to find that there were crowds of people of all ages and both sexes either attending to the graves or lying on the grass.

Eric and Edna belonged to that class, most remote from the working class, the middle class. Their social standing was such that they neither associated with it, nor yet employed it. If they had, they would have known that this cemetry [sic] is a very popular resort on fine evenings for those who have relatives buried there.

Mr Kearney's grave was in the Eastern corner of the cemetry [sic], a part which at that time was almost empty. Even there they found that they were in full view of large numbers of people; so, at Eric's suggestion, they decided to cut across the Railway line, which runs alongside the cemetry [sic], and return home by the old Dundonald Road.

They had gone through several fields when Eric, who all the time had been trying to lead the subject along suitable tracks, suggested that they should have a short rest. They sat down on a grassy bank, comfortably warm and glad of the rest. Summer was in June that year, yet there was still a good touch of Spring freshness in the air.

"What are your plans for the future?" asked Eric.

Edna sighed and threw herself back on the bank with her hands behind her head.

"I wish I only knew," she said, "jobs are so difficult to get nowadays."

"Edna," said Eric, determinedly, "Why should you do anything at all? My father has got heaps of money; he is going to take me into partnership next year and then I'd easily be able to………… Edna…." He was nervous when it got to the point.

Edna had been lying flat on her back with her eyes closed. Now she opened them and smiled lazily. It was one of those smiles that says everything and invites everything. Eric's shyness dropped from him like a glove and he accepted the invitation.

……………………………………………………………

It was a long one; or rather they were long ones; for there were several and first ones usually are. There was a sudden noise close to them and they drew apart hastily. A bull was staring over a gate at them. Before their startled gaze it snorted and turned away with a disapproving look.

"You nasty old polygamist," said Edna. "You've got about fifty wives and you don't love any of them."

"I suppose we had better be going," said Edna rather reluctantly. "I said I wouldn't stay too long."

They got up slowly and walked past a farm house and up a lane until they came to the old Dundonald Road.

They were walking in silence with their arms linked, when Eric suddenly spoke.

"Darling," he said, "When are we going to get married?"

"Darling," She replied, with equal suddenness and greater vehemence, "We shall never get married. I should never have allowed you to kiss me to-night. There is a reason, I can never tell you what it is, but it makes it absolutely impossible for us ever to get married. I love you intensely, and I always will love y………………"

"Darling," he said, "Nothing, whatever it may be, can stand between……………"

"Eric," she said, cutting him short with a force that made him quail, "I must never marry you; I must never have children, and it is wicked for you to try and make me."

They walked the rest of the way home in comparative silence.

When they reached the Kearneys' gate they said, "Good-night," and
Eric was surprised at his own boldness when he added, "Darling."
It was unnoticed for he said it so quietly that Edna never heard it.

"Well, dear," said Mrs Kearney, "And did you see your poor
father's grave?"

"Oh Yes Mother, I did," replied Edna after a momentary hesitation as she realised that she had not seen it at all.

"And did it look nice?" She continued laboriously.

"Do you know," said Mrs Kearney, to Harry, "I thought Edna
seemed very queer to-night. Did you notice it?"

Harry being only a brother had hardly noticed his sister at all.

"It must have been the effect of seeing her fatherMs [sic] grave
so soon after his death. It must have been awful for her finding him
like that dead in the office." It was not often that Mrs Kearney was
sympathetic.

As he went home Eric racked his brains to solve the question
of Edna's curious behaviour. He remembered that inviting smile,
that seemed to give, that did give everything to him. Then it was
suddenly withdrawn. Was it because he was an agnostic and she
was a Christian. That must be it, he thought. Well, he knew that
he could never become a Christian. The only way was to make her
an Agnostic like himself.

The plan came to him next night at the gospel hall. He was
rather fond of going to gospel meetings of all kinds. Partly because
he thought he might get something that would help him, partly
because they amused him, and partly because he was fond of argument.

He stood with his mouth tightly shut during the hymns at the
begining [sic] of the meeting. He was not going to say what he did
not believe. He had his own code to live up to and he did not rely
on any imaginary spiritual help. He always felt proud of the fact
that he was fighting his way alone through the universe; not only
in this world but the next.

Hell. The sermon was about Hell. The preacher believed in Hell.
People like Eric, he said, were going there. Eric half believed in it
himself.

The congregation was attentive. The sermon was vivid and

exciting. Those who were not saved began to tremble apprehensively; those who were licked their lips over the downfall of the wicked. The sermon began to draw to a close. The preacher having painted the downfall of the wicked was pointing out the way of salvation.

Eric neither licked his lips nor rolled his eyes. He was not frightened by this picture of Hell, though it did interest him. Nor was he amused for he did not try to disguise the fact that he had come with a definite purpose. These Christians possessed something that he craved for; yet how they got it he did not know for to him their religion seemed infinitely foolish. Presently they would argue with him about it and he would shock them with what they would describe as blasphemy.

The preacher was working himself into a frenzy and the screech of the voice awoke Eric from his dream.

"Salvation," he cried, "How shall I find it?" I will find it in this book, the Book of Books (He waved it above his head), The Word of God, The Bible (Here he crashed it down on the desk in front of him). I read, and what do I find?"

He licked his fingers copiously all over and, using both hands, turned over the pages of his Bible with immense rapidity. Then he raised his head with a shout and, as it seemed to Eric, pointed his finger straight at him.

"Young man or young woman sitting down there to-night (His finger darted about the hall so that all were included in that terrible gesture) there is no time for delay. Behold the Bridegroom cometh like [a] thief in the Night. He might come to-night. Then to-morrow would be to [sic] late and you would go down to Hell-Fire!"

A shiver passed throught [sic] the audience and the preacher subsided having done his duty nobly. One of the select band established on the platform rose to his feet.

"We will now," He said, "Join in a few minutes silent prayer, during which time anyone (And I do pray there will be a few) who has been saved to-night through the words of our brother Mr Lace will have an opportunity of making a declaration."

He was mistaken, however. Another brother, who had no previous chance, and who was evidently intended to have none, took the opportunity to rise up and break into a long winded prayer. A sidesman suddenly stopped his saintly-posed walk up and down the aisle and approached Eric meaningly. To his disappointment the prayer, which he had thought good for another five minutes at least, suddenly came to an end. He remained hovering in the background while an announcement was made from the platform.

"We will now join in singing hymn 396, during which time all those who wish may leave the hall; but I would earnestly request that all those who can will remain, so that those who have been saved to-night may be given a further opportunity of declaring their faith."

He scowled at the little man, who had spoilt the first opportunity. The little man smiled back with Christian benevolence.

Immediately after the hymn there was another prayer. A man, who was unmistakebly [sic] a small grocer, came and sat down beside Eric. He had a very dried bacon look, yet he lost no time in getting down to business.

"Young man," he said, "Have you been saved?"

"What exactly do you mean by that?"

There was a pause and Eric saw that several of the platform party were looking at him between their fingers. He glared back at them and they hastily continued with their praying.

"When I was a young fellow like you," said the sidesman, "I said to myself, 'What do I care about God and what has he done for me?' I began to go to dances and to the theatre and the hippodrome. The [sic] my conscience began to prick me and one day when I was going into the hippodrome God stopped me and I went into the tent mission instead.

"Well I remember that night. I never knew the name of the minister and I've always regretted it ever since. As I was going to say a man came up to me, just as I came up to you to-night, and he says to me, 'Are you saved?'

" 'No,' said I, 'I am not.'

" 'Do you want to be?' says he.

" 'Yes,' said I, 'I do that.'

"Well then we both went down on our knees and asked God to

show me the way to salvation, through Christ Jesus, his Son. So he came and took all my sins away.

"That's how I was saved. Now could you not just kneel down and ask God to save you, just as I did."

"Do you mean to say that you never sinned any more after that[?]" said Eric, though he knew perfectly well what the answer would be.

"Oh no," said the grocer, "I sin too sometimes; but then I just kneel down and ask Christ to forgive me my sin and he does.

"Now why don't you do just the same. Christ died on the cross for you just as much as he did for me. Come on with you now. You needn't try to pretend with me. It is not so very long since I was a young fellow myself. I know just what you are feeling like. Just kneel down with me now. Come on now."

Eric, however was not to be rushed like this. So he asked, "What does it feel like to be saved?"

There was a pause while the man thought of words to express the greatest feeling of his life. It was a somewhat unusual question. He must express himself well. He was dealing with a difficult customer. Eric did not show the usual anxiety and obedience in being saved.

"Have you ever felt a tremendous longing to be young again?" said the man at last. "I know that you are not very old, but what I mean is, have you never wished that you were quite young and innocent? Have you never wished to feel that you were beautiful, clean, pure, and free from all sin, or taint of sin? That is what being saved does for you. It washes all your sins away. If you ask Jesus that is what he will do for you."

He returned to the same point with unfailing precision of a circular tour.

"How can I ask him," said Eric, rather testily, "When I am not sure that I believe in him at all?"

"You have only got to believe to be saved," said the grocer simply; as if believing was just a matter of making a decision.

"How can I believe, when I don't believe?["] Said Eric.

"Do you believe that there ever was any man called Christ that lived here one [sic] Earth?"

"Yes," admitted Eric, "I believe that there was a man called Jesus Christ, who went about on Earth for some years preaching and teaching that he was the saviour of mankind. I do not believe any further than that. I do not believe that he was God."

Several of the people on the neighbouring benches, who had been leaning forward, hearing, as they thought, the declaration of a newly saved convert, now sank back with dismay as they heard this blasphemy.

"You must either believe that Jesus was the worst or the best man that ever lived," continued the grocer, heedless of the interest of the surrounding audience, to which he was well accustomed. "Do you think that he was an imposter?"

"Yes," said Eric, "I do. At least I believe that he was self-deceived."

"Oh, well," said the man, "I can't convince you against your will. Read your Bible yourself and may be you will come to believe. May be I will see you here again sometime. I hope so."

Eric shook his head warmly. He was a decent soul and he was trying to do him a good turn.

He looked round the hall and saw that several other young men and boys were getting questioned as he had been. Indeed the real object of the prayer and the after-meeting was to allow this questioning to take place. It is true that a man was praying from the platform during most of the time for the benefit of those that were already saved. The majority of the people, however, were either being saved, trying to save someone else, or listening to someone else being saved.

"It was towards the close of the prayer that Eric had his great idea. The best way to make Edna become an Agnostic, or rather to make her lose faith in Christianity, was to make her sympathetic with his point of view. If she saw a number of people against him in an argument she would surely tend to support his views, even if they were not her own.

That would be easy to arrange. He would take her to a coffey-crush. What his particular coffey-crush was designed for we will see in another chapter.

It did occur to him that the problem would be solved if he became a Christian, but he turned the idea down as an impossibility. It was hard luck on Edna he reflected losing what she valued so much. Yet he could not do without her.

Chapter 3.

Edna Learns Her True Value.

The business had been sold. Edna thought that they should have got more than a thousand pounds for it. Harry was anxious to get his share of the money quickly and was pleased to get a buyer so soon.

Now Edna would have to support herself and she imagined that she would be able to do it very easily. She had estimated that she was worth about £175 per annum. She felt quite willing to take £150 or even £140 to start with. This estimate was based on another. Harry and she had calculated that they could run the business so as to bring themselves in about £400 per annum, though their father had made much more out of it. The business had sold for £1000, which was equal to £50 per annum. That meant that of the profits from the business Harry and she must have been capable of earning at least £350. Half of that sum was £175. Q.E.D.

It was just over a fortnight since her father's death. This morning she was going into town to see if she could get a job. So she caught the 9-45 train at Bloomfield station. She had been going to catch the 8-30 her usual business train. Only she remembered that the higher lights in business did not come into town till about ten o'clock.

In the train she had another inspiration and decided to put off calling in the various offices to which she was going until eleven o'clock. It usually took businessmen about an hour to deal with their correspondence she remembered. They were members of the Linen Hall Library and she decided that she would put in an hour there before going to McKenzies. She thought McKenzies would be a good place to try, for she knew that her father had been employed there.

As she went across the Queen's Bridge she decided that if she got a job she would give the one-legged beggar a florin. It was not that she thought he needed the money, for he had a well fed look. She thought it would be nice to see his look of surprise, for she felt sure that he had never received so much at one time.

She thought not for the first time how really beautiful was this scene; the bright colours of the steamers['] funnels, the thick blue colour of the water, and the distant hills emerging from their morning haze. She noted that the Liverpool boat had been changed from grey to black. It was an improvement she decided, even though it had been beautiful before. She wondered rather idly which of the three it was, Monarch, Queen, or Prince?

Appendix III

'The Pear Tree' by Forrest Reid, undated MS. sent to Stephen Gilbert.[1]

THE PEAR TREE.

(S.G.)

YOUR hands, I think, were not made for picking and stealing,
Or plucking the strings of a fiddle, or mending a clock,
But to hold in their grasp and to shake the boughs of a pear tree,
While I stand below,
And you look down at me, laughing and calling through the
      green leaves.

To the damp, long, tangled grass the pears drop down;
The branches sway and sweep in the air with a noise like the
      rushing of wind;
Soft little thuds sound in the grass, while your voice shouts from
      the tree-top:
'How many? Two?—Three? Any luck? Any good?'
Old Roger sits patiently waiting and hoping for sticks.

The pear tree, all stripped of its fruit now, is silent and naked.
Dark and asleep it stands, a grey sky above it.
Clouds are caught in its branches and raindrops glisten;
And the bleached winter grass is sodden and matted below.

I saw it to-day—a pear tree, but not my pear tree.
My pear tree is growing within me, its branches grow green in
      my heart.
You shake them and call, 'How many? One fell close by Roger!'
And Roger will wait, and you laugh and look down through
      those branches
For ever and ever:—a boy, and a dog, and a tree.

F. R.

1 Special Collections, Queen's University Belfast, MS45/1/14/72.

Appendix IV

'For a Birthday' by Forrest Reid, MS. poem sent to Stephen Gilbert.[1]

FOR A BIRTHDAY.

No new gift can I give you:
All that I had I gave you—
Gave you and give you still:
Now I have nothing to bring
To lay at your feet.

Drooping and faded:
The flowers that I gathered this morning
Are drooping and faded:
Dusk turns to night.

Dearest boy of the spring-time,
Stephen with hair of sunlight
And eyes like the sky,
What can I send with my love song?
I have nothing to send you:—
Nothing but love.

F. R.

22nd July 1935.

1 *Special Collections, Queen's University Belfast, MS45/1/14/23.*

Appendix V

'S.G.' by Forrest Reid, undated MS. poem sent to Stephen Gilbert.[1]

S. G.

Stephen, to me you have brought all
    That sunshine and the morning bring
When dew is shining on the grass
    And woods beat with the heart of spring.

The sky is in your young blue eyes,
    The sunlight in your yellow hair,
And when your voice and laughter sound,
    Echoes of wind and stream are there:

And sometimes when your mood is stilled
    Your face grows thoughtful, grave, and kind,
And through your eyes a spirit peeps,
    Gentle and shy. If I could find

Some way to draw that spirit close,
    What would it speak and say to me?
What dreaming wake of fairer scenes,
    Memories of immortality?

F. R.

1 Special Collections, Queen's University Belfast, MS45/1/14/73.

ALSO AVAILABLE FROM VALANCOURT BOOKS